FRILL KILL

Frill Kill

LAURA CHILDS

**WHEELER
CHIVERS**

This Large Print edition is published by Wheeler Publishing, Waterville, Maine, USA and by BBC Audiobooks Ltd, Bath, England.

Wheeler Publishing, a part of Gale, Cengage Learning.

The text of this Large Print edition is unabridged.

Other aspects of the book may vary from the original edition.

Set in 16 pt. Plantin.

Printed on permanent paper.

LIBRARY OF CONGRESS CATALOGING-IN-PUBLICATION DATA

Childs, Laura.
    Frill kill / by Laura Childs.
      p. cm. — (Scrapbooking mystery)
      ISBN-13: 978-1-59722-666-0 (softcover : alk. paper)
      ISBN-10: 1-59722-666-1 (softcover : alk. paper)
      1. Women detectives — Louisiana — New Orleans — Fiction.
    2. New Orleans (La.) — Fiction. 3. Large type books. I. Title.
    PS3603.H56F75 2008
    813'.6—dc22   2007038115

BRITISH LIBRARY CATALOGUING-IN-PUBLICATION DATA AVAILABLE

Published in 2008 in the U.S. by arrangement with The Berkley Publishing Group, a member of Penguin Group (USA) Inc.
Published in 2008 in the U.K. by arrangement with Penguin Group (USA) Inc.

U.K. Hardcover : 978 1 405 64390 0 (Chivers Large Print)
U.K. Softcover : 978 1 405 64391 7 (Camden Large Print)

Printed in the United States of America
1 2 3 4 5 6 7 12 11 10 09 08

*This book is dedicated to
my friend Pat Hawley*

ACKNOWLEDGMENTS

Many thanks to all the fine folks at Berkley Prime Crime who help make each book possible; to my agent, Sam; to Dan for his considerable marketing and design help; to Bob (my Batman); to Jennie and Elmo, always my first readers; and to Lance for all his fine work.

CHAPTER 1

"A loup-garou!" exclaimed Carmela Bertrand. "You've hired a werewolf to work in your shop?" Carmela pulled her eyes from the handsome young man who was dealing out tarot cards and turned to face Ava Grieux, her best friend and owner of the Juju Voodoo Shop. Just twenty minutes earlier, Carmela had run her fingers through her short, toffee-colored bob and highlighted her pale yet flawless complexion with a dab of NARS Orgasm blusher. Then she'd flipped the lock on her scrapbook shop and slipped through the dark streets of New Orleans's French Quarter to attend Ava's open house tonight. With Halloween barely a week away, Ava's quaint little store was jammed to the rafters with magic charms, amulets, saint candles, masks, and potions. And with candles blazing, red wine flowing freely, and a table heaped with barbecued ribs, Cajun chicken wings, hot crabmeat dip, and sliced po'boy sandwiches, she'd drawn an enormous throng of people.

"He's no werewolf," Ava was telling Carmela. "Gypsy, maybe — werewolf, no." Ava eased a hand down her crushed red velvet dress, smoothing invisible wrinkles as she watched her new employee skillfully work the jostling crowd. "He's fantastic," she enthused. "People simply *adore* him. And he's only been here a few days."

Carmela and Ava watched as three female customers huddled together, giggling at the floor show.

"Ladies, step a little closer, and see what fascinating twists and turns your future may hold," said the gypsy in a low voice that drew them in. Or maybe it was the fact that his black leather pants fit like a second skin, while his fur vest hung open, exposing a bare chest. Ringed fingers continued to summon his audience with hypnotic charm.

"All he needs is a bandana tied around his black hair and a gold earring," said Carmela with a bemused expression. This guy was good, she decided. A veritable magnet. In fact, she fervently wished she could summon customers into Memory Mine with as much panache. Sales of scrapbook supplies were good, but business could always be better.

Ava's new tarot card divinator continued to work his wiles.

"Let me read the tarot cards and answer your questions," he intoned. "Gaze into the crystal ball and venture a peek at the future. See if you'll meet that tall, dark stranger — your soul mate." The gypsy's black eyes glanced up, met Carmela's blue-gray eyes, and held her riveted in place as he cajoled his next customer into a reading.

Carmela let out the breath she'd been holding and realized she'd been hanging on his every word. Hmm. Interesting. And when, indeed, *would* she meet her soul mate? Her ex-husband Shamus certainly didn't measure up to that description. Shamus was charming, handsome, and scion to the überwealthy and decidedly strange Meechum family, who laid claim to New Orleans's chain of Crescent City Banks. But Shamus was also about as trustworthy as a sidewinder. Yes, he'd lured Carmela back into a few months of reconciliation this past spring. Had thrilled her with tender lovemaking, romantic cuddling, and whispered endearments. But all that had pretty much fizzled out. Of course, Shamus's wining and dining of other women had been a serious contributing factor. What could she say? The man had roving eyes and a callous heart.

"Don't you wish my fellow was into scrap-booking?" asked Ava as she shook back a tangle of auburn hair that swirled about her face.

"I doubt preserving memories is high on his list of priorities," laughed Carmela. "Making memories is more like it. So what's his name? Zandor? Apollo? Cupid?" Carmela was suddenly aware of the intense aromas of sandalwood and musk incense that permeated the shop. Could feel heat radiating off the people who pressed closely around her.

"His name is Giovanni," purred Ava, sensuously rolling each syllable.

"Are you conjuring Eartha Kitt?" Carmela chuckled.

"Vhat ever do you mean, darlink? Meow." Ava clawed playfully at the air.

"Ah," said Carmela. "Playing the cat woman who could scratch his itch. Tsk, tsk. And you're old enough to be his —"

"Careful!" Ava's long, sculpted fingernails looked lethal in the flickering candlelight.

"Sister?" finished Carmela.

"I can accept that," said Ava. "After all, he's only twenty-five, and I'm only, dare I say it, twenty-nine. So he's a titch young to accommodate my champagne and caviar tastes." They both fell silent as they watched

Giovanni cup his hands together, whisper a few words, then slowly release a snow-white dove. Applause rose all around them; the crowd was definitely eating this up.

Giovanni's dark eyes scanned the crowd. "Who's next for a tarot card reading?" he asked. Then, ignoring pleas from the women closest to him, he snaked one strong arm out and grabbed the wrist of a young blond woman.

The woman Giovanni selected was thin and angular, dressed in skintight faded blue jeans and a yellow silk halter top. The man she'd been standing with, a man considerably older than she, shook his head in protest as Giovanni reeled her in possessively.

"Who's the girl?" asked Carmela.

"That's Amber Lalique," said Ava. "The fashion model. That fellow she was standing with, the one who looks supremely unhappy right now, is Chadron."

"The designer?" exclaimed Carmela. She gazed at the man in the black shirt and white slacks. He had a high forehead, slicked-back hair, and a somewhat prominent nose. Chadron was a bit of a celebrity in New Orleans. A former art gallery owner, he'd made a smooth transition from selling oil paintings to creating elegant haute couture. Carmela had heard that Chadron had even taken his collection to New York and London this year. And he'd opened a smart-looking atelier just a few blocks over on Royal Street that went by the name Moda Chadron.

"See," Ava exclaimed triumphantly. "A lot of hip, hot people showed up here tonight. Over there is Toby Dumas, the jazz musician. And there's that new sculpture gallery owner, Riley Boyer, who specializes in west African artwork."

But Carmela's eyes were drawn back to Giovanni. His dark head was bent to meet Amber's blond head as they huddled together at the small table in the dimly lit reading room.

"He's smooth as silk," said Carmela, as the crowd of people suddenly shifted in front of them, cutting off their view.

"Ain't he just," said Ava. She tapped Carmela's arm. "C'mon, *cher,* let's go help ourselves to a little liquid refreshment. I am feeling parched!"

They pushed their way through the shop, past the shrunken head display and racks of velvet amulet bags, and elbowed their way to the refreshment table.

"Who did you get to dress up in the Pierrot costume?" asked Carmela, gazing at the sad painted clown face of the character made famous in the commedia dell'arte.

Ava shook her head. "No idea. Not one of my people."

"You really did draw a huge crowd," marveled Carmela. Music blared loudly, and she recognized the familiar strains of the Bienville Zydeco Band.

Ava nodded as she grabbed a bottle of red wine and poured out two generous glasses. "Free food and wine will do that. Plus, New Orleans *is* the Halloween capital of the world, and folks do love to celebrate a good holiday."

That was for sure. In the weeks preceding Halloween, the ghost walks, haunted house tours, and cemetery tours ratcheted up to a fever pitch, fueled by people's bizarre and insatiable desire to be scared out of their wits. The French Quarter played right into this Halloween mania, too. Gift shops and restaurants decorated their establishments with images of ghosts, ghouls, and vampires. Bookstores displayed their vampire lore front and center. A big gala was planned for Halloween night down near Jackson Square, complete with food booths, music venues, and a torchlight parade.

Even some of the museums had gotten into the spirit. The normally staid Hermann-

Grima House had draped their historic interiors in typical 1800s mourning fashion.

"You're gonna make a fortune," said Carmela. The crowd milling at the checkout counter was ten deep. Ava's young employees seemed hard-pressed to keep up with the customers who thrust skull candles, silk charms, leather masks, and Visa cards at them.

"Let's hope so," said Ava fervently. The not-so-distant memory of Hurricane Katrina still hung over New Orleans. It had been many months since their beloved city had been ravaged beyond belief. Business had come back, but it had been a slow, painful process.

Carmela took a sip of wine and fanned herself. "Warm in here," she said. "So many people."

"Let's go outside," suggested Ava. "Cool off a little."

They pushed their way back through the crowds and out the back door into a little cobblestone courtyard with a pattering fountain. For tonight's event, Ava had strung the venerable live oak tree with orange twinkle lights and white gauzy ghosts, and she had rented glass-topped tables and French bistro chairs. A couple dozen guests had already found their way out there, so Carmela and Ava made a beeline for the last available table.

"I should check on the dogs," said Carmela. Two dogs, Boo, a girly-girl Shar-Pei, and Poobah, a mutt Shamus had found on the streets, lived with her in the garden apartment just across the way. Though cramped and possessed of antediluvian plumbing, the place was cozy and oozing with French Quarter charm. And with Shamus acting so stupid and crazy and divorce looming on the horizon, the apartment gave Carmela a sense of independence she ravenously craved.

"Your pups are fine," said Ava, waving a hand. "But check out those ratty-looking guys over there. I think the tattooed and pierced contingent has just arrived."

"Crazy," agreed Carmela, who'd never quite seen the merit of perforating your ear twenty times or tattooing barbed wire or Japanese *kanji* around your bicep.

"As long as they're here to spend money," sighed Ava.

A man seated at one of the distant tables stood up and waved at them. "Ava!" he called.

Cursed with a touch of night blindness, Ava peered over at him. "That's not one of my old boyfriends, is it?" she muttered to

17

Carmela. "Tell me it's not that motor head Clayton. The one with the rebuilt Corvette."

Carmela gazed across at the man. He was mid-forties, exceedingly well dressed, and good-looking in a slightly fey sort of way. "Don't think so," Carmela told her. "It's not grease monkey Clayton anyway."

The man ambled over to their table. His cream-colored jacket and slacks were exquisitely tailored of heavy, elegantly draped silk. "Hi, dawlin," he said to Ava as he eased an arm around her shoulders and delivered air kisses.

"Ah, Gordon," said Ava, now that she'd finally recognized him. "Carmela, meet Gordon van Hees. He's Chadron's business partner."

"How do," said Carmela.

"Delighted to meet you, love," said Gordon, leaning over and giving Carmela a quick peck on the cheek.

"Gordon's asked me to decorate the Moda Chadron atelier for their big Halloween runway show next week," explained Ava.

"So you're part of that crazy celebration, too?" asked Carmela. All of the French Quarter businesses had been asked to participate. The French Quarter Halloween Bash was being touted as another way to draw visitors and bolster the image of New Orleans as a prosperous, recovering city.

"I don't know how interested Halloween revelers will be in haute couture," said Gordon with a shrug of his shoulders and an exaggerated eye roll. "But we shall find out." He gazed across at his table. "Oops, have to run. Chadron's taking us all for drinks at Bon Tiempe to celebrate a big order we just received. Tootles, ladies." And Gordon was off.

"I've got to hustle along, too," said Carmela.

"I have those ceramic skulls you ordered," said Ava. "If you want to grab them."

"Rats," said Carmela. "I forgot all about those stupid things." She'd promised her soon-to-be-ex, Shamus, that she'd pick up a couple dozen skulls for him. Shamus was a card-carrying member of the raucous Pluvius krewe, and that group of party-hearty fools was planning to roll three floats in the Halloween parade.

"C'mon," said Ava. "They're just taking up space in my office."

The two women ducked back inside Juju Voodoo, where the crowd had thinned out considerably, and Carmela followed Ava into her cramped office. Saint candles sat on floor-to-ceiling shelves, a clutch of shrunken heads swayed provocatively as they hung from the ceiling, Day-Glo voodoo posters littered the walls.

"Nice," said Carmela as she batted away fake spiderwebs. "Sophisticated and smart, but without that decorator look."

"We got a special on Saint Martha," said Ava, nodding at her shelf of saint candles. "Unfortunately, the dear lady hasn't been all that popular."

"What's she patron saint of?" asked Carmela.

"Dieticians," laughed Ava, as she shoved a giant cardboard box into Carmela's waiting arms.

"Ugh," grunted Carmela. "Heavy."

"You want me to help you schlep that across the courtyard?" asked Ava. " 'Cause I sure will."

"No, I'll be okay," said Carmela. "You've still got well-wishers and probably a million things going on here. Besides, I'm just gonna carry these down to my car and stash 'em in the trunk. Then I can drop 'em off at the Pluvius den first thing. Be rid of this whole entire project. Be rid of Shamus, too."

"I hear you," said Ava. She put a hand on Carmela's shoulder as her friend muscled the box through the doorway, then headed toward the back of the shop. "Bet you'd like one more peek at Giovanni," Ava teased.

"Nothing wrong with that," Carmela shot back.

But when she rounded the display of tiki torches and gazed into the reading room, it was empty. Giovanni was gone. Probably finished for the night, Carmela told herself. Or up front enjoying a glass of wine and a plate of smoky, sweetly sauced ribs.

Outside on the patio now, Carmela found it empty. *Funny,* she thought to herself, *it was jammed out here just ten minutes ago. Guess things really are winding down.*

Carmela thought briefly then of just crossing to her apartment, putting the key in the lock, and calling it a day. Dump Shamus's skulls by the front door, deal with the darn things tomorrow.

On the other hand, mornings were always a time of stress for her. Between hot rollers, feeding dogs, brewing coffee, and selecting the eye shadow du jour, she always seemed to run a perpetual fifteen minutes late. And she'd promised Shamus she'd deliver the stupid skulls. So . . .

Adjusting the box in her arms, Carmela ducked through the stone archway at the back of the patio and headed down the alley.

■ ■ ■ ■

Carmela wasn't at all keen about keeping her little car in a garage down the street, but she didn't have much choice. Her building complex didn't have a garage, and leased parking spaces were always at a premium in the French Quarter.

As Carmela's footfalls echoed down the alley, shadows stretched out from the buildings that buttressed up against it. And Carmela proceeded cautiously. It was one thing when you had two alert dogs walking beside you. Or if you were unencumbered and striding down the alley confidently, one finger poised on a can of pepper spray. But tonight she felt like a pack animal. Slow-moving and overburdened.

With each stride, the unwieldy box banged against Carmela's legs. And her eyes darted into each nook and cranny. She'd never felt completely safe walking down any dark alley. And, for some reason, this one seemed particularly menacing tonight.

Just up ahead loomed the rusty hulk of a Dumpster. Carmela decided to pick up her pace, give it a wide berth. Just twenty more feet, and she'd be at her garage stall. Then she could flip up the door, switch on the dim overhead light, dump the box, and hustle her buns back home. And then she was going to —

Scrtch scrtch.

Carmela stopped dead in her tracks. She'd heard something. In fact, the sound she'd heard was definitely coming from behind that damn Dumpster.

Oh crap, she thought, *now what do I do?*

Mustering all her courage, Carmela called out, "Who's there?"

And was suddenly rocked to the core when she heard a gargled, slightly strangled sound.

Is someone hurt? she wondered, her mind thunking into overdrive. *Is someone crying for help?* Because there definitely *had* been a strange sound, an almost plaintive cry.

Tiptoeing closer, Carmela peered around the Dumpster as her ears picked up an almost imperceptible *scuffle.* Something moving against cobblestones. And then something akin to a low growl.

Everything inside her told her to get away from there.

But for some reason she remained glued in place. For some reason her brain said, *Injured animal.*

Carmela Bertrand, rescuer of cats and dogs, fund-raiser for terns and egrets, petition-signer for Louisiana turtles, suddenly had it in her mind that an injured creature was back there.

Then, just as she bent forward, a flash of white fluttered up in front of her!

A dove? she thought in the split second her brain began to comprehend what was going on. *The same dove Giovanni had produced to please the crowd?*

But wait, her brain told her. *This dove's wings are tinged with red!*

Terror gripped her then, but still Carmela bent forward to look. And as she did, it seemed her eyes must be playing tricks on her. Because there, among the heaps of broken bottles and rags and flap of dirty newspapers, lay the twisted body of a young woman. A young woman with blond hair, a yellow silk halter top, and blood all around her. Lots of blood.

Oh no!

The box Carmela had been clutching suddenly slipped to the pavement. As its seams burst open, white skulls seemed to fly out everywhere. A ghastly punctuation to the death and the horror of the moment.

And then, as Carmela's brain was still playing catch-up to what happened, she was hit from behind.

Not hit, her scrambled brain told her as

she tumbled forward, *more like tackled.* By someone big. And strong. And very, very determined.

Cobblestones rushed up to greet her as Carmela fell sideways with full force. She was cognizant of the side of her head connecting with cement, her breath being knocked out of her, and someone — or some*thing* — jumping on her back. Then, just as fast, the presence was gone.

Gasping for breath, head hammering with pain, Carmela was aware that a light had gone on in the second-story window above her. That a window had creaked up.

Will they call 911? she wondered. Then she struggled to try to make her brain function. She knew some horrible event had taken place behind that Dumpster and that she had to get away. Now!

Flailing about helplessly, Carmela managed to prop herself up on one arm, then pull herself to her knees. Just as she was puzzling out what to do next, Giovanni suddenly loomed in front of her. Reaching out, he grasped her arms and pulled her effortlessly to her feet!

Gazing into Giovanni's dark, intense face, Carmela saw a swirl of long hair, caught the scent of his fur vest. Terrified, she threw back her head and let loose a bloodcurdling scream.

"It's okay," Giovanni told her. But to Carmela, his voice sounded deceptively soothing.

"No!" she cried.

"It's okay," he tried again, releasing her arms, holding his hands up in front of him.

But Carmela was making little moaning sounds in the back of her throat, backpedaling away from Giovanni as fast as she could. Praying that someone — anyone — would come to her aid! Then the heel of Carmela's shoe caught between a pair of uneven cobblestones, and her knee twisted painfully. Arms flailing, she wrenched herself about, trying to save herself, then crashed down hard once more. And as consciousness seemed to wink away, like a candle guttering in the wind, Carmela's last terrifying thought was, *Please keep him off me!*

CHAPTER 2

Blue light bars pulsed, voices barked orders, someone was urging Carmela to open her eyes.

She gave it a try, managed a gentle flutter of eyelashes.

"That's it," coaxed a kindly voice. "You're okay, just a few scratches and a bump on the noggin."

Carmela eased her eyes open to find a worried pair of brown eyes staring intently at her. "Who are you?" she croaked. Her throat felt dry, her lips parched.

"Barney," said the man. His finger tapped the front of his light blue uniform. "New Orleans EMS at your service."

As memories suddenly flooded back to her, Carmela clutched Barney's arm. "I'm still in the alley?" she asked.

He nodded.

"What's . . . where's . . . ?" began Carmela.

"Where's Amber?" asked Ava, kneeling down next to Carmela. She shook her head sadly. "Gone."

But that's not what Carmela was asking about. She tried again. "Where's . . . uh . . . ?" *What was his name again?* she wondered. "Where's Giovanni?"

Ava patted Carmela on the shoulder. "He's fine. Giovanni's right over there."

"What?" said Carmela. She twisted her head too fast, was suddenly overcome with a wave of nausea.

"Whoa, take it easy," said Ava, settling a blanket around Carmela's shoulders.

Carmela clutched frantically at Ava's hand. "Ava, I think Giovanni . . ." Carmela's eyes sought out the nearby Dumpster with its hubbub of activity. "I think he might have . . ."

"Oh honey, no," said Ava. "Giovanni said he was trying to *help* you."

Carmela was suddenly taken aback. "Really?" she asked as she drew a few shaky breaths. "Are you sure?"

"Oh, *cher,* you can't possibly think Giovanni would . . ." Now Ava turned to stare at the furor that surrounded the Dumpster. Bright lights had been brought in, police and paramedics milled about, black and yellow crime scene tape seemed to crisscross the alley everywhere. An ambulance had been backed directly up to the Dumpster, a gurney unloaded. Lights blazed from the second- and third-floor apartments that lined the alley, and scores of gawkers peered down.

Carmela gingerly touched a sore and scuffed part of her arm. "It was like a bad dream," she murmured. "And I thought Giovanni had . . ." Her voice trailed off. "Where is he?" Carmela asked again.

"Over there," gestured Ava. "Talking to the police. Well, actually he's talking to that detective we know. The one who's relatively cute and is kind of a sharp dresser."

"Edgar Babcock?" said Carmela. She glanced over, saw his tall and lanky form, his ginger-colored hair. Babcock was sort of attractive in a tough-guy kind of way. He was also uncannily smart and dogged in his pursuit of crime. As luck would have it, they'd had run-ins with him before.

Barney clicked on a miniature flashlight and shone it in Carmela's eyes. "Look this way," he told her.

Carmela glanced left, then right.

"Head still hurt?" Barney asked.

Carmela lifted her shoulders, rotated her head. Pain seemed to radiate everywhere. "Not too bad," she said.

"You might want to go to the emergency room and have a CT scan," Barney suggested.

"I really don't need to do that," said Carmela. She could just imagine the scene. Since she was still on Shamus's medical plan, the hospital would call him. Then he'd want to come down there, swagger about, and put his two cents in. No thanks. That was the last thing she needed right now.

"You sure you're okay?" Ava asked gently.

"What I'd really like to do is go home," insisted Carmela. She glanced down the alley, saw Babcock and a uniformed police officer talking to Giovanni. The way they were all posturing, the situation looked vaguely hostile.

Ava got to her feet and walked over to them. Carmela watched from a distance.

"You need to come downtown with us," Babcock was saying in his louder, more authoritative cop voice.

Giovanni nodded unhappily.

Ava stepped forward protectively. "Are you arresting him?"

"No, ma'am," said the uniformed officer. "We just need to take a statement. It's routine."

Ava eyed them both carefully. "You're not going to beat him with rubber hoses or shine bright lights in his eyes, are you?"

The officer pretended to look shocked. "No, ma'am. Of course not."

"Very well," said Ava.

"Oh for goodness sake," Babcock exclaimed in what was a very exasperated tone.

But Detective Edgar Babcock was far kinder when he questioned Carmela. "What exactly did you see?" he asked her. Ava stood by, ready to lend assistance.

"A bird flew up, and then I noticed the body," said Carmela.

Puzzlement swam in Babcock's brown eyes. "A bird?"

"Like a dove," said Carmela. "No, not like a dove. It *was* a dove." Her eyes met Ava's, wide with surprise now, but Carmela didn't elaborate any further. "Then after someone knocked me down, Giovanni came along, and I guess" — Carmela drew a deep breath — "I guess he sort of saved me."

"He didn't attack you?" asked Babcock. "You didn't see him with the girl?"

Carmela stared at Ava again. "No."

"And what was it the other officer said you heard?" asked Babcock.

"Kind of a scratching, scuffling sound,"

said Carmela. "And then . . . maybe like a growl?"

Babcock stared at her placidly. A single eyebrow lifted. "A growl?"

"Like the sound an animal might make," said Carmela. She stared at him, feeling the throb of a whopper headache coming on. "Am I making any sense at all?"

"Possibly," allowed Babcock. He didn't look happy.

"Of course, you are, darlin'," cooed Ava.

"Here's the thing of it," said Edgar Babcock slowly. "There are what look like teeth marks around the victim's neck. Like . . ." He hesitated, choosing his words carefully. "Like . . . gnashes. Like an animal tore into her."

"Dear Lord," breathed Ava as she crossed herself.

Carmela's mind suddenly flashed back to the old black-and-white film, *The Wolf Man.* Her earlier mention of a werewolf had probably shaded her memory, had planted a trick image and colored what she saw and heard tonight.

"And what else?" asked Babcock.

"Whoever — whatever — kind of jumped on top of me and knocked me down," said Carmela.

Tears oozed from Ava's eyes. "You poor,

poor dear."

"Action news, let me pass," a woman's brash voice suddenly demanded.

A blue-uniformed officer stepped into the woman's path and blocked her advance as well as that of her cameraman. That didn't seem to faze the pair in the slightest. The light atop the mobile camera suddenly blazed like a lighthouse beacon, throwing out a glare of white light that blinded Carmela, Ava, Babcock, and everyone in their immediate circle.

"Do you know who I am?" asked the woman, thrusting a microphone forward. "I'm Kimber Breeze. WBEZ-TV. I have every right to be here, so kindly step out of my way."

Slightly cowed, the officer gave way, and Kimber Breeze surged forward, leading with the padded shoulders of her bright red power suit. Her skirt hugged her hips, and her long legs slid down into a pair of stiletto heels. Kimber's sleek, blond mane was teased into a seriously big do and flowed around her head like a halo. But this woman was no angel; she was the fiercest reporter on the air.

"Ma'am," the police officer tried again. "These people have had a rough night, and the paramedics and detectives need to finish with them. You'd best let this go till tomorrow."

"Tomorrow's too late," snapped Kimber. "The news waits for no one." She swiveled her head toward her cameraman. He was big, blocky, and built like a linebacker. "You sure you got the body shot, Harvey?" she asked.

Harvey responded with a tight nod.

"Good," said Kimber. "Then we'll interview the wits." She held up her index finger and made a twirling motion. "Roll tape."

Detective Babcock suddenly swung into action. "Hey news lady!" he barked. "This is a crime scene. You need to step way back behind the yellow tape."

Kimber ignored him completely as she pointed one red-tipped finger toward one of the smashed skulls. "Be sure to get a shot of that," she instructed Harvey. Then her eyes fell on Carmela, still clutching a blanket around her shoulders. Kimber lifted her chin and pressed forward like some kind of news automaton.

"You're Carmela Bertrand?" Kimber asked, consulting a page of hastily scrawled notes. "You were attacked here tonight?"

The reporter caught Carmela completely off guard.

"No," said Carmela. "Well, sort of," she corrected. "Maybe." Then she blinked, frowned, glanced at Ava for help.

"Carmela's just fine," said Ava. "It was the other girl who didn't fare so well."

"That's an understatement," muttered Carmela.

"The murdered girl," said Kimber, still focusing intently on Carmela. "Do you know who she was?"

"Amber Lalique," piped up Ava.

Kimber's eyebrows shot up. "The fashion model?"

"I guess so," said Carmela.

"But *you* were also the intended victim of this French Quarter stalker," Kimber said to Carmela.

"Enough," said an irritated Babcock. "You guys got your sound bite. Now back off and let the police do their job."

"Sir, it's our duty to let the public know what's happening," protested Kimber. "How else can we help protect them?" Her words sounded noble, but her attitude didn't ring true. Ambition burned in Kimber's eyes and in her voice.

"Out!" thundered Babcock. And this time Kimber and her cameraman did back off. But Kimber, glaring back over her shoulder, looked positively livid.

CHAPTER 3

"Have another piece of pie," urged Ava.

"I've already had two pieces," said Carmela.

"But it's peanut butter pie," cajoled Ava. "From the Bon Ton Bakery."

They were sitting in Carmela's apartment, trying to depressurize from the evening's unsettling events. Ava had hastily wrapped things up at her shop, then headed over to Carmela's. Now she was attempting to pour copious amounts of red wine down Carmela's gullet and force-feed her peanut butter pie. Carmela wasn't protesting all that much.

"The right food can cure whatever ails you," proclaimed Ava. "Stress, depression, even a bad love life. I read the scientific details in one of those magazines at the supermarket checkout. They said the world's brightest doctors and researchers concur with that theory."

"I think they were referring to antioxidants and heart-healthy foods," said Carmela. "You know, like broccoli and soy and whole grains."

"Yeech," said Ava, making a face. "Who wants to eat that crap when you can feast on the likes of fried oysters, étouffée, and po'boys?"

"We're still young," said Carmela. "We can get away with eating that stuff. Give it another twenty years or so, and then our poor arteries will probably be clogged with that bad goo you're always hearing about. You know, cholesterol."

"In twenty years my poor ankles will probably get as fat as my calves," sighed Ava. "I'll have those old lady cankles. Everything all swollen and merged together."

Carmela was starting to feel a whole lot better. She lay sprawled on her leather chaise with Boo and Poobah curled at her feet, being the sweet little doggy darlings they always were. An ice pack was easing the pain in her twisted knee. And Ava was keeping her well-fed and sublimely amused. In times of stress, Ava generally resorted to food and humor. Never a bad antidote.

"You think your guy Giovanni will be okay?" asked Carmela.

"I tried to impress upon Lieutenant Babcock that Giovanni was a good kid. That he'd never, ever be involved in anything like this attack tonight."

Carmela shook her head. "At first my jumbled brain made it seem like Giovanni was the one doing the attacking. But then, when you explained it all . . . when you said he was trying to help me . . . I figured that had to be right."

Ava nodded. "That *is* right."

"I don't know how to explain the dove, though," said Carmela.

"Probably just escaped," said Ava. "Fluttered away on its own."

"And the growling I heard?"

"You've got to put those bad memories out of your mind, *cher.* Stop driving yourself crazy."

"I suppose," allowed Carmela.

"You know what we should do?" proposed Ava. "We should turn on the TV. That awful, pushy newswoman said her report would play tonight." She nudged an elbow toward Carmela. "We're probably breaking news." Ava sounded almost enthusiastic. "Maybe they'll even have footage of my shop!"

Carmela reached behind her head, fished around for the remote, then pointed it at the television. She clicked, and the TV hummed with electricity and music. Quickly punching in Kimber's station, Carmela jacked up the volume.

"Holy smokes," exclaimed Ava, "it's on now!" She hunched forward, elbows on knees, anxious to watch the news report.

A TV graphic that said *"Special Report"* leapt across the screen as lights zoomed around Kimber Breeze's big hair. The microphone was held firmly in her fist, her long red fingernails pulsated like blood with each flash of lights.

"The murder of a young woman occurred in the French Quarter tonight," began Kimber. "The name of the victim is being withheld pending notification of the family." She paused dramatically. "But we can tell you this . . ."

Carmela and Ava strained forward to hear.

"The young woman had her throat virtually ripped out. It was, as one police officer described, an animal-like attack."

"What!" shrieked Carmela.

"Where on earth did she get her information?" wondered Ava.

"Babcock wouldn't have told her *that,*" said Carmela. "He always plays it close to the vest."

The station cut away from Kimber to footage of a gurney being loaded into an ambulance. There was no mistaking the fact that a body was sheathed beneath a white blanket.

"Whoa," said Ava. "They got a shot of the body."

"That's in awfully poor taste," echoed Carmela.

But what came next really stunned the two women. Now the station cut to a shot that showed the front of Ava's store.

"The alley behind the Juju Voodoo Shop is the site of this most recent murder," continued Kimber as she stood in front of the brick facade with its graceful arched window. "Ava Grieux, the proprietor of this quaint establishment, hired the suspected killer only days ago. The man has been taken into custody after another woman, Carmela Bertrand, was similarly attacked."

"She's accusing Giovanni?" shrilled Ava. "That's so not right!"

Carmela and Ava exchanged nervous, startled glances, then their eyes returned to the newscast.

Kimber was back on-screen. "Ms. Bertrand is the owner of Memory Mine, a scrapbook specialty store, and is the wife of local banker Shamus Allan Meechum of the Crescent City Bank Meechums."

"Uh-oh," said Carmela.

"The shit's hit the fan now," declared Ava.

The phone rang suddenly.

"What was I just saying?" said Ava. "The sh—"

"Shamus?" said Carmela, picking up the phone.

An angry male voice burst from the earpiece.

Carmela moved it away from her ear. "Yes, I'm watching it right now," she said, rolling her eyes at Ava.

Footage of Carmela standing in the back alley wrapped in a blanket suddenly flashed on the screen.

"Mother of pearl!" exclaimed Carmela. "Do I really look that bad?" Her free hand felt the top of her head and found that her hair, a short, choppy do to begin with, was actually standing on end in several places.

"It's not so bad," whispered Ava.

Then the camera pulled back to include Carmela and Ava in a two-shot.

"Yikes!" screamed Ava. "I look like the bride of Frankenstein!"

As Shamus continued his hissy fit in Carmela's left ear, she mouthed, *You look fine,* to Ava.

"Bullshit," muttered Ava.

Carmela absently combed fingers through her hair, trying to make amends for the tangles and damage, knowing it was too little, too late.

Shamus's rants and raves continued to pour from the phone. "How could you be involved in such a thing?" he roared. "Why are you so darned intent on bringing shame to our family name? What will our investors think?"

"I have no idea," said Carmela. *Nor do I really care.*

"And what's this about an animal-like attack?" demanded Shamus. "Are Boo and Poobah there with you?"

"No, Shamus," said Carmela. "They're out roaming the back alleys of the French Quarter, ripping people apart." She paused. "Of course, they're here now, you idiot!"

"Thank goodness *something* is going right," spat Shamus.

"I'm so pleased you're concerned about *my* welfare," Carmela snapped as Shamus finally ran out of steam and had to pause to grab a gulp of air. And what was his sudden concern about besmirching the family name, anyway? Hadn't Shamus — her Shamus — skipped out on the business not so long ago? Hadn't he pleaded the Gauguin precedent so he could go take artsy-fartsy photos in the Baritaria Bayou? Yup, that sure as heck was the same Shamus.

Ava reached over and patted Carmela's arm knowingly. She'd always thought Shamus was a little shit. His phone tirade merely confirmed it.

Shamus's voice rose again and spilled from the telephone receiver. Both Boo and Poobah's ears pulled back. They hung their furry little heads and slowly slipped off the couch.

Carmela knew how they felt. She wanted to join them.

"That's quite enough, Shamus," snapped Carmela. She abruptly hung up the phone and went over to where the two dogs were huddled. Gathering them gently into her arms, she stroked their soft fur. "Boo. Poobah. It's okay. Daddy wasn't yelling at you. He's just mad at *me* again." They gazed at her with sorrowful brown eyes, licked her hand.

Why couldn't Shamus ever be this contrite? she wondered. *Of course, these animals are smart. These animals are even paper-trained.*

On television, Kimber Breeze was wrapping up her report. "Recapping tonight's big story, a murder has taken place in the French Quarter, raising stress levels to an all-time high." A shot of the broken skull, looking ominous and ghostly, came on the screen, then the visual switched back to a

43

close-up of Kimber. "Local banker Shamus Meechum's wife, Carmela, was also attacked. Ava Grieux refused to comment on why she hired the alleged killer in the first place. This is Kimber Breeze reporting live. Back to you, Stan, for our Halloween weather forecast."

Carmela clicked off the television and closed her eyes as the phone shrilled again. She reached down and yanked the cord from the wall. She fumbled for her cell phone in her purse and turned that off, too.

Ava struggled to catch her breath. Everything about the broadcast had turned sour. "How can that woman just *say* that?" she asked, pointing to the television. "She completely fabricated her story . . . implied Giovanni was a *killer.* And she all but condemned my *shop!*" Ava looked stunned.

"Face it, we're big news," sighed Carmela.

"But she screwed up every single detail," sputtered Ava. "She said I hired a killer. She said you were attacked by Giovanni. Everything . . ." Ava's hands churned in the air. "Everything is completely wrong! I mean, is that even legal?"

"She's very sly," agreed Carmela. "Kimber Breeze knows just how to phrase things so they're loaded with innuendo. But she's careful enough so nothing comes back to haunt her."

"If it wasn't for her looks, she wouldn't even be in front of a camera," scoffed Ava.

"You're probably right," agreed Carmela.

"I heard she was a weather girl up in North Dakota and had to leave the station in disgrace. Then somehow she turns up here and lands a prime reporter job," huffed Ava.

"Why do people like that always land on their feet?" wondered Carmela.

"Someday she's going to land on that big bottom of hers," sniffed Ava. "And I hope I'm there to see it."

"I hear you," said Carmela. She was feeling pretty glum herself.

But Ava was on the verge of working herself into a frenzy. "After this claptrap broadcast I'm terrified about what might happen to my business. What if people are afraid to set foot in my shop?"

"As crazy as it sounds," said Carmela. "This could actually be *good* for business."

Ava chewed at a fingernail. "You think?"

"Call it the train wreck factor," said Carmela. "People always want to visit the scene of the crime, stare at a burned-out building, see the nasty consequences. People are generally fascinated with other people's bad luck. Publicity, even negative publicity, draws attention."

Ava eased herself out of her chair. "You're makin' me feel so much better, *cher.*"

Carmela stood up and put her arms around her friend. "Glad to hear it. Now you better totter off home. Something tells me you're going to be very busy tomorrow."

"Lots of cleaning and restocking," said Ava. "Hey, you gonna be okay? How's your head?"

"Better."

"Really?" asked Ava.

"No problem," said Carmela, sounding far heartier than she felt.

"Well, scream if you need me," said Ava. "And I'll come a-running." Ava's apartment was directly above her voodoo shop.

They walked slowly to the door, where Boo and Poobah snuffled, wagged tails, and administered good night kisses to Ava. Ava leaned forward and grabbed Boo's muzzle in her hands, then kissed her on her fat Shar-Pei nose. "Don't pay any attention to that silly old daddy of yours. 'Cause your mommy sure doesn't."

"Thanks," said Carmela. "I think."

"Night, night," said Ava. "Be sure to bolt the door after I leave."

Carmela watched Ava's slender form run down the steps and across the courtyard.

No shadows or shapes followed her. As promised, she threw the dead bolt and pulled the curtain tight.

There, she told herself, *snug as a bug.* Carmela glanced around her apartment, drawing comfort from the belle epoque decor she'd managed to pull together on a shoestring budget. Knocking crumbling plaster off the walls had revealed century-old brick walls. And forays through French Quarter antique shops had yielded a wonderful brocade fainting couch, an ornate gilded mirror, marble coffee table, and some excellent etchings of antebellum New Orleans. Bits and pieces of antique wrought iron were hung on the walls to hold her collection of antique children's books. And recent additions included a small mahogany dining table and a silver candelabra she'd pinched from Shamus's Garden District house. It was cozy, it was snug, it was home. And right now, it was just perfect for one person and two dogs.

Carmela was just starting to drift off to sleep when Boo stood up on the end of the bed. Uttering a low, throaty growl, Boo stared intently out the bedroom window. Carmela hadn't pulled those curtains completely closed, preferring to let the outside wrought-iron lamp function as a sort of

47

nightlight.

Easing herself up onto one elbow, Carmela strained to see what her little dog was focused on. She knew the wrought-iron bars on her windows would protect her. Nothing could get in. She told herself that again. Nothing could get in.

A shadow seemed to rise up and hover in the air. Then it shimmered slightly and was gone.

Boo and Poobah suddenly dove under the comforter, snuggling their warm, furry bodies up against Carmela. Still jittery, she pulled the down coverlet up over their collective heads and took slow, deep breaths, until finally her nervousness fell away and she winked out completely.

CHAPTER 4

It was early, 8:00 a.m., when Carmela unlocked the door to Memory Mine and softly inhaled the scents inside her shop. *I love the smell of glue sticks in the morning,* she told herself. It was a silly little nonsensical thing that always made her giggle. And today giggling helped her feel almost normal.

Usually, her assistant, Gabby, was the first one in each morning. Turning on lights, putting on a pot of chicory coffee or Earl Grey tea, getting everything ready for the coming business day. Carmela was the one who usually came straggling in at quarter to nine. But not this morning. Today she was the one eager to get going, anxious to jumpstart the day so she could feel normal again.

Flicking the lights on, Carmela's eyes fell upon a collection of miniature paper theaters. Those little half-completed objects made her smile again. Her regulars were always pressing her for new and creative projects, projects that incorporated scrapbooking, paper arts, rubber stamping, embossing, tag art, and even calligraphy. And after a little consideration, Carmela had come up with these crazy little paper theaters.

First made popular in the eighteenth century, paper theaters re-created opera sets, Punch and Judy shows, fairy tales, tales of Greek mythology, Wild West shows, children's stories, and pretty much anything you could think of.

Gabby had turned a fourteen-by-fourteen-inch wooden box into a Venetian theater, complete with marbleized columns, tiny velvet curtains, movable pieces of scenery, and a top cornice that included a small clock flanked by gilded masks. Her cast of miniature cardboard characters included clowns, minstrels, circus performers, and magicians.

Carmela herself had taken a cardboard gift box with top flaps, flipped it on end, and was working on turning it into a *Theatre de la Vampyr.* Looking very much like a triptych now, she had added a purple velvet backdrop, black and silver paint, and a miniature lamppost. Spooky castle turrets topped the box, along with some gargoyles she'd sculpted out of plastic modeling clay. She was going to add wax seals, purple tassels, and miniature iron gates to the proscenium and was searching for some bits of black lace to really stylize it.

Five people had already asked if they could buy it when she was finished. But it wasn't for sale. When the little theater was completed, Carmela planned to put it on display in her front window. She hoped it would serve as a novelty to hustle up business for her new Dream Weaver classes, a series of classes that incorporated scrapbooking, fibers, original illustration, and paper arts.

Carmela was, of course, always on the hunt for hot new scrapbook and craft ideas to keep her loyal customers interested, as well as hopefully attract new customers. A couple months ago card making had been huge. Now her customers were delighted with making paper theaters. In a couple months they'd all be on to something new.

Three years into her endeavor, Memory Mine was producing a steady profit. There had been a big hiccup after Hurricane Katrina, of course, but now things were once again moving forward.

Carmela walked past the racks of paper, rubber stamps, ink pads, and cutting tools.

Past the big wooden table they'd dubbed craft central. Pens for calligraphy, fibers for decoration, and packets of beads and charms were enticingly displayed. Leather-bound albums waited to be stamped with gold lettering and thus become new family heirlooms.

Heading into her little office, Carmela immediately noticed the red blinking light on her answering machine. She wondered who could have called late last night or so early this morning.

Hmm. Maybe . . . Shamus?

She figured he was probably the culprit. Shamus had undoubtedly continued to call her apartment last night long after she'd yanked the phone from the wall. Then he'd probably called here early this morning looking for her.

The early bird gets the . . . blame?

Carmela locked her purse in the bottom drawer of her desk and pondered pressing the *Play* button.

But did she really want to start her day with a screeching torrent from Shamus? The answer was a resounding no. After last night's madness, she wanted to savor these early minutes of calm. And maybe enjoy a nice cup of tea.

She was heating water when the handle

on the front door jiggled impatiently. Carmela leaned left so she had a straight sight line through her store and saw that somebody was definitely trying to open the door. *Why can't people read?* she wondered. The store hours were clearly stenciled on the glass.

Now the person was rapping with their knuckles. Inquisitive eyes peered in above the giant purple sign that said *Closed.*

Carmela resisted the urge to duck and hide. It was too late now, of course. Whoever was rapping on the front door, annoying the crap out of her, had clearly seen her. The lights were on, and she was pretty much out there in plain view.

Knock, knock, knock. The person rapped on the glass insistently.

"Hello? Hello? I see you in there," a male voice called.

Carmela sighed, deciding she was going to make this quick, send this guy on his way. She strode to the front of the store, ready with a sharp retort. Honestly. Couldn't he read?

"We're not open yet," Carmela called as she gazed through the etched glass. Then she did a serious double take when she suddenly recognized who was out there tippy-tapping at her door. It was Giovanni. Ava's

Giovanni.

But he's knocking on my door, so it looks like he's my Giovanni right now.

As if they possessed a will of their own, Carmela's fingers turned the dead bolt lock and pulled open the door. *What was she doing letting him in?* she wondered. Was she crazy or what?

Or what.

"Come in," she told Giovanni, holding the door open and letting him slide by. She was not unaware of Giovanni's impressive stature or his seemingly rock-hard body. *Do I really trust this guy?* a little voice inside her head whispered. *Good question.*

Giovanni avoided eye contact as he stepped inside and now stood worrying his hands as Carmela relocked the door.

She turned and gazed into dark, brooding eyes. *Why had he turned up here?* she wondered. *What did he want?* "Are you okay?" she finally asked him.

Giovanni nodded in the affirmative. "Okay. Yes. And you?" One hand reached up to touch the back of his head. "Your head?"

"A little sore. The police just let you go?"

"They did. But it was a long, difficult night."

This was a different Giovanni from last

evening, Carmela decided. Last night he'd appeared self-assured, bold, almost seductive in dealing with Ava's customers. Then, in the alley, he'd seemed cooperative with the police. This morning he seemed tired and worn, yet jangling with nervous energy.

"There's a place in back where we can sit," Carmela told him. She motioned with her fingers, and he followed her docilely.

They sat facing each other in Carmela's cramped office, and Carmela scrunched up in her chair, not really wanting to touch knees with him.

"You're wondering why I'm here," began Giovanni. He ran a hand through his tangle of dark hair, trying to calm the mess. Yesterday his hair seemed to snap with electricity; today it hung flat. "I just came from the police station and needed to talk seriously with you."

Carmela chewed at her bottom lip for a few seconds, making up her mind. Then she finally said, "I guess I have you to thank for last night. You sort of saved me. At least I think you did."

Now Giovanni's dark eyes drilled into her.

"You scared him off," added Carmela. "Whoever *he* was."

"And you, in turn, saved me," Giovanni replied quietly.

Carmela's brows knit together. "What are you talking about?"

"Last night the police were ready to haul me off and put me in leg irons. Accuse me of cold-blooded murder! You were the one who told them I was innocent. That I arrived on the scene *after* poor Amber had been attacked."

"I said that?" asked Carmela. Funny, she didn't remember being quite so eloquent. In fact, her recollection of herself was that of a babbling, crying mess of goo. She thought for a moment. "You knew her. Amber."

"Yes, of course," said Giovanni. "She'd been to see me before for readings."

"Tarot cards?" asked Carmela.

Giovanni shrugged. "I do a little palmistry, too. And astrology."

"But you pulled her into the reading room last night."

"Because I wanted to talk to her."

"About . . . ?" said Carmela.

Giovanni ducked his head. "Her future, of course."

Carmela's stomach suddenly rumbled. "Are you hungry?" she asked him.

"Starved," said Giovanni.

"I think I have some crackers and cheese. And maybe a day-old muffin. Or maybe it's two days old."

"Doesn't matter," said Giovanni.

"And I was just about to make a cup of tea. Would you like some tea?" Then Carmela remembered his age. "Or how about a can of soda? That I know we have." His presence here was definitely flustering her.

"You're very kind," said Giovanni, as Carmela scrounged about in their little refrigerator. She found half a sandwich, a container of yogurt, and a baggie of crackers and cheese. There was always food left behind after one of their scrapbook crops.

Carmela carried everything to the large craft table and pulled off a square of paper towel for him. "Eat," she commanded.

As Giovanni chewed and munched and washed everything down with big swigs of soda, Carmela returned with a granola bar and a steaming mug of tea. A string and tag hung over the side. Not really a proper cup, she told herself, but it was all she could manage at the moment.

Giovanni sat back and spooned his yogurt in a little slower. "I came here to see if you'd help me," he said.

Carmela stared at him over the rim of her mug. "Me help you?" Her voice rose in a sort of squeak.

"Ava told me all about you. She said

you're her very best friend in the entire world."

"Okay," said Carmela, wondering where this was going. Kind of fearing the worst.

"And that you're extremely smart."

"Smart as in . . . ?"

"Figuring things out," said Giovanni.

A warning bell sounded inside Carmela's head. "No, no, not really," she said. "Ava likes to *pretend* I've got some strange intuitive power. That I can charm bees or bring dead ficus trees back to life. But I'm really just a very average, ordinary human being."

"Sure you are," said Giovanni.

"Let me ask *you* something," said Carmela. "And I would really appreciate your giving me the straight poop on this. What exactly were you doing in that alley last night?"

"I guess I was just in the wrong place at the wrong time," said Giovanni.

"That answer may have worked swell with the police," said Carmela, "but it doesn't satisfy me one bit. You were following Amber, weren't you?" *Amber,* thought Carmela. *The lovely fashion model who ended up with a poor, wrecked body. Terrible. Unspeakable, really.*

"Yes, I was following her," whispered Giovanni. "But not with any intention to harm her. I'd never do anything like that."

"But you obviously wanted to talk to her again," pressed Carmela. "Away from Ava's shop."

Giovanni swallowed hard and gazed into Carmela's eyes. "The thing is, Amber is . . . was . . . my brother's girlfriend," stammered Giovanni. "Or rather, ex-girlfriend. They broke up a couple months ago."

"Your brother's girlfriend!" exclaimed a startled Carmela. "Did you tell that to the police?"

Giovanni's eyes slid away from her.

"You didn't tell them?" exclaimed Carmela. "Are you serious? That's withholding evidence!"

"It's not in the realm of evidence," said Giovanni. "It's merely information."

"Call it what you want," said Carmela, "but it's extremely relevant. So you have to tell the police. Listen, I have a sort of acquaintance there. Lieutenant Edgar Babcock . . . well, you met him last night."

Giovanni licked his lips nervously. "If I throw out my brother's name, then he becomes a suspect, too."

Carmela stared at Giovanni. "Is your brother . . . um . . . what's his name?"

"Santino."

"Was Santino — and I don't mean to suggest anything here — was he angry over the breakup? Upset?"

"Upset, yes," said Giovanni. "But not in a way that he'd do anything crazy. Santino is extremely mild-mannered. Very gentle. He's my older brother, and I absolutely look up to him."

"Does Santino live around here?"

Giovanni shrugged. "Mostly he's off traveling. Santino's a performer with Cirque de Bella Luna."

Carmela had heard about this group. They were a European-style traveling circus, similar to Cirque du Soleil, that played to sold-out crowds throughout the southern United States.

"So why did Amber and Santino break up?" asked Carmela.

"For one thing, Santino was always traveling. Always on the road."

Carmela waggled her fingers, urging him to be more forthcoming. "And what else?"

"They had their . . . differences. And Santino recognized that Amber was well on her way to becoming an international model. So he thought maybe he wasn't good enough for her anymore."

"So he called it off?"

"Actually, she did."

Carmela thought about this for a moment.

Unrequited love could trigger extremely powerful emotions, could create an enormous wall of anger and resentment.

"Where's Santino now?" asked Carmela.

Giovanni shrugged. "Don't know."

"Don't you think we should find out? Wait a minute . . . Did Cirque de Bella Luna have a performance last night?"

Giovanni nodded. "Yes. Probably."

"So there you are," said Carmela. "Your brother, Santino, has a ready-made alibi. If the police decide to check him out, he's covered."

"In which case, we don't even have to bring it up," said Giovanni. "Santino's relationship with Amber is a nonissue." He leaned back in his chair, crossed his long legs.

Yeah, that could be, thought Carmela. Although withholding that kind of information from the police still didn't feel completely legitimate to her. "But you still have to tell Santino the bad news about Amber," said Carmela. "Right?"

Giovanni looked pained now. "That I must do." He ran the back of his hand across his chin. "Now will you do something for me?" he asked suddenly.

"Maybe," hedged Carmela.

"I started to ask you this before . . . Will

61

you call Ava and see if you can get my job back? I really like working at Juju Voodoo. I do more than just read tarot cards and perform magic tricks, you know. I've got experience in retail sales, and I've done some bookkeeping."

"What makes you think your job's in jeopardy?" asked Carmela.

"Isn't it?"

"Are you kidding me?" said Carmela. "Didn't you hear Ava last night?"

Giovanni shook his head. "With the police barking questions at me, most of it was a blur."

"Ava was singing your praises. In fact, she views you as my savior." Carmela allowed a few degrees of warmth to creep into her voice.

"Hallelujah!" said Giovanni. He leapt from his chair, almost knocking it over backwards.

"So if I were you," instructed Carmela, "I would get my butt over to Ava's shop and start helping her put things back together. It's probably a crazy mess from last night, but I'm positive you've still got a job there."

"Thank you," said Giovanni, striding toward the front door. "Thank you a thousand times!" He stopped abruptly, turned back to gaze at Carmela. "Since you know this police lieutenant, you'll help insure I'm in the clear, won't you?"

Carmela sighed. "No promises, but I'll do what I can."

"Thank you."

"No problem," said Carmela, although everything about Giovanni did seem problematic. She watched as he unlatched the door, threw her a friendly wave, then disappeared.

Carmela stood there a few moments, trying to comprehend everything Giovanni had revealed to her. He knew the murdered girl, Amber. His brother knew her. But Giovanni had been adamant that neither of them had been involved in last night's vicious attack. Carmela wanted to believe Giovanni. But she'd have to reserve judgment on the brother, Santino. After all, *someone* had brutally attacked Amber. *And what about the man Amber had been standing with earlier?* Carmela wondered. *The designer, Chadron.* When Giovanni had grabbed Amber's arm and pulled her into the reading room, Chadron had seemed awfully unhappy.

Carmela wandered through her shop, stopping to adjust a rack of cutting tools, arranging an assortment of colored pens at the front counter. She reached over to lock the door again, and was startled when a shadow suddenly filled the window.

Has Giovanni come back?

Squinting into the sun's glare, trying to peer between the scrolling etched letters that spelled out Memory Mine, Lieutenant Edgar Babcock's face suddenly appeared.

Carmela had figured he'd stop by, and now she dreaded his questions. In fact, she wished Babcock had shown up a few minutes earlier. Then he could have turned his high-powered microscope on Giovanni instead of nattering away at her.

Pulling open the door, Carmela said, "You should have been here a minute earlier."

"Why?" asked Lieutenant Babcock as he eased himself in.

"Giovanni was just here."

"What?" came Babcock's startled reply.

"Don't look so stricken," said Carmela. "He only came to talk. You just missed him."

Babcock ducked his head outside and glanced up and down the street. "I don't see him. And I know I didn't pass him on the street." He gave an absent frown.

Carmela hadn't noticed which direction Giovanni had gone. But she figured Babcock *had* to have seen him leaving her shop. How many guys in leather pants and fur vests went strolling around the French Quarter at nine in the morning? Besides,

Giovanni had just gone out the door seconds earlier. He couldn't have simply vanished into thin air, could he? He didn't possess *that* kind of magic, did he?

"Tell me he didn't threaten you." Babcock's hand reached down to the cell phone at his hip and started to pull it from its holster.

"Not at all," said Carmela. "In fact, you're completely overreacting. Giovanni stopped by because he was worried Ava wouldn't want him working at her shop anymore. He thought she might be suspicious of him, in light of last night's attack."

"Mm-hmm," said Babcock. "And is she?"

"Not really," said Carmela.

"And what about you?" asked Babcock.

Carmela decided to dodge that question. "What about *you?* Are you any closer to fingering a suspect?"

"Working on it," said Babcock. "Or rather our crime scene team is busy analyzing things. We found a poker chip along with some rather strange evidence."

"You mean the marks?" asked Carmela. "The bite marks on the girl's neck?"

"That and some rather unusual hairs. Which, by the way, don't appear to be human," said Babcock, staring intently at Carmela.

She suddenly thought of Giovanni's fur vest. "Can you have them analyzed?"

Edgar Babcock drew in a breath, let it out slowly. "That's the general idea, but between you and me, the NOPD still isn't back one hundred percent since Katrina. Including our crime labs."

"Nothing's truly back to normal yet," said Carmela. "Maybe it never really will be." She picked up a spool of gauzy ribbon and fumbled with it. "What was that poor girl doing in the alley, anyway?"

"Her car was parked there," said Babcock.

Carmela nodded. "Have you notified Amber's family?"

"How did you know the victim's name?" asked Lieutenant Babcock.

"Er, I think Ava must have mentioned it," said Carmela. "And it was on the news."

"Not last night it wasn't," said Babcock.

"This morning then," said Carmela.

Babcock peered at her, obviously suspicious. "You sure about that?"

Carmela let loose a deep sigh. "You know how *news*people are," she said. "Particularly that Kimber Breeze. Always prowling around, ferreting out little details. Pretending to weave together a plausible story but usually jumping to conclusions. You know the type."

66

"Yes," said Edgar Babcock, staring at her. "I surely do."

CHAPTER 5

"Carmela? What are you doing here so early?" Gabby's pleasant voice echoed through the scrapbook shop, instantly calming Carmela's nerves. Then she remembered she had to tell Gabby about last night. And suddenly she felt jittery again.

"Trying to update my day planner," Carmela yelled back. She grabbed the book, flipped quickly through pages. And of course couldn't locate today's date.

"Did the pumpkins arrive?" Gabby pulled a silk scarf from around her neck and folded it carefully. She dropped the scarf and her car keys into her purse and put it in Carmela's desk. Then she buttoned the top button of her pastel yellow twin set, swept back her brownish-blond hair, and focused soft, brown eyes on Carmela.

"Uh . . . pumpkins?" said Carmela, trying to cover up the fact that she'd somehow landed on July Fourth. She'd forgotten all about the pumpkins. They were supposed to decorate a few for customers and a dozen or so for the French Quarter Halloween Bash.

"They're not here?" Gabby's brows knit together as she immediately reached for the phone. "I need to call Broughton Foods right away. They promised a delivery *yesterday.*"

"Wait a minute," said Carmela, happy to have an excuse to close her book. She slid out of her chair and walked the few steps to the back door, a big black metal contraption. She flipped open about a dozen different dead bolts, then muscled the door until it gave way with a loud *whoosh.* A gigantic wooden crate, piled high with bright orange pumpkins, sat on their back step.

"They're here," said Carmela. "They just got delivered to the back door." The alley behind Memory Mine, though dark and dank, could be a fairly busy thoroughfare. Between Cat Daddy's, the bar next door, and the newly opened frame shop on the other side of them, there were always deliveries of beer, liquor, fresh oysters, linen mats, and fine art. Quite an interesting combination, but somehow not all that strange, considering it was the French Quarter.

Gabby's face appeared in the doorway. "Thank heavens," she said. "We've got to get started on these puppies right away." She looked around, wrinkled her nose at the bags of garbage that littered the alley. "We should try to move the pumpkins inside. This alley gives me the creeps."

Carmela handed Gabby a nice squatty pumpkin with a twisted stem, while she grabbed a taller pumpkin. She knew she had to tell Gabby about the nasty trouble in *her* alley last night, but dreaded doing so. Gabby was the wife of Stuart Mercer-Morris, the self-proclaimed Toyota King. Stuart had never been happy about his wife working in the French Quarter, which he deemed as "filled with tourists, topless bars, grifters, and unsavory sorts." Carmela had once pointed out to Stuart that the French Quarter was what attracted most people to New Orleans. Sure, the Quarter could be bawdy, rollicking, and, during Mardi Gras, a trifle profane. Sure, they threw ladies' underpants from the Pluvius floats during Mardi Gras. But when Lent came, everyone reverted to fairly pious behavior and walked around with little daubs of ash on their foreheads.

Gabby carried her pumpkin inside and dropped it on the big wooden table where it landed with a solid *thud.* "I'm going to do this one right away," she said.

Crash! Bang! The shop's front door suddenly burst open.

What the . . . ?" said Carmela, quickly stepping inside to see what was going on.

"Carmela!" shrieked Tandy Bliss as her heels hit the wooden floor like Spanish castanets. "Are you even *alive?*" Tandy's tight red curls bounced with every step. Her skinny fifty-something frame radiated nervous energy from every pore. "I caught the news last night and tried to call, but your phone just rang and rang!" She stopped directly in front of Carmela and put a hand to her bony chest. "I was so doggone *worried.* That news report said you were *attacked* last night!"

"What?" exclaimed Gabby.

Oh great, thought Carmela. *So much for my quiet chat with Gabby.*

Attacked!" continued Tandy. "I was beside myself all night. Hysterical one might say." She put both hands on Carmela and turned her from side to side, studying her like she was a store mannequin. "That's funny, I don't see any marks," said Tandy, looking puzzled and maybe even a little disappointed.

Carmela was amazed that Tandy's rapid-fire delivery could be maintained on so little oxygen. Didn't the woman ever stop to breathe like normal hyperventilating human beings?

"Tandy, I'm fine," Carmela assured her friend, glancing over at Gabby's shocked face. "That reporter got everything wrong. I'm okay."

Tandy looked like she didn't quite believe Carmela. "What about Ava? Is she fine, too? I know her open house was last night. Guess things got rowdy and completely out of hand, huh?"

Carmela grasped Tandy's arms and squeezed them gently, trying to loosen the woman's grip on her. "That reporter, Kimber Breeze, didn't know what she was talking about. No one gave her any real facts, so she basically made up a story."

Tandy looked sublimely confused now. "So no one was killed last night?"

Carmela drew a deep breath. "Unfortunately, that was the only part of the news story that *was* correct."

Gabby's hand rose to her mouth, and she sat down hard on the edge of Carmela's desk.

"Gabby?" said Carmela. "Are you going to be sick?" Gabby's face seemed to be transforming itself from shocked white to a bilious shade of green. Carmela reached for the wicker wastebasket, then just as quickly abandoned it. *Nope, that won't work.* She grabbed a plastic bucket from atop a file cabinet and slid it under Gabby's chin. "Okay, let'er rip if you have to."

Tandy switched her focus to Gabby. "Are you okay, honey? You're not gonna pass out, are you? Here, bend forward and stick your head between your knees. Pretend you're doing tantric yoga or something." Tandy reached up to swoop Gabby's hair out of the way, but Gabby stopped her.

"I'm not going to be sick," Gabby mumbled. "I'm just . . . *stunned.* How did I miss all this?"

"It was on the news," said Tandy, trying to be helpful. "WBEZ."

Gabby's eyes sought out Carmela. "And just when were you going to tell me about this attack business?"

"Trust me," said Carmela. "I was gearing up for it."

"Tell me now," demanded Gabby. "Tell me everything."

"Uh-oh." Tandy's head swiveled like a submarine periscope. "Better hold off on that story for a couple minutes. Here comes the rest of the brigade."

Now Baby Fontaine and Byrle Coopersmith were clumping their way into the shop. Craft bags slung across their shoulders like pack animals, they were in a blind panic, as well.

"Poor Carmela!" said Byrle as she spotted her friend.

"We tried to call," wailed Baby, "but your phone just rang into oblivion."

Carmela winced. She should have left her phone plugged in so her friends could call. What had she been thinking? Then the memory of Shamus's angry words echoed inside her head, and Carmela knew she'd done the right thing. *Begone Shamus, you little devil.*

"Carmela's fine," said Tandy, immediately taking charge. "But someone did get killed!"

"You *knew* that poor woman?" Baby shrilled at Carmela.

"Knew *of* her," said Carmela. "Her name was Amber something. She modeled for Chadron, that local designer."

"I know Chadron rather well," said Baby in a strangled tone. "I bought several pieces from his spring collection."

Now all four women stared at Carmela with expectant faces, waiting for her to spill the complete story. So Carmela sat them all down at the big wooden table, each in her usual place, and proceeded to give them a blow-by-blow account of last night's tragedy. When she was finished, they pummeled her with a multitude of questions. But Carmela really couldn't provide many answers.

"So Ava still has this Giovanni character working in her shop?" asked Gabby.

Carmela nodded.

"And he's really as good-looking as you say?" asked Baby. "But in a sort of dangerous way?"

That question merited a shrug from Carmela. She hadn't realized she'd played up Giovanni's good looks so much.

But Tandy was extremely skeptical. "How do you *really* know this Giovanni person isn't the killer?"

"Because I'm pretty sure he frightened the real killer away," said Carmela.

Tandy shivered. "You *think* he did. I say Ava's plum crazy to keep that guy on."

"I agree," murmured Gabby. "And I'm glad I wasn't here by myself when he showed up this morning. I would have been scared out of my mind!"

"But you wouldn't have known anything about him," Carmela pointed out.

"Still," argued Gabby, grabbing a jar of paint and unscrewing the lid, "I'm sure I would have had a bad *feeling*."

Once Carmela's friends had finally quieted down, she slipped back into her office to make a call.

Ava answered on the first ring. "Juju Voodoo, if it's tragic or magic, you'll find it at Juju. Unless you're a scummy reporter."

"Love the way you answer the phone," said Carmela. "Highly imaginative."

"We aim to please," said Ava. "And, *cher,* you smart trick, you were so right! There was a huge gaggle of customers waiting on my doorstep this morning. And the phone hasn't stopped ringing. Our charms and amulets are selling like crazy, and the skulls — those beautiful, crazy skulls — are completely sold out! Plus my hand-made masks seem to be a huge hit as well. Ooh, hold the phone a sec, will you?"

There was a *clunk* as Ava set down the phone, then Carmela could hear her friend's voice. *"Miguel, those skeletons are meant to dangle from the ceiling; don't just drape them on the shelf. They have to look more lively, for heaven's sake. Well . . . not exactly alive . . . but you know what I mean."*

"I'm back, *cher,*" said Ava.

"I take it Giovanni showed up?"

"He's doing a reading even as we speak." Ava sounded delighted. Beyond delighted, in fact.

"He was terrified you wouldn't want him back."

"That's what he told me. And you were so sweet to talk to him this morning, to reassure him." Ava dropped her voice to a loud whisper. "Carmela, darlin', I think Giovanni's gonna be one of my biggest draws!"

"Go figure," said Carmela.

"People are *fascinated* with him. I don't know what it is, but . . ."

"Did he tell you about his brother Santino?"

"No. I don't . . . oops, gotta run. The TV people just showed up."

"Not Kimber Breeze, I hope!" said Carmela, horrified.

"Nope," said Ava. "Different station. WJ somethin' somethin'. They called earlier, asking if we'd let 'em do a live remote. Don't ya love it?"

Carmela would have. If only a young woman's blood hadn't been spilled last night.

Midmorning, and the women at Memory Mine had definitely settled down. Tandy was working on a Hansel and Gretel paper theater, Byrle was doing a scrapbook page on her grandchildren, and Baby was stringing faux pearls on thin wires, creating elegant cobwebs for her Saturday night Halloween party.

When the delivery boy from Creole Coffee came chugging in with their take-out order of hot, steaming chicory coffee, Baby pulled a white bakery bag from her giant Gucci tote. "Got some cookies here," she announced. Opening the sack, she pulled out a sugar cookie in the shape of a black cat. Covered with black squiggly frosting, it sported large orange eyes.

"Yum," said Tandy, digging into the sack. Her cookie was a white ghost with raisin eyes and black licorice mouth. "Halloween is gettin' to be more popular than Christmas."

Byrle grabbed the bag and pulled out a witch cutting across a crescent moon on her broom. "Who takes the time to make these?" she marveled. "So elaborate. They must take forever to decorate."

"I bet a scrapbooker makes them," said Tandy. "Good attention to detail, lots of creative tricks." She passed the bag to Gabby, who shook her head and passed it on to Carmela.

Carmela accepted the bag and reached in. A werewolf cookie emerged. The black eyes, brown furry face, and white fangs seemed to leap out at her. Something pinged inside her brain. She jiggled a foot, hunched her shoulders. She remembered the awful feeling last night, when she'd been struck hard from behind and shoved down. She thought about what Lieutenant Babcock had said about bite marks and strange hairs. And the tiny hairs on the back of her own neck rose in fear.

"Your cookie okay, honey?" asked Baby, glancing up.

Carmela stuck it in her mouth and bit down before the werewolf could bite her.

Carmela was standing behind the front counter, setting up a display of embossing powder, when she recognized a familiar form strutting across Governor Nicholls Street, making a beeline for her front door.

She slipped around the counter and turned the latch. *Way too many visitors today,* she thought to herself.

Shamus's face loomed in the window. Handsome, with flashing brown eyes, he was the proud possessor of a lazy yet devastating smile. But today his tall, athletic body seemed contorted by anger.

"Carmela, I want to talk to you," he shouted through the glass.

Carmela touched her index finger to her lips and shook her head.

He batted at the door. "C'mon, babe, open up."

"Forget it," she called back. "I don't want to talk to you. Besides, you're not talking, you're shouting."

Shamus's fists hammered against the front door, and the entire storefront seemed to shiver and shake.

Carmela could feel her face redden. She knew everyone was watching her, could feel their eyes on the back of her head. She was embarrassed by Shamus's bad behavior. Always had been, even though *he* was the one who ought to be embarrassed.

Holding up a hand to try to calm him, Carmela unlatched the door and slipped outside. Warm air greeted her. It had turned into a glorious day. Brilliant sun streamed down, the mercury had climbed to almost seventy degrees. A slight breeze riffled the potted palms and green awnings of Glisande's Courtyard Restaurant across the way.

It was too bad Shamus had to show up and ruin everything.

"What the hell's going on?" demanded

Shamus. "Why did you hang up on me last night? And why are you involved in some fashion model's murder?"

"I'm only peripherally involved," began Carmela, but Shamus didn't give her much chance to finish.

"Why on earth was your face on that awful news program? Meechums don't appear on the news. It's considered vulgar."

Vulgar, thought Carmela. This coming from a man who used to brag about spitting beer from the roof of his frat house. And who, she was pretty sure, had cheated on her more than once.

"Shamus," said Carmela, trying to be reasonable, "it's too early to have a knock-down, drag-out fight. And why on earth are you acting so wacko? Did you just down a twelve-pack of Hostess Twinkies or something? Are you on some sort of sugar high?"

"I want an explanation!" continued Shamus. Veins stood out around his temples, and Carmela could see them pulsate with each beat of his heart. "In fact, I *demand* an explanation!"

"Goody for you," said Carmela. "But listen to me, please. I only said a couple of words to that female reporter. And since the police wouldn't let her near the murder scene, she had to report something."

"They showed a freaking body bag," shrilled Shamus. "And the most grizzly close-up of a busted-up skull! It was enough to give me nightmares!"

"Oh," said Carmela. "I meant to tell you about that. You know those skulls you wanted for your Halloween floats?"

"Wait a minute," cried Shamus. Are you trying to tell me that was one of *my* skulls? Are you serious? Where are the rest of them?"

Carmela stared at him. "I have no idea. Probably picked up as souvenirs by morbid gawkers."

"But I *paid* for those skulls!" complained Shamus.

"Shamus, get over it. They were just cheap ceramic things from Ava's shop. Probably . . . probably the police tossed 'em in a box for evidence or something. I don't know."

"Can I get 'em back?" asked Shamus. "We need them for the float. And they better not be all cracked and broken."

"I'm sure they're just fine," said Carmela. "They're very hardheaded."

"Don't try to make this into some kind of joke," huffed Shamus.

"Then don't get your underwear in such a twist," Carmela shot back.

"I just *hate* the idea that you were right there when that model was murdered!" said Shamus. "And that the suspect is actually one of Ava's employees! Please tell me he's not still working there."

Carmela shifted from one foot to the other. "Well . . . he's not really a suspect anymore."

Shamus stared at her with burning eyes. "I forbid you to have anything to do with Ava! Or her employees!"

Carmela's composure suddenly evaporated. "You *forbid* me? I don't *think* so, Shamus!" White-hot anger exploded inside her head. "Besides, we're getting divorced. Remember?"

"Damn it!" said Shamus. He kicked the front door, causing it to rattle noisily.

"Stop it," commanded Carmela. Out of the corner of her eye she suddenly caught movement as a white van zoomed round the corner. As it sped toward them, Carmela recognized it as a news van. The satellite dish fixed to its roof, the WBEZ call letters emblazoned across the hood.

Carmela reached out and put a hand on Shamus's shoulder. "Don't," she warned. She wanted to tell him to ease off, to not make a fool of himself. But she couldn't seem to get the words out fast enough, and the white van had already squealed to a halt and Kimber Breeze was jumping out like a paratrooper, microphone in hand. Kimber's hips swayed confidently; her golden mane of hair made her look like a lion stalking its prey. Her linebacker cameraman, Harvey, followed hot on her heels.

"Shamus," began Carmela. "That news . . ." But she still wasn't spitting it out quick enough. Shamus kicked her door again, causing it to vibrate like mad. Then, slowly, a spiderweb of cracks began to radiate out from the point of impact.

"You got that?" Kimber Breeze asked her cameraman.

"Oh yeah," said Harvey. His eye was pressed against the eyepiece; the camera lens was aimed squarely at Shamus's offending foot.

"Damn, I think I might have broken my toe!" cried out Shamus.

"Serves you right," admonished Carmela.

"Thank you, Lord, for such glorious theater!" intoned Kimber Breeze. Then she jammed her microphone directly in Shamus's face. "Shamus Meechum, I have a few questions for you."

Shamus glared murderously at Kimber, both anger and pain reflecting in his eyes. Then he held up a hand to cover his face.

"No comment," he mumbled.

No comment? thought Carmela. *This is the first time Shamus hasn't wanted to open his mouth to spew forth his expert opinion.*

"You're here to check on your ex-wife's safety?" asked Kimber.

"She's not my ex-wife," snapped Shamus.

"We're still married," said Carmela. Even as the words burbled out of her mouth, she wondered why she said them. Why she felt the need to clarify their marital status. Especially when their divorce was definitely in the works. Especially when she'd just tossed that fact in Shamus's face.

"You must be terribly concerned about the attack last night," continued Kimber. "Do you think it was because of your Crescent City Bank connection? Will you consider hiring private security to guard your wife?" She fired questions with machine gun precision.

Shamus glared at Carmela. "You did this on purpose."

Carmela threw up her hands, acknowledging their ridiculous situation.

"I'll talk to you later," Shamus snarled at Carmela. Then he spun on his heel as best he could and limped off down the street with as much dignity as he could muster.

Gee, I wonder if his toe really is broken?

wondered Carmela.

Kimber stalked Shamus for a few steps, then paused. She turned in midstride and, like a shark smelling blood, headed back toward Carmela.

Seeing Kimber coming at her, Carmela jumped back and immediately bumped into Gabby and Tandy, who had come to inspect the damage to the front door. "Get back, get back," she warned her friends.

The women scrambled back while Carmela stood her ground.

Kimber grinned and continued her report. "Carmela Bertrand, proprietor of Memory Mine scrapbook store, was violently attacked last night. Carmela, what can you tell us about those harrowing moments? And what do you remember about your alleged attacker?"

Carmela faced the camera. "Sorry, but the police asked me not to say anything that could jeopardize their investigation."

"Ms. Bertrand, can you comment on the extent of your injuries?" Kimber's voice sounded concerned, but her eyes buzzed over Carmela like a mosquito searching for blood.

Just a little wounded pride as of today, thought Carmela.

"No comment," responded Carmela.

Kimber's voice rose. "The public has a right to know what's going on in this neighborhood," she pressed. "If anyone else is hurt or murdered, their blood will be on *your* hands."

Carmela stared at Kimber. She looked like an imperious Disney villainess. Wide-eyed, hair flowing like fire, voice menacing as she wielded her microphone like a scepter. In fact, Carmela could almost hear Kimber shouting, "Off with her head!"

CHAPTER 6

"What do you think?" asked Gabby, proudly holding up the sign she'd been laboring over for the past hour. *No Cameras or Microphones Allowed in This Store* was embossed in large gold letters on dark green chipboard.

"You should also specify *reporters,*" said Tandy as she looked up from her project. She was the only one left at the back table. Baby and Byrle had taken off just before lunch.

"I like it," said Carmela. "I'm not sure it's going to slow down Kimber Breeze, but I do like it."

"Honey," said Tandy, holding out half a sandwich. "You should eat something." They'd sent out for sandwiches and salads earlier, but Carmela just wasn't hungry. She was still feeling jittery from everything that had gone on.

"Your little theater looks great," said

Gabby. She'd just hung her sign in the front window and was now inspecting Carmela's *Theatre de la Vampyr.* "Very moody and spooky."

"It still needs something," said Carmela, studying it with an appraising eye. "I haven't quite captured the decayed, decadent look I was hoping for."

"Looks good to me," said Gabby. "Although I can't say I know anything about authentic vampire theaters. If there even are such things."

"Are you kidding?" Tandy's voice floated at them from the back of the store, rising in a squawk. "This is New Orleans. There's gotta be something like that here. Lord knows, we've got everything else."

The bell over the front door tinkled, and two women came rushing in. "We finally found you!" exclaimed one. "We've been walking all over the French Quarter, and we finally located your store."

"Are you visiting from out of town?" asked Gabby.

"Tulsa," said the other woman. "And we need *lots* of supplies. And some really interesting paper if you've got it."

Gabby grinned. "We can sure help you there. Right now we've got tons of new vellums and an assortment of hand-made, screen-printed papers that are to die for."

"Don't forget to show them that new Contem-Pro line with the distressed finishes," said Carmela as she reached to grab the phone that had just started ringing. Suddenly, they were busy again! Feast or famine, as always.

But it was Ava, not an inquisitive customer.

"Edgar Babcock just showed up here and is nosing around," she said without preamble.

"What's he want?" asked Carmela.

"Begging me to have dinner with him tonight at Galatoire's."

"Get out!" said Carmela. "Come on, what's he really doing?"

"Browbeating Giovanni."

"Seriously? Listen," said Carmela. "I didn't get a chance to tell you before, but Giovanni's brother used to *date* Amber."

"What!" Ava's voice was so piercing Carmela had to hold the phone away from her ear. "Are you kidding me?"

"I'm dead serious," said Carmela, instantly wishing she hadn't used that particular phrase.

"Well, that's not so good," said Ava. "I sure wish Giovanni would have told me about this brother of his." For the first time, she seemed to have doubts about Giovanni's veracity.

"Santino," filled in Carmela. "That's the brother's name. Apparently this Santino is a performer with the Cirque de Bella Luna, so he may already have a good alibi for last night."

"Great," said Ava, sounding glum. "Just a minute, *cher* . . . Hey, you be careful there. Those masks are utterly priceless! Well, actually they're priced at thirty-five ninety-nine, if you want to buy one."

"What's going on now?" asked Carmela.

"Babcock's got this ragtag CSI crew combing through my shop, and this idiot just tried to take a snip off one of my masks."

"Did he say what they were looking for?" asked Carmela.

"Some sort of evidence, I guess," said Ava. "I heard one little nerd mumble something about hair and fibers."

"Have they found any?" asked Carmela. *That's what Edgar Babcock said to me earlier,* thought Carmela. *Something about strange hairs.*

Ava snorted. "Tell me you're not serious. This place is a walking hair and fiber gallery. I've got shrunken heads with horsehair, some amulets with goat hair, drums made

91

out of some kind of South American lizard. You could train entire classes of zoologists or would-be CSI detectives here. Oh crap, now Babcock's heading back toward me. He must be finished talking to Giovanni. What should I *do?*"

"Use your considerable arsenal of feminine charm to confuse and confound him until we can figure things out," advised Carmela. "In other words, flirt."

"I think he's more interested in *you,* cupcake," breathed Ava. " 'Cause he's sure been asking lots of questions."

"He always asks questions," said Carmela. "Too many for his own good."

"Listen," said Ava. "Get over here soon as you can, okay? We need to put our heads together on this thing."

Carmela sighed. "On my way."

"Head line, life line, heart line," said Giovanni. The tip of his index finger traced the various lines that intersected Carmela's palm. "This one is really quite interesting."

"Which one?" asked Carmela.

"The heart line."

"Is there a problem?" she asked skeptically. "Am I destined for a quadruple bypass or something?"

"No," said Giovanni slowly. "You see how

the line is quite long and curves upward?"

Carmela gazed at her palm, as Giovanni's finger traced again, tickling her ever so slightly.

"That means you're a warm, some might say romantic, person. With a very giving nature."

"Uh-huh," responded Carmela. This guy was just full of it, wasn't he?

"But you see these little lines just below the base of your little finger?" asked Giovanni. "More than one line is indicative of more than one marriage."

"I could have told you that," said Ava, standing at the door of the reading room. "Carmela's moving on, right?" She sat down at the little table and gazed across at her friend.

"Right," agreed Carmela, even though she was secretly dying to hear more.

But now Ava was all business. "Giovanni, darling," she said, "it would have been nice if you'd mentioned your brother, Santino, to me earlier."

"I mentioned it to Carmela," he said.

"But you didn't tell *me*," she said.

"Look," said Giovanni, "Santino used to *date* Amber. But he didn't murder her!"

"How do we know that?" asked Ava. She stared at Giovanni with hard, slightly suspicious eyes.

"We just *do*," said Giovanni. "Santino's not like that. He's not a killer. I'd pledge my life on it."

Ava slumped in her chair. "Cripes, what a mess," she said.

Now Carmela turned her full attention to Giovanni. "How well did you know Amber?" she asked.

"Not very well," said Giovanni.

"And why were you trying to catch up with her last night?" asked Carmela. "In the alley?"

"I told you before; I just wanted to talk to her."

"Nice try," said Carmela, annoyed at the way Giovanni always seemed to give half answers to important questions. "What were you going to talk to her *about?*"

Giovanni stared at the wooden table for a few moments. "A couple things."

"Like what?" pushed Carmela.

"She was unhappy about her tarot reading."

"Why?" asked Ava.

"It was very jumbled," said Giovanni. "Something about cross-purposes and mismanaged finances. I had trouble making sense of it."

"Come on now," said Ava. "This is *me*

you're talking to. I make my living from this stuff. And, as far as I'm concerned, tarot readings are like telephone astrology or Internet biorhythms. For entertainment purposes only."

"But there's often an underlying message," said Giovanni.

"You ever play poker, Giovanni?" asked Carmela.

He frowned. "Huh?"

"A poker chip was found on the ground next to Amber. You know anything about that? You're pretty good with cards, after all."

"*Tarot* cards," said Giovanni.

"Still," said Carmela, "they're cards. Suits of cards."

"Does Santino play poker?" asked Ava.

"Not that I know of," said Giovanni. He tried to look earnest, mostly looked nervous.

"What else did you want to talk to Amber about?" asked Carmela.

"Santino asked me to talk to her," said Giovanni.

"He wanted you to intercede for him?" asked Carmela. "You mean like a Cyrano de Bergerac–type scenario?"

"But without the big nose?" said Ava.

Giovanni nodded. "Sort of."

"So Santino was still in love with Amber,"

said Ava.

Giovanni nodded again. "Very much. I have to tell you . . . when I broke the news to him this morning, he was utterly devastated."

"You called him at home?" asked Carmela.

"On his cell phone," said Giovanni. "He's still on the road with the circus."

Carmela thought for a moment. "So you sort of arranged to have Amber here last night?"

Now Giovanni looked downright sheepish. "I sent one of the invitations to Moda Chadron, where she was working."

"You stole one of my invitations?" screeched Ava.

"Not exactly," responded Giovanni. "Gordon van Hees was already on your list. I just sort of readdressed the invitation so everyone from Moda Chadron was invited."

Ava tapped her long, polished nails against the table. "Interesting." She stared at Giovanni, then switched her gaze to Carmela. "So where does that leave us?"

"Here's the thing of it," said Carmela. "Edgar Babcock is heading this murder investigation, which means he's not about to leave any of us alone." She pointed a finger at Giovanni. "Babcock is going to be on your case night and day because you're still his prime suspect."

"Until we tell him about Santino," said Ava.

"But Santino's innocent," protested Giovanni. "*I'm* innocent."

And Babcock's going to keep hounding me for details," said Carmela. "Because I had the unfortunate luck to actually be at the scene of the crime."

"Even though you didn't really see anything," said Ava.

"Doesn't matter," said Carmela. She gazed at Ava. "You're going to stay embroiled in this, too."

"I know," sighed Ava. "And it's starting to get old fast. So the thing is, what do we do now?"

"I think we should try to do a little investigating of our own," said Carmela.

Giovanni rocked back in his chair, lifting the two front legs up off the pegged wood floor. "You're kidding," he said. He turned to Ava. "She's kidding, right?"

Ava shook her head. "Carmela's completely serious. I've seen her this way before."

"Flummoxed?" said Carmela. "Whipsawed by indecision?"

"No, honey," protested Ava. "I really like

97

what you're proposing here. The thing of it is, you're real good at figuring things out."

"So you *are* going to help me," said Giovanni. "And Santino, too."

"I don't know how helpful we'll be in producing an outcome," said Carmela. *Or a verdict of innocence,* she thought to herself. "But we'll snoop around. See what we can find out."

Ava shook her finger in front of Giovanni's nose. "And that means you better start coming clean with us," she warned. "No more holding back information!"

"I still have my job here?" he asked in a tentative voice.

"Only because I want to keep an eye on you, buster," said Ava. "Now why don't you hustle yourself up to the front of the store and help unpack those new feng shui wheels that just came in!"

"Okay," said Giovanni, getting up from the table and backing tentatively out of the room. "And thank you, thank you for believing me."

"Enough," said Ava. She reached over and pulled the door closed, then shook her head.

"You might be taking a real chance, keeping him on," said Carmela.

"I might be," allowed Ava. Then she shrugged. "Aw, what the hell, I'm a risk taker from way back. So where do we start? *How* do we start?"

Carmela thought for a few seconds. "Do we know where Santino is right now?"

"I checked Cirque de Bella Luna's Web site just before you got here," said Ava. "They're playing up in St. Tammany Parish."

"Then that's where we start," said Carmela.

CHAPTER 7

Carmela caught sight of the circus tent even before she negotiated the turn off Highway 6. A giant golden pouf of nylon rose out of the dark pine forest like some kind of bizarre spaceship. Lights shining inside gave it a golden tinge, like an enormous puff of meringue that had been quickly toasted under a broiler.

Bumping down a narrow lane, it seemed incongruous that there'd even be a circus out here. But when they rounded a grove of trees, the land widened out to reveal a parking lot filled with cars, the large main tent, and a small caravan of silver Airstream trailers.

"Kind of spooky out here," said Ava as she stepped from the car.

Indeed, the air was cool, and faint night sounds carried on the breeze: the low hoot of an owl, small animals skittering in the nearby forest.

"But setting up out here does lend the feel of a traveling European circus," said Carmela. "Like a caravan of gypsies encamped on the edge of the Black Forest."

Once inside the tent, the women were pleasantly surprised. Seating was on plush red velvet theater-type chairs. And the place was small enough so that everyone had a good view; no nosebleed seats here.

Vendors brought around steaming cups of coffee, hot cinnamon doughnuts, and traditional Louisiana bourbon balls.

And once the circus started, with the strutting ringmaster, his capering assistant, and the small but well-rehearsed brass orchestra, the evening seemed magical.

A troupe of Chinese acrobats were dazzling in their red spangled tights as they seemed to defy gravity. Hurtling upward toward the overhead lights, they seemed to twirl and tumble forever. Then, like agile cats, the acrobats landed on the shoulders of their compatriots.

"I wish the stud muffin was here to see this," chortled Ava. The stud muffin was Ryder Bowman, Ava's sort-of boyfriend and the millionaire owner of Shipco International.

"Where is he again?" asked Carmela.

"Peru," said Ava. "Lima, Peru. Negotiating some kind of shipping contract with a fruit company. Oh, speaking of fruit . . ."

A juggler had entered the main ring and was artfully juggling a watermelon, an orange, and a grapefruit. After he amused the crowd with his antics, he pulled out a gleaming saber and showed off his swordsmanship.

"A juggling act that turns into a fruit salad," laughed Ava. "That's pretty neat. You know, I haven't been to a circus since I was a kid. And then it was a fairly standard circus with trapeze artists and guys getting shot from cannons, and clowns and all."

"Clowns," said Carmela. "I'm not a big fan of clowns."

"Nobody is," said Ava. "Remember that creepy movie we watched on the Friday night *Creature Feature* where the wacky, possessed clown had razor-sharp teeth?"

"Please," said Carmela. "Don't remind me. I had nightmares for an entire week."

"But don't you love being scared, too?" asked Ava. "Just a teensy weensy bit?"

"Maybe," said Carmela, reaching for her program. "When I know who's doing the scaring. Say, when does Santino come on, anyway?"

"Dunno," said Ava. "What's he do, anyway? Trapeze act or something?" She'd just purchased a huge bucket of kettle popcorn, what she'd laughingly referred to as the bimbo bucket, and the two of them were munching it down like crazy.

"Probably," said Carmela, settling back in her seat to watch.

Then the lights gradually dimmed until the ringmaster stood in the center, a single bright spotlight highlighting him.

"Ladies and gentlemen," he began. "Your attention please. We request that everyone remain seated during this next presentation." The ringmaster took off his top hat and walked to the edge of the ring, pointing it at the crowd. "No talking, no unnecessary movements. Please just remain in your seats and stay as still as possible."

"What's goin' on?" whispered Ava.

Carmela shook her head. "Some kind of magic act, maybe?"

Just as Carmela uttered those words, the spotlight and overhead lights blinked out completely, and the entire tent was plunged into total darkness. From across the ring, a woman gave an excited little shriek, and others around them laughed nervously.

"And now," called the ringmaster's disembodied voice, "I bring you Santino Stavrach, king of the canids."

"It's him," exclaimed Ava. "Santino's on now."

"Shh," said Carmela, wondering why the ringmaster had been so adamant about the crowd remaining silent.

Slowly, almost imperceptibly, two small blue spotlights began playing on the ring, and the orchestra struck the opening chords of a lighthearted theme by Prokofiev.

"What's going on?" asked Ava. All around them were whispers and expectant rustles. They weren't the only ones who were curious about what was up next.

And then, as the blue spotlights continued to flutter around the ring, small flashes could also be seen. It was, Carmela thought, almost as though a trained team of fireflies had come out and were circling the ring in a low-flying pattern.

A hush swept the crowd now.

"What are those little flashes?" asked Ava as the footlights that circled the ring began to glow.

Carmela stared, not quite believing what she was seeing. As more lights came on to illuminate the ring, they slowly revealed a pack of furry animals circling within it. *Those are eyes, not fireflies,* she told herself.

And then, as the music built, a key light

was thrown on a man that now stood in the center of the ring. Dressed in black leather riding boots, black slacks, and a red silk shirt, he posed with his arms open wide.

"What kind of dogs are those, anyway?" asked Ava, peering down. "They seem so well-trained, chasing each other around like that."

"They're not dogs at all," said Carmela, her eyes fixed on the blazing eyes, chiseled snouts, and luxurious tails of the lithe, sinuous creatures that circled the ring. "They're wolves!"

"You want a cup of this black bean soup?" asked Carmela. They were back at her apartment, digesting what they'd just seen, planning to digest some real food. The circus fare they'd partaken of earlier just hadn't done it.

"Love some soup," said Ava. She was sitting at the dining table, flipping through one of her favorite tabloids.

Carmela pulled open the freezer door and scanned the contents. There were frozen chicken necks for the dogs, a frozen piece of king cake that had to be at least eight months old and could probably be passed off as permafrost. *Ah, here they are.* "And maybe a sour cream muffin, too?" she asked.

"Bring it on," said Ava. "I'm starvin' to death."

"You downed an entire bucket of kettle corn," Carmela told her.

Ava flapped a hand. "No nutrition. If a food doesn't have nutrition in it, my body doesn't accept it as food."

Carmela stared at Ava as she heated up the soup. "How does that work?" she asked. "Share your secret of eating food but not paying the price."

Ava yawned. "Has to do with my metabolism, I think. And my proprietary digestive system. Kind of complicated. I could actually be a medical miracle." Ava continued to flip through her tabloid. "Hey, you have to take a look at some of these candid photos that are in here. They oughta call this the cellulite issue. Julia, Pam, Jennifer . . . put them in a revealing bathing suit, and most of these stars don't look any better than we do!"

"That's heartening," said Carmela.

She spooned bean soup into bright green ceramic bowls, topped each serving with a dollop of shredded cheese, then placed the bowls in the center of bright yellow plates. Those went onto a giant wicker tray. And once the microwave *dinged* and the sour cream muffins were properly defrosted and warmed, she carried everything to the table.

"Did you make these muffins, or did your momma bring 'em by?" asked Ava, slathering on butter and taking an enormous bite.

"My momma did," said Carmela. "But I've got the recipe, and I promised myself I'm gonna learn to make them, too."

"Good," said Ava. She broke off a couple bits, slipped the pieces to Boo and Poobah under the table. " 'Cause these are really wonderful."

They continued to spoon up their hot soup, enjoying it immensely.

"So what do you think?" asked Ava, finally.

"About the wolves?" said Carmela. They had talked about the wolves on the ride back to New Orleans. The fact that Edgar Babcock's forensic people had found strange hairs on Amber had been a major concern. That and the fact that Carmela had *thought* she'd heard a kind of growl last night.

"What I think is, we're going to have to tell Detective Babcock," said Carmela.

Ava nodded. "I was afraid you were going to say something like that."

"Santino could be guilty," said Carmela. "Or have served as some kind of accomplice."

This time Ava sighed. "Maybe so, although

it doesn't feel completely right."

"Murder never feels right," said Carmela.

"What about Giovanni?" asked Ava. "You think he still bears watching?"

"Yes, I do. Your boy, Giovanni, has a tricky way of dodging certain questions."

"So I've noticed," said Ava. "You think it's from six hundred years of persecution as a Romanian?"

"No, I think it's because he doesn't like answering questions," said Carmela. "And that white dove thing still freaks me out."

"He had one of those little plastic dog carriers full of them," said Ava. "So one could have fluttered away."

"Point taken," said Carmela. She stood up, grabbed the remote, and clicked on the television set. "I want to see if Shamus made the news."

"Oh, the door-kicking incident you told me about," said Ava. "Yeah, that'd be a hoot if they showed that footage. Serve him right."

They half-watched the news as the anchorman chattered about Hurricane Katrina rebuilding still going on, how the Tulane football team was faring, and the big plans for Wednesday night's Halloween Bash in the French Quarter.

Which seemed to segue neatly into a

special report by Kimber Breeze.

"Here she is," exclaimed Ava, pointing at the exploding graphics on the screen. "The old bat herself."

And then Kimber Breeze was babbling on about last night's murder in the French Quarter and how the police weren't one bit closer to solving it.

"The victim, we have learned," said Kimber, "was Amber Lalique. Miss Lalique was a high-fashion model employed at the Moda Chadron atelier. Earlier today we tried to interview Ms. Carmela Bertrand-Meechum, the other woman who was attacked, but she refused to speak with us."

"Here we go again," said Carmela.

"We also spoke briefly with her husband, Shamus Meechum, of the Crescent City Bank Meechums, and he expressed deep frustration that the police are not any closer to solving this heinous crime."

Accompanying Kimber's lies was footage of Shamus kicking Carmela's front door.

"Oh, Shamus is not gonna like that one little bit," said Carmela. "He's probably screaming at his lawyers already."

"Shamus looks older on camera," remarked Ava. "You be sure to tell him I said that."

"My pleasure," said Carmela, turning

back to watch this strange segment unfold.

"At this time," said Kimber Breeze, dropping her voice to a conspiratorial stage whisper as she stared directly into the camera, "police are telling us their best suspect so far is an unnamed employee at Juju Voodoo . . ."

"There's another ten grand in free advertising," mused Ava. Then she hesitated. "Although it's not so great for Giovanni."

"Ssh . . ." said Carmela. "I want to hear this.

Kimber's broadcast continued. "WBEZ has been fortunate to obtain confidential information from an investigator who was actually present at the crime scene . . ."

"Uh-oh," said Ava.

". . . And we have confirmed the fact that unusual fibers or perhaps hairs were found on or near the victim, possibly taking the investigation in an altogether different direction, indeed."

"Shit," said Carmela.

Now the camera moved in on Kimber, and she focused on conveying her most worried and perplexed look. "*Unusual* hairs," she repeated. "Not human and not typical of your common everyday dog, cat, or rodent." She paused. "With Halloween just around the corner, it would appear some unknown presence might be stalking the residents of New Orleans!"

CHAPTER 8

"Wolves," said Edgar Babcock, staring at Carmela in disbelief. "Wolves."

Carmela nodded. It was 9:00 a.m. Friday morning, and they were sitting under one of the green and white striped awnings of Café Du Monde. Carmela had chosen this as their meeting spot because it seemed like neutral territory. Not her office where Babcock could hunker down and stay forever, not police headquarters where he could browbeat her or bring in police reinforcements.

Then again, there was the chicory coffee and beignets to consider. That was a selling point for meeting here, too. Three to an order, nestled in a little cardboard container, there wasn't a tastier, sweeter, more lethal doughnut to be found. Beignets were, literally, tasty little gut bombs.

Carmela took a giant bite of a beignet, cognizant she'd just given herself a powdered sugar mustache.

"Wolves," Edgar Babcock muttered again.

Carmela nodded, shoving a trio of beignets across the table toward him. There was no reason she should gain ten pounds from eating here and Babcock should remain trim.

"This is truly bizarre," he said.

She smiled at him. "Welcome to my world."

"And you say this Santino Stavrach is the *brother* of the Giovanni character who works for Ava."

"The one you hauled in for questioning. The one you wanted to arrest."

"Maybe I should arrest them both," said Babcock.

"Have you got enough evidence to make it stick?" Carmela asked.

Babcock stared at her unhappily. "You watch too many cop shows on TV. That's the trouble these days. Too damn many people watching too damn many cop shows on TV."

"Don't forget the lawyer shows," said Carmela, taking another bite. "Those are the shows that teach us how little we really have to reveal to cops."

"I suppose I should be grateful you even told me about this," said Babcock. "That you didn't keep it under wraps."

"I thought about remaining quiet about Santino's existence," said Carmela. "Until I started checking a little more thoroughly. And found out about the wolves."

"Don't keep doing that," snapped Babcock. "Don't investigate on your own."

She ignored that last comment. "And, by the way, I *do* feel moderately guilty about getting Santino into hot water."

"Oh, he's in hot water all right," said Babcock harshly. "Along with Giovanni. Giovanni should have revealed all this information about his brother the very first time we talked to him."

Now that Carmela had Edgar Babcock somewhat allied on her side, she decided to discreetly push him a little for information.

"What's this thing about the weird hairs?" she asked.

Babcock snorted. "You watched Kimber Breeze's report last night." He leaned down, looking fairly dismayed, and brushed a layer of powdered sugar off one high-gloss wingtip.

"I really tuned in to see Shamus make an ass of himself," said Carmela. "And I'm happy to say I wasn't disappointed."

Babcock shook his head. "I've no idea how Kimber Breeze found out about those strange hairs we found at the scene."

"You didn't release that information to the press?" Now Carmela was brushing powdered sugar off her camel-colored sweater. And making a real mess of it.

"Of course not," said Babcock.

"You mentioned it to me."

Babcock nodded. "And I assumed complete confidentiality." He cocked an eye at her. "Which I got, right?"

"There has to be a leak in your department," replied Carmela.

Babcock nodded. "Obviously someone couldn't keep his mouth shut or else just ran to the TV station and yapped. I've heard rumors that Kimber's got paid spies but haven't been able to confirm anything." He popped a white plastic lid onto his coffee container, signaling he was about ready to leave.

"Really," said Carmela. She thought for a couple moments. "I suppose it's all about TV ratings, isn't it? The more people watch and are entertained, the higher the fees WBEZ can charge its advertisers. It all comes down to revenues."

Babcock cocked an eye at her. "Did you major in business or something?"

"Graphic design," said Carmela. "But for the last three years I've been getting my BF."

"Bachelor in fine arts?"

"Baptism by fire," said Carmela. "I've had to learn tax laws, dicker over building leases, deal with a shady vendor or two, do my own marketing, and try to make sure gross sales exceed overhead."

"And recover from a hurricane," said Babcock.

"And recover from a hurricane," agreed Carmela. "Although we all had to do that."

"How much help did you get from your husband?" asked Babcock.

"On the business? Nothing. Nothing at all."

"Glitter pumpkins," said Tandy, adjusting her bright red half glasses. "What on God's green earth are glitter pumpkins?"

Carmela had newspapers spread out on the craft table and had just sprayed three of the pumpkins a candy apple metallic red.

"It looks like a pretty start," allowed Tandy, "but I've no idea where you're going with this."

"It's not too tricky," explained Carmela. "I just took red metallic paint and spray-painted the pumpkins on top and about three-quarters of the way down. Now I'm going to take this gold glitter paint pen and draw some loops and swirls randomly around the circumference of each pumpkin." She took the pen, made a freestyle wave pattern around the midsection.

"I like that," declared Tandy. "Fun."

"Baby's planning to use these on her buffet table," explained Gabby. "As part of her centerpiece. Her party colors are red, gold, and orange."

"Do you know what her menu is?" asked Tandy. One penciled eyebrow rose in a questioning gesture.

"Funny you should mention that," said Carmela. "I just ran a sample menu sheet through the printer a little while ago."

"Ooh, let me look," said Tandy, reaching for the fluttering piece of paper that Gabby was handing her.

Carmela did another row of loops and swirls around the pumpkin, giving the plain-Jane vegetable a glitzy new look. "So . . . ?" she said. "What do you think of the menu?"

"Fantastic," enthused Tandy. "Chicken jambalaya, baked shrimp casserole, and Cajun meatloaf. Now isn't *that* interesting."

"Take a look at the desserts," urged Carmela. Desserts were something she had more than a nodding acquaintance with.

A grin spread across Tandy's thin face. "Pralines, Louisiana pear cake, and rice custard. To die for! Tell me Baby's not doing this all herself."

"She's using that new caterer, Dunbar & Deeds," said Gabby. "From over on Magazine Street."

"Looks like it's going to be one heck of a *fais do-do,*" said Tandy, using the Cajun phrase for *party.*

"Carmela," said Gabby, "Ava's on the phone.

From the look of urgency on Gabby's face, Carmela figured Ava must be upset.

"You okay?" she asked as she snatched the phone up in her office.

"They took Santino into custody," said Ava. "And his poor little wolves have been impounded."

Carmela drew a deep breath. "We knew this was going to happen," she said. *What other possible outcome could there have been?* she wondered. *Especially after my meeting with Babcock this morning.*

"Giovanni is absolutely hysterical," said Ava. "Says he's way too upset to do any readings. And to tell you the truth, I feel pretty crappy, too."

"I'm not thrilled about our decision either," said Carmela. *But what could I do? I had to tell Babcock, didn't I?*

"Listen, I had an idea," said Ava. "I'm supposed to meet with Gordon van Hees

118

over at Moda Chadron today? 'Cause I'm supposed to be doing the decorations for their Halloween Bash fashion show?"

"Yeah?" said Carmela, sensing the stirrings of a plan.

"Why don't you tag along with me? Maybe we could ask a few questions, find out a little more about Amber. We really don't know much about her, after all."

"And Giovanni hasn't exactly been forthcoming," said Carmela.

"So you want to come along?" asked Ava.

"Why not?" said Carmela.

CHAPTER 9

While Ava dashed upstairs for her meeting with Gordon, Carmela wandered through Moda Chadron, coveting the gorgeous haute couture pieces that were on display. First she fell in love with a petal-pleated pink organza dress. Then a plunging gown with a full, crinkly skirt caught her eye. Then she decided she just couldn't live without the asymmetrical-cut black dress, no matter what it cost.

Carmela plucked the price tag from where it was tucked inside the neckline and peered at it. Hmm. On the other hand, maybe she *could* live without the dress. It was sexy and scintillating, yes. But affordable? No. Not in the least. So maybe she'd have to satisfy her designer fix by shopping at The Latest Wrinkle, her favorite little resale shop over on trendy Magazine Street.

Now that Carmela had established that Moda Chadron's lofty prices were completely beyond her range unless she reconciled with Shamus and his money (and she'd sooner gnaw off her own foot than let that happen) she focused on the atelier itself. Housed in a magnificent brick building that had once been a warehouse, Moda Chadron projected an elegant, rarefied air. Chadron, the man behind the spectacular designs and the rehabbed building, had chosen soft dove gray as his key color. That subtle and soothing tone was carried throughout. In the whisper-soft carpeting, a grouping of upholstered brocade chairs, and the silk draperies that hung at the tall windows and ended in a little puddle on the floor.

Within the atelier itself were dozens of racks of clothes, antique cabinets filled with camisoles, scarves, and lingerie, and a scatter of marble pedestals that displayed humongous floral arrangements that lent a jungle effect. At the far end of the room, just to the left of the circular staircase, was a long, gleaming white desk where the sales associates congregated. Behind that were oversized fitting rooms. Soft music — Carmela was pretty sure it was Mozart — played on the stereo, and the front door opened constantly to let in well-heeled customers.

Some twenty minutes later, Ava came tripping down the carpeted staircase from the second-floor business office and design studio. She had Gordon van Hees firmly in tow.

"We meet again," said Gordon, extending an outstretched hand to Carmela. "Although so much has happened since." He gazed about Moda Chadron, let a tone of dismay creep into his voice. "Amber's death has put us all in a sad, contemplative mood."

"She seemed like a lovely girl," said Carmela.

Gordon nodded. "Amber was gifted with a natural talent for the runway, and she was smart. Just amazingly bright. She'd been a business major at Tulane, you know."

"I didn't know that," said Carmela.

Ava jumped in, trying to lift them all out of their suddenly somber moods. "I told Gordon that you've agreed to assist me with the decorating," she said, nudging Carmela.

This, of course, was news to Carmela. "I'd . . . uh . . . love to," said Carmela, slightly taken aback. *Do I even have time for this? I sure hope so!*

"Excellent, excellent," said Gordon. "We're looking for over-the-top spectacular, so don't be afraid to take chances. I'm a huge proponent of pushing the envelope.

Sometimes I even have to nudge Chadron a bit — play Pierre Bergé to his Yves Saint Laurent."

"Got it," said Carmela, looking around, wondering how on earth they were going to transfer this lovely shop into a venue with a spooky, over-the-top theme.

"And please, dear ladies," continued Gordon. "Do shop around. And if you should see a creation you simply can't live without, there's a chance I might be able to arrange a sizable discount."

"Really?" squealed Ava. "Then we better take a closer look. C'mon, Carmela."

They waved good-bye to Gordon.

"Sizable discount?" whispered Carmela. "I already know what I want. There's this black —"

"Honey," interrupted Ava, and she was practically drooling, "I want it all!"

While Ava tried on a blue silk dress with a tight, Renaissance-inspired bodice, Carmela happened to strike up a conversation with one of Chadron's regular models, a young woman by the name of Yasmin. It didn't take Carmela long to elicit a few details from her.

"So you knew Amber?" asked Carmela.

Yasmin nodded. Tall, impossibly skinny, she sported dark, close-cropped hair. The kind of haircut Ava always referred to as a "collaborator" cut. Referring, of course, to the French women who'd had their heads shaved at the end of World War II as punishment for fraternizing with Nazi officers.

Overhearing Carmela's questions, Ava came sashaying out of the dressing room to ask a few questions of her own. "Do you know if Amber was seeing anyone?" Ava asked Yasmin.

Yasmin shrugged as she considered the question. "There was this one guy by the name of Remy."

"Remy," said Ava, digesting the name. "He works here?"

Yasmin gave a disdainful laugh. "No way. But I know he's the manager at one of the nearby costume shops."

"The big one here in the French Quarter?" asked Carmela. "Or the one over in Faubourg Marigny?"

Yasmin shrugged. "Maybe . . . here in the Quarter? Why do you want to know?"

"We're just looking into things," said Ava. "A friend of ours is sort of implicated in Amber's death, and we're checking all the angles."

"Okay," said Yasmin, fingering the multiple layers of leather cords strung with tiny charms that hung around her thin neck.

"That's cool."

Carmela studied the girl. She figured Yasmin probably lived on Marlboro Lights and bottled water. And an occasional hunk of Bibb lettuce thrown in for dessert.

"So Amber was dating this guy Remy?" Carmela asked.

"I don't know if you'd call it *dating,* per se," said Yasmin. "She went to a party with him once or twice."

"At the costume shop?" asked Ava.

Yasmin frowned at them like they were idiots. "No, some big mansion in the Garden District. Some fat cat's place."

"That's a pretty nice part of town," said Carmela. "Did you ever tag along?"

Yasmin looked colossally bored with their questions. "Yeah, I guess. Maybe like once," she answered. "But those parties weren't exactly my scene."

"You remember exactly where this house was?" Carmela asked.

Yasmin brushed a minuscule piece of lint from her long, lean skirt. Carmela figured she was wearing one of Chadron's creations, a little piece of silk knit that sold for thousands.

Yasmin closed her eyes, leaned back against the wall, and thought for a moment. "Maybe on Iberville?" she said. "I know it was right near the cemetery."

Carmela figured that Yasmin had to mean St. Louis Cemeteries No. 1 and No. 2. She had no idea who resided on Iberville Street. But she knew someone who might know: Baby Fontaine. Baby knew everybody who was anybody in the Garden District.

Five minutes later, Ava had poured herself into a green strapless chiffon gown and was admiring herself in a three-way mirror, tossing her hair, doing graceful little pirouettes.

"That dress looks utterly spectacular on you," said an enthusiastic male voice. "Please tell me you're planning to buy it."

Both Ava and Carmela whirled around to find Chadron, the designer himself, smiling with admiration.

"Buy, no," said Ava. "But I'm sure as heck going to try to *finance* it."

Chadron's smile turned slightly hesitant.

"Oh, hey," said Ava. "We're just kind of goofing around here. I'm Ava Grieux, and this is Carmela Bertrand. We're doing the decorating for your Halloween fashion show. I just had a meeting with your partner."

Chadron stared pointedly at Ava. "Oh my goodness," he said, putting a hand to his face in an old Jack Benny–type gesture. "Oh

126

course. You're that darling girl who runs the magic shop."

"Voodoo shop," corrected Carmela.

"Yes," said Chadron. "Of course. That was the night . . ." Chadron shook his head at the too-painful memory. He touched his fingers to the bridge of his nose, pinching it gently. "Such a terrible, terrible tragedy. We all loved Amber so much. She was such a beautiful, talented girl."

Now Chadron reached for Ava's hand in a sympathetic gesture. "We *do* know each other, don't we?" Chadron turned to gaze at Carmela. "And you're Ava's friend."

"Carmela," repeated Ava.

"Carmela," echoed Chadron. "And you do . . . what?"

"I own the scrapbook shop over on Governor Nicholls Street," said Carmela. "Memory Mine."

Chadron rolled his eyes. "Oh, for heaven's sake. Of course you do! That *darling* little shop with all the lovely, lovely paper and bits of fiber." Now he grabbed Carmela's hand and patted it. "Talented, talented," he told her.

"Losing Amber must be very hard on you," said Carmela. "And on your business."

"Simply awful," agreed Chadron. "She

was like *family.* Everyone who works here is like family."

"Do you know . . . have the police learned anything new?" asked Carmela. "Do they have any suspects yet?" She knew exactly who Lieutenant Edgar Babcock and his investigators viewed as suspects, but she wondered if Chadron knew as well.

Now Chadron looked even more saddened. "A detective has been over here several times, asking questions, looking around. But I must say, he's been incredibly tight-lipped when it comes to revealing who they view as suspects." Chadron shifted his gaze back to Ava. "Is that fellow still working for you?" he asked. "The first one they questioned?"

"You mean Giovanni?" said Ava. "Yes, he is. But we're positive he had nothing to do with it. He was actually a friend of Amber's."

"A friend," murmured Chadron. "Yes, I suppose Amber had lots of friends. Young people always do."

"We've been admiring your designs," said Carmela. Seeing Chadron's obvious distress, she decided to change the subject to something a little more neutral. "They're absolutely fantastic!"

Chadron crossed his arms and grimaced.

"You think so, really? Because I have these absolutely *crippling* bouts of self-doubt."

"We saw the article about you in the *Times-Picayune* a couple months ago," said Ava. "About taking your collection to New York."

"Those tents at Bryant Park!" exclaimed Chadron. "Such a madhouse. An absolute madhouse. And those crazy New York women. So skinny, must live on nothing but air."

"It must be thrilling to show your collection alongside major designers," said Carmela. "Plus you must garner tons of orders from New York's finest stores."

"Bergie's," Chadron stage whispered. "Bloomie's."

"Congratulations," enthused Carmela.

"Now if I can just get some local publicity for my little atelier," said Chadron, making an expansive gesture over his shoulder. "I'd love to bite off a piece of the local market, so to speak."

"Chadron," called one of his salesclerks. "We're ready for Mrs. Todman's fitting."

Chadron made a rueful face at Carmela and Ava. "I must be demented," he told them. "Trying to service my clients *and* committing to this runway show Halloween night. And all because the French Quarter

Merchants Association was fishing around for something new. I had to go and stick my dainty foot right in it."

"You can count on us to come up with some moody decor," said Ava.

"Thank you," said Chadron. "It's comforting to know there's *someone* I can count on." He hesitated for a moment, then peered at Ava with a speculative look. "I have to ask . . . have you ever done any modeling?"

"Who, me?" said Ava, clearly pleased. "Just swimsuits and evening gowns in beauty pageants. Of course, I was runner-up in the Miss Teen Sparkle Pageant and then festival queen at Pickled Watermelon Rind Days. In fact, I still have my tiaras."

"You're tall enough, thin enough," mused Chadron. He took a step back, giving her a serious appraisal. "Not as young as I usually prefer . . ."

"Watch it," said Ava. "I'm not *that* old."

"Yes," said Chadron, absently. "I do need two more models, and I think one of them could be you."

Ava rested a hand on her hip and struck a casual pose. More like a slouch, really. "You realize I'm just an amateur," she told him, obviously thrilled to be singled out.

"We'd have to do something about your

130

hair, of course," said Chadron.

Ava peered at him nervously. "What did you have in mind?"

Chadron pulled his face into a thoughtful grimace. "Tease it into a gigantic bird's nest, pile in strings of pearls and bunches of grapes, then spray it all silver."

Carmela winced. "Sounds pretty extreme."

"We're actually hoping for bizarre," agreed Chadron.

"Then I'll do it!" exclaimed Ava. "On one condition."

"What's that?" asked Chadron.

"Carmela models, too."

"What!" Carmela and Chadron exclaimed together.

"She's a natural," Ava pointed out. "Pretty, slender, *très* sophisticated."

But Chadron wasn't quite buying it as he gave Carmela a speculative look from head to toe.

"Plus Carmela knows lots of ladies who buy expensive clothing," added Ava.

"On the other hand," said Chadron, looking thoughtful, "you might be perfect after all. Tell me, dear, can you manage four-inch stilettos without clomping like a Clydesdale or breaking your pretty neck?"

"I think so," said Carmela, still not believing Chadron would seriously consider using her as a model. Models were really tall girls, and she was barely five six.

"Excellent," said Chadron. "Now, the real question is, can you get those lovely friends of yours to attend my runway show?"

"Probably," said Carmela.

Chadron waved both hands in a kind of benevolent fashion designer blessing. "Then it's settled," he pronounced. "Your fitting is Monday at 5:30 p.m."

CHAPTER 10

Grand Folly Costume Shop glowed like a theater marquee as overhead pinpoint spotlights bounced and reflected off racks of glitzy, glamorous costumes. Sequins, spangles, and gold lamé seemed to be the watchword. On shelves overhead, plastic, faceless heads showcased hats, wigs, tiaras, and crowns of every style and color. Amid all this faux splendor, the smell of mothballs, cigarettes, and cleaning fluid hung redolent in the air.

"You think this is a good idea?" asked Carmela. She wasn't sure they would be able to waltz right in and locate Remy.

"It's worth a try, *cher*," replied Ava. "Besides, we need costumes for Baby's party tomorrow night."

"I thought you were going to wear your Cleopatra costume," said Carmela. "The one with the little rubber asp sewn right into the bodice. And I had my Spider-

Woman thing all planned out."

Ava shrugged. "As far as I'm concerned, old Cleo's been there, done that. I say it's time for something new. And after trying on all those couture dresses at Moda Chadron, I'm definitely in the mood for something supersexy."

Carmela took in the hodgepodge of inventory. "If we can possibly find it," she said.

A young man stood at the counter, sorting through a pile of costumes. His black hair was pulled back into a ponytail that fell below his shoulders, and his nails were painted black to match. Ripped jeans, a sleeveless black AC/DC T-shirt, and a wide belt studded with silver completed his outfit. He looked up as Ava and Carmela moved toward him, looking around, fingering various costumes.

"Comment ça va?" he asked in a Cajun French accent. How's it going?

"We're here to find a costume," said Ava, flashing one of her dazzling, high-voltage smiles.

Unswayed, the man behind the counter just stared back at her.

Ava approached the counter and leaned forward. "So, how exactly does your system work?"

The man scratched his head and yawned.

"You look around, find what you want."

Ava was going to say more, but Carmela cut in. "Do you have any Venetian-style costumes? You know, Italian gilt robes and masks?"

"Beth!" the man yelled suddenly, startling Carmela and Ava.

A soft voice floated back, muffled, obviously coming from the rear of the store. "Remy, what do you want? I'm helping someone." Anger and frustration seemed to taint the girl's words.

"Costumes are all over the place, dressing rooms are in back," Remy told them. "You got questions, go back and ask Beth. She'll help." He reached over toward the cash register and picked up a pack of Marlboros. "I'll be back. *Excuse mon.*" And he left.

Carmela and Ava exchanged conspiratorial glances.

"That was him!" hissed Ava. "Can you believe Amber actually went out with him?"

"I can't believe *anyone* would go out with him," said Carmela. "He seems rude, crude, and . . ."

"Probably lewd," finished Ava. "So now what?"

"Look around, I guess," said Carmela. "Try to talk to him when he comes back."

"Maybe we should ask this Beth about

135

him?" said Ava.

"Excellent idea," said Carmela. Glancing around, she noticed that the costumes seemed to be arranged by category. Movie star, showgirl, monster, historical, and so on. Elbowing her way down one narrow aisle, she saw that Las Vegas showgirl outfits filled almost two full racks. Curious, she pulled out one of the outfits for a better look, then decided she could probably read her watch through the flimsy flesh-colored body suit. *Yikes, who wears this stuff?* she wondered.

The next section contained hangers with G-strings, sequined thongs, and some unusual fringed items that Carmela couldn't figure out *how* to put on. Maybe a puzzle master or a contortionist could solve the mystery, but her perceptual skills were starting to ache, just looking at them.

Carmela glanced up to see Ava racing toward her carrying a full-length gown. A feather boa fluttered over one shoulder.

"Look at the great costume I found!" Ava plucked at Carmela's sleeve, urging her toward the back of the store. "I just gotta try this on!" she whispered excitedly.

Beth, a tired-looking young woman with pale skin and bright pink hair, was stacking boxes at the back of the store. "You want to try that on," she said to Ava, more a statement than a question.

"Love to," said Ava. She turned to Carmela. "And Carmela, I expect you to try something as well."

"Carmela?" came a sudden, screeching voice from behind a dressing room door. "Carmela?"

Carmela and Ava stared at each other in horror.

"Is there a parrot in here?" Ava asked Beth.

Her pink hair moved back and forth imperceptibly. "Nope."

"An escaped banshee, perhaps?" persisted Ava.

Beth squinted at her. "You mean like a ghostly presence?"

"I was thinking more in terms of ghastly," replied Ava.

There was a loud rustle, then a flimsy, slatted wooden door crashed open to reveal an enormous woman encased in a tight, spangled dress. Glowering at them with hard, dark eyes, the woman's hysterical voice shrieked, "Carmela? Carmela? What are *you* doing here?"

"Glory?" said Carmela, not quite believing her eyes. Glory Meechum was Shamus's older sister and the matriarch of the Meechum family. She was overprotective, over-bearing, and, tonight, quite bizarrely over-dressed. Usually clad in splotchy print dresses or boxy suits, this strange apparition of Glory in a Halloween costume seemed to throw Carmela for a loop.

Glory's hard eyes flitted across Carmela, openly conveying hostility and scorn. Glory had never liked Carmela, had never approved of her marriage to Shamus. A couple years ago, when Shamus had abandoned his bank job as well as his wife, Glory had taken it upon herself to personally toss Carmela out of Shamus's Garden District home. And she'd been gleeful in the process.

The moment of shocked silence was broken as Ava let loose a derisive hoot.

Quick as a cobra, Glory's eyes latched on to Ava. And then the costume she had in her arms. Glory wore, or was attempting to wear, the same Mae West costume.

"You said mine was a one-of-a-kind original," Glory snapped to Beth as the costume she wore bulged and strained at the seams.

Caught in what appeared to be rather soft middle ground, Beth gave an indifferent shrug. "It is." Beth's radar told her *something* was amiss; she just didn't quite comprehend the exact details.

"Then what's that costume in her arms?"

demanded Glory.

Beth gazed at the dress Ava was clutching. "Ma'am, that dress is in an entirely different size. Yours is the only one we have in your size."

Glory's face flamed red. "And what exactly do you mean to imply with *that* comment?"

"We only have a few costumes in your size," said Beth. "There just isn't much call for them."

Carmela figured the girl must have a death wish. Glory looked like she was working up to an incredible head of steam. And when she exploded . . . watch out!

Glory pointed a trembling finger at Ava. "I *forbid* you to try on that costume!" she thundered.

That was all Ava needed. "I'll try on anything I darn well please," she responded. Glory's hand tried to bat at Ava, but Ava was far too agile and promptly ducked into one of the fitting rooms.

Glory pounded on the door. "Get out here, missy! You hear me?"

Carmela watched this bizarre drama unfold around her. She wasn't sure what to do next. Support Ava? Ava seemed to be doing just fine on her own. Calm Glory? As if that would ever happen.

Like a willful five-year-old, Glory stomped her foot and retreated to her own dressing room.

Good, thought Carmela. *Problem solved.*

But of course it wasn't. Because not more than two minutes later, Glory came flying out, clutching her precious Mae West costume. She grabbed Beth, spun her around, and breathlessly asked, "How much for the gown if I buy it outright? And the other one, too?"

"Ma'am," said Beth, snapping her gum. "We only *rent* here. We don't sell."

Glory's eyes narrowed. "What if items are lost or damaged? Then what do you do?"

"We deal with that as it happens," Beth said slowly. Then she glared at Glory. "But you'd better not have any funny ideas about stealing. Or malicious destruction of property."

The front door opened, letting in a gush of fresh, cool air.

"Remy," said Beth. "Talk to this woman, will you? She wants to *buy* the Mae West costumes."

Remy slipped behind the counter, and Glory hustled toward him. "Are you the manager?" she asked, her voice rising to the point of belligerence.

Curious now, Carmela eased her way

between a row of Peking opera costumes and a clutch of cowboy costumes to see what was going on. As she pushed aside costumes to peek at Glory, her hand brushed against a leather vest trimmed in fur.

Fur, thought Carmela, suddenly. She wondered if this could be the source of the strands of hair found at the murder scene. Should she pluck a few hairs and turn them over to Edgar Babcock? Or just send him over here?

Carmela glanced around, suddenly noting that *lots* of costumes contained fur trim. There were Henry VIII costumes, Viking costumes, and even Wookie costumes. *Better just send him over here,* she finally decided, then crept toward the front desk to see what was going on with Glory.

In the end, Glory got her way. Sort of. She bought her costume at what Carmela hoped was a greatly inflated price and paced nervously while Remy hung the fabric on a padded hanger, then zipped a plastic bag around it.

As Glory flung the bag over one arm, she caught sight of Carmela watching her. "Carmela," she said, a nasal quality to her voice. "I'm only going to say this once. I don't want Shamus's name or our dear family's name mentioned on the news again. Do you hear me? I don't want your silly exploits to reflect on the Crescent City Bank."

"Then you must have loved last night's news, Glory," said Carmela. "That little segment of Shamus kicking my front door . . . shattering the glass. How's his poor toe by the way? Broken, I hope?"

Glory ignored Carmela's words as she continued her tirade. "Our family has honor as well as pride in this city, and I don't want you bringing shame to our family. The social circle my family belongs to understands how marrying the wrong sort can cause problems. But I'm sick of their pity when it comes to the likes of you."

As Glory slammed out the front door, she was aware of Remy staring at her.

"Who dat?" he asked. Curiosity flickered in his dark eyes. "She sure make the *misère*."

Carmela shrugged. "Sister-in-law. And, yes, she can cause trouble."

"Look like she got it in for you."

"Glory's got it in for a lot of people," said Ava as she came up behind Carmela. Then she squirted past her friend and spun around to show off her costume. Looking very much like a Hollywood goddess from the twenties, she purred, "Well, come up

142

and see me sometime." Hips swaying provocatively, she allowed one curvaceous leg to escape the slit that ran up the side of the dress.

"Marvelous," said Carmela. "You'll be the hit of the party."

"When I'm good, I'm good, but when I'm bad, I'm better," said Ava in a perfect Mae West imitation. She strode toward the counter, whipped her feather boa at Remy. "Hey, big boy, didn't I see you at my place the other night?"

He stared at her, a silly smile creeping across his face. "Huh?"

Ava dropped the accent. "Weren't you at Juju Voodoo the other night, Remy? Didn't you stop by my open house?"

"Not me," said Remy. His eyes continued to rove up and down Ava's exquisite form. "Sorry I missed it."

"We were positive we saw you walk in with the pierced and tattooed crowd," said Carmela.

Remy carefully arranged his face into a blank stare again. *"Non,"* he said.

" 'Cause your friend Amber was there," said Carmela. "Remember poor Amber?"

Remy's face darkened, his hands twitched nervously, and he suddenly focused on the twisted pile of clothes that sat on the counter. "My eye!" he spat out.

"What's this *my eye* business?" asked Ava, once they were outside the costume shop. "What the heck does that mean?"

"It's slang for *no way*," said Carmela. "But I'm definitely thinking *way*. Remy for sure knew Amber. We just have to figure out how well."

"And when he saw her last!" added Ava.

CHAPTER 11

Carmela sat at her computer, an eye on the front door, tippy-tapping out E-mails to her friends, inviting them all to attend Wednesday night's runway show at Moda Chadron.

Gabby had loaded all the decorated pumpkins into her Toyota Land Cruiser and was running some over to Baby's house, the rest to the French Quarter Merchants Association office. So Carmela was alone at Memory Mine, sending her E-mails, keeping an eye on Boo and Poobah, who had accompanied her to work this Saturday.

She hit a few more keys, glanced down at her list. *There, that's the end of it,* she thought. *Unless . . .* A wicked idea plucked at the cortex of Carmela's brain. *Unless I invite Glory, too. Should I? Could I? Am I really that nasty?*

The notion of Glory Meechum sitting in the audience while she and Ava sashayed down the runway wearing gorgeous haute couture creations almost made Carmela giddy. So she quickly typed in Glory's E-mail address at the bank, then hit Send.

There, it's done. Love it!

The front doorbell chimed as it opened. Boo and Poobah immediately rose to their feet, eager to rush out and greet their first visitor.

"Boo, Poobah," Carmela said in a cautionary tone. "What did we talk about earlier?"

The dogs gazed at her with worried expressions. *Talk?* They seemed to say. *We talked about something? Hmm, can't remember what that could've been.*

"You promised to be good dogs and stay in my office," Carmela reminded them. "On the rug."

Boo and Poobah looked a little sheepish now. It was all coming back to them.

Carmela watched as a woman wearing oversized sunglasses and a headscarf paused just inside the front door and glanced around. She looked sharply to make sure it wasn't Kimber Breeze come calling in some sort of disguise. But, no, this woman was shorter, stockier, and definitely a lot more timid.

"Welcome to Memory Mine," said Carmela, rising from her seat and walking toward the woman. "Can I help you find

146

something?"

"Excuse me," said the woman, staring intently at her now. "You don't know me, but I need to talk to you." Her words sounded slightly desperate, and her voice was hoarse. As the woman removed her sunglasses, Carmela could see that her eyes were rimmed in red and her face was blotchy, like she might have a bad head cold.

Before Carmela could say anything, the woman continued, "The police told me that you . . . you . . ." The woman paused and drew a deep breath. "That you were the one who found my daughter." Then her voice broke, and she was unable to continue.

Her daughter? thought Carmela. And then the image of poor Amber in her yellow silk halter top lying behind the Dumpster filled Carmela's mind. *Good lord, Amber was this woman's daughter?*

Carmela scurried forward to meet the poor woman. "Why don't we sit in my office and talk," she suggested, ushering her toward the back. "I'll fix you a nice cup of tea."

"You don't have to go to all that trouble," the woman sniffled. But she went along anyway.

Carmela guided her to a chair, shooing away Boo and Poobah, who were both extremely curious. "I think we could both use a cup," Carmela told her. She reached across her desk and retrieved a box of tissues, set it next to the woman.

A few minutes later they were both sipping away.

"You're . . . Carmela," said the woman. "I saw you on the news."

Carmela nodded. "Carmela Bertrand. I own Memory Mine. As you can see, my hobby has become an obsession, albeit a paying one."

"And you're probably wondering why I'm here," said the woman.

Carmela took another sip and nodded, although she had a pretty good idea. This was becoming Grand Central Station for the Amber Lalique murder investigation.

"Amber . . . my daughter . . ." But the woman burst into tears, unable to continue.

Carmela handed the woman a tissue. *Now what do I do?*

"You don't have to explain," said Carmela, gently. "Take your time. I can't imagine what you're going through. It must be very difficult . . . after such a loss."

The woman took a deep breath and seemed to pull it together. "I'm sorry, I'm Margaret Guste. My husband and I live north of here in Hermitage."

"But Amber's last name was —"

"Lalique," said Margaret Guste. "I know; she changed it."

Carmela nodded, trying to give encouragement to the woman.

"Not so long ago Amber was in her second year at Tulane," said Margaret. "Then, when it was shut down after Hurricane Katrina, she kind of drifted away from the idea of a college education. And by the time classes were back in session, Amber was already working as a model. Flying off to, you know, New York and Paris." Margaret blew her nose loudly. "Once Amber saw Europe and made some money of her own, college became a pretty tough sell."

"I can imagine so," replied Carmela.

As more tears slipped down Margaret's cheeks, Carmela handed over the entire box of Kleenex. This was definitely a sad, tragic story. But what could she do?

"I understand you were . . . there," said Margaret. "You saw it all happen."

"Not really, Mrs. Guste," said Carmela. "Everything happened so fast — a blur, really. I didn't really see anything concrete, nothing that could help the police, anyway. And once I saw Amber, I tried to run for help . . . and then Giovanni . . ."

Margaret Guste inhaled sharply at hearing the name.

"You okay, Mrs. Guste?"

"I was told this Giovanni person was the prime suspect in Amber's murder," said Mrs. Guste.

"Who told you that?" asked Carmela.

Rather than answer, Mrs. Guste just daubed at her eyes.

"I believe there are actually a number of suspects," said Carmela.

"Do you have any idea what my daughter was doing in that back alley?" Margaret asked.

Carmela nodded sadly. "Just going to her car." She paused. *Should I ask her? Why not?* "Mrs. Guste, do you know if your daughter was seeing anyone in particular?"

"No idea," said Margaret. She pressed a clean tissue firmly against her lips, then pulled it away. "Do you think she suffered?"

Silence stood between them. *What can I tell her?* wondered Carmela. *What I saw was horrific.* "It happened so fast. So, no, I don't think she suffered."

Margaret Guste nodded. "The police haven't told me a whole lot. I suppose they're trying to spare my feelings."

"I think they're trying to solve Amber's murder," Carmela replied gently.

As if on cue, Boo nosed forward and lifted

a dainty Shar-Pei paw toward Margaret Guste.

Margaret accepted Boo's paw and shook it. "Nice doggy," she said.

"That's enough, Boo. Now please lie down," said Carmela.

"I was hoping you might come to Amber's funeral," said Margaret. "It's this Monday. In Hermitage. It's a bit of a drive, but . . ."

"Of course, I'll come," said Carmela. *And I'll be interested to see who else attends,* she thought to herself.

"Bless you," said Margaret in a tear-choked voice.

The next hour was a blur of activity as customers swarmed Carmela's shop. Two women, who regularly drove down from Baton Rouge, came bustling in, looking for chipboard tags, embossing paste, and some of the new embroidered papers.

Another customer had been looking high and low for accordion books. Luckily, Carmela stocked three different kinds.

And still there were people clutching water-damaged photos. They'd heard from friends how Carmela had worked miracles on hurricane-ravaged family photos. Of course, now the photos were completely dried and hopelessly stuck together in massive gobs. All Carmela could do was resoak the photos, try to carefully peel them apart, chemically treat them, and then hope for the best. She wasn't always successful, but most people were willing to trust their precious mementos to Carmela's skills.

Just as they seemed to enjoy a few moments of calm, just as Carmela was rewarding Boo and Poobah with some homemade biscuits, Lieutenant Edgar Babcock came tromping in.

"You've been to see Remy Chenier," he said in a not-so-friendly tone.

"How did you know?" asked Carmela.

"Because I'm a homicide detective," said Babcock, "the operative word being *detective.* Thus, it's my job to detect and discover these things. The question is, how did *you* know he was worth talking to?"

"One of the models at Moda Chadron mentioned it," said Carmela. "Apparently Amber went out with Remy a couple times."

"Which model?"

"Ah . . . I think her name was Yasmin."

"What else did this model tell you?" asked Babcock.

"Nothing, really," said Carmela.

"And why didn't she talk to me?"

"No idea," said Carmela. "Maybe she wasn't even there when you dropped by for your daily browbeating." She picked up a spool of ribbon, unfurled a foot or so, and snipped it. "Did you, um, happen to notice all the fur-trimmed costumes Grand Folly had on display?" she asked.

Babcock gave an imperceptible nod.

"Did you test any of the fur?"

"What do you think?" he shot back.

Carmela gazed at him, trying to gauge his true meaning. "I think you did, but that you're stumped," she said finally. "That's why you're so darn cranky."

"And I think your gal pal Ava is trying to protect someone. I just haven't figured out whether it's Giovanni or his crazy brother, Santino. The one who runs with the wolves."

"Listen," said Carmela, "don't jump to too many conclusions. Fact is, we've never even *met* Santino."

"I find that hard to believe."

"It's the truth," said Carmela. "Well, half truth, anyway. We saw Santino perform at Cirque de Bella Luna, and that was it. But you know all about that."

"Is that where Santino is now?" asked Babcock.

Carmela was getting frustrated with Edgar Babcock's questions. "I have no idea. And why do you keep shouting questions at *me?*" The stress in her voice drew the dogs

153

over, but Babcock chose to ignore them as they circled around.

"Because you seem to be one step ahead of this investigation, and I don't like it at all," said Babcock, raising his voice, sounding frustrated as hell.

Hmm, thought Carmela, *am I really?* The notion scared her as well as thrilled her.

"Let me ask you a question," said Carmela. "Those wolves that you impounded. Santino's wolves. Did you run tests on their hair?"

"Of course, we did," huffed Babcock. "And they're not a match — yet."

"So where does that leave you?" asked Carmela.

Babcock shook his head, like he was chasing away a cloud of angry bees. "The bite marks," he growled. "That's what's got us puzzled." He looked down at Boo and Poobah, who had positioned themselves between him and Carmela. "Are these guys always so protective?" he asked.

"They have been lately," said Carmela.

"Hello, little darlings," cooed Ava as she pushed her way into Carmela's shop. "Yes, I brought wondrous treats for you, but kindly give me a minute to get organized, please."

Dressed in tight jeans, a glitter skull T-shirt, and stiletto heels, Ava looked like the poster girl for a rock group. In reality, she'd just returned from a quick shop at the Saturday Market in the Warehouse District. The one at the corner of Magazine and Girod.

"Look," said Ava, dumping out a brown paper shopping bag full of goodies on Carmela's front counter. "Loot. I bought boiled peanuts, homemade carrot chips, a jar of rémoulade sauce, an a couple ooey gooey bars. Oh, and duck sausage."

"I surely do love duck sausage," said Carmela. Boo and Poobah's eyes had grown large, and their noses moved in a symphony of sniffs. Obviously, they were raving fans, too.

"They were selling rabbit sausage, too, *cher,* but I didn't know if that was your thing."

"No, duck's the best," said Carmela.

Ava knelt down and fed Boo and Poobah bits of carrot chip. "Here you go, my babies. Tasty and healthy for you." Her fingertips scratched the wrinkles atop Boo's head, and the little dog stretched her neck up in her canine version of contentment.

"Those little theaters are just adorable," said Ava, noticing the shelf of half-constructed theaters. "Y'all are so creative."

"You're the one who was tapped to do decorations for Moda Chadron," said Carmela. "So you better start conjuring some fancy ideas, too."

"That's why I pulled *you* in," laughed Ava. "I might have the raw materials in my shop, but you're the one who's got the creative brainpower to pull it all together."

Carmela picked up a sketch pad and made a couple broad strokes with a fat ink pen. "I did have one idea," she told Ava.

"Shoot," said Ava, still ministering to the dogs. Now Poobah had muscled in for more munchies and scratches.

Carmela continued sketching. "What if we cut free-form ghosts out of white chiffon fabric. And cut eyeholes and mouths, too, to make them look scary and ethereal. Then, if we suspend our ghosts upside down from the ceiling, they should sort of waft in the breeze as people pass by beneath them."

"Very good," said Ava. "Now if we can come up with another dozen ways to creepify Moda Chadron, I'd say we're in business!"

CHAPTER 12

Opulent and at the same time slightly decayed, the Garden District is one of the most photographed, beloved, and coveted neighborhoods in all of New Orleans. The homes, which include Italianate, Greek Revival, and Moorish-style mansions, are the ne plus ultra of the Southern belle époque.

Tonight, carved jack-o'-lanterns flickered up and down Third Street, one of the toniest of drives. Their smiles, scowls, and wacky expressions glowed in the dark, lighting the way for all the Halloween revelers who were getting a jump-start on the holiday.

"That's the house right there," said Carmela, leaning forward. "You see the lamppost with the witch hunched around it?"

The cabdriver slowed down as his eyes took in the decked-out neighborhood. "Wowee," he exclaimed. "Is this the party you're goin' to? Someone sure spent a purty penny to decorate the neighborhood."

"Right here," said Ava, as he eased the cab to the curb in front of a stunningly large Italianate house. "This is Baby's place."

"I wish I had the night off," said the driver. "I'd sure enjoy escortin' two fine ladies to that par-tay." He turned around and smiled, revealing a missing tooth and looking for all the world like a jack-o'-lantern himself.

Carmela glanced at his picture and cab license in the plastic protector: Jake Bujold. "Jake, we'd love to invite you in —"

Jake raised a hand and stopped her before she could continue. "Ma'am, I wasn't fishin' for an invite. I need to drive the drunks home tonight. Someone has to help keep the streets safe." He peeled off a business card and handed it back to Carmela. "But just in case you ladies need a ride home later, give a holler."

"We might do that," said Carmela as she paid the fare, then slipped out of the cab after Ava.

"Hurry up," called Ava. She gave a quick shimmy to adjust her dress, pulled herself to full Amazonian height on four-inch spiked stiletto heels, and headed for the front entry, where two valets were manning the double doors.

Carmela caught up with her. "This is gonna be good," she enthused.

Ava wiggled her hips again and tossed her feather boa around her shoulders. It poufed out, releasing a few errant feathers into the dark night and causing Carmela to sneeze.

"Bless you," said Ava.

"I need all the blessings I can muster," muttered Carmela. She was beginning to get cold feet about her costume. "I'm not completely sure this costume was the best idea in the world."

"Honey, you look adorable," cooed Ava. "You're the cutest little Spider-Woman I ever laid eyes on."

"You think?" said Carmela. Her black, form-fitting bodysuit had a red hourglass sewn on the front with decorative white stitching that ran across the rest of her body like spiderwebs. A loose-knit black shawl entwined with black plastic spiders was draped across her shoulders. More spiders were entwined in Carmela's hair, and her glass ring was imbedded with a preserved spider.

"The only thing is . . ." began Ava.

"What?" asked Carmela, feeling slightly paranoid now, worrying that the costume might be a little *too* form-fitting.

"Think about it, *cher*," giggled Ava. "Look at the message you're sending. Whoever mates with you *dies* afterward."

"Huh," said Carmela, as they made their way inside. "I should be so lucky."

"Oh my," said Ava, her head twisting from side to side, trying to take it all in.

"Easy," laughed Carmela. "You're starting to look like that kid from *The Exorcist*."

"Everything's just so . . . so gorgeous and glam!" exclaimed Ava, continuing her unabashed perusal of Baby's house. "Splendiferous, in fact."

Always known for her over-the-top decor, Baby Fontaine had completely redone her entryway since Hurricane Katrina had wrought some roof and water damage. Pink silk had been replaced by Prussian blue textured wall covering. Shining brass sconces flanked a wall mirror with Rococo brass frame and inlay of tortoiseshell. Carved cypress moldings crowned the entry room. An enormous crystal chandelier dangled above a huge circular staircase that curled up to the second floor. The overall effect was very *Gone With the Wind*.

"Welcome," said Del. Dressed as one of Napoleon's officers, Baby's husband sped across the parquet floor, then greeted them with a sweeping bow.

"Ain't you the chivalrous gent," said Ava, flipping her boa at him.

"I'm crazy about your Mae West look," he told her with a grin, then turned to survey Carmela's costume. "And our own itsy-bitsy spider, too." He dropped an arm around each woman's shoulder and propelled them into the main salon, which was jam-packed with guests oohing and aahing over each other's costumes. "Come join the party. And I guarantee, it's quite a party."

"Give a man a free hand, and he'll run it all over you," quipped Ava in a Mae West accent.

"Love it," roared Del as he turned them loose and went back to his meet-and-greet duties.

"Are you going to keep that up all night?" asked Carmela as they melted into the crowd of revelers. She wondered just how many Mae West bon mots Ava had memorized.

"Just aiming to get into character," replied Ava. "And make myself a little more approachable, too."

"I wouldn't worry about that," replied Carmela with a smile. "When you walk into a room, most of the men's tongues tumble out of their mouths. When I enter, all the strange men slither out of the woodwork."

As if on cue, Shamus suddenly materialized right before Carmela's eyes.

"Hello Carmela," he said, hobbling toward her, a white plaster cast on one foot.

"See what I mean?" sighed Carmela. She leveled an unhappy gaze at her soon-to-be ex, wondering what *he* was doing here. Wasn't this supposed to be a Shamus-free zone? "And what exactly are you supposed to be?" Carmela asked him, taking in Shamus's dark blue knit cap, matching knit sweater, and stretch ski pants. She decided that Shamus looked like a cross between a gimpy cat burglar and a deranged member of the Bulgarian ski team.

"What do you think I am?" said Shamus, sounding more than a little huffy.

Ava jumped in for a little fun of her own. "Snow bunny? Chalet lizard?"

Shamus glared at her.

"You two enjoy," said Ava. "Marriage may be an institution, but I'm too young to be committed." She waggled her fingers at Shamus and was off.

"Good luck with Glory," Shamus called after her in an acerbic tone. "She's wearing the same costume, you know."

Ava stopped dead in her tracks. "Not quite," she called back. Then she grabbed a flute of champagne from the tray of a passing waiter, downed it completely, and grabbed another one before the stunned waiter could take another step.

Carmela stifled a laugh.

"Nice to see you laugh," said Shamus. He peered at her, this time offering a warmer gaze.

Carmela allowed a cautious smile back. After all, it was only two days ago that this very same man had been a ranting, panting nutcase. "How's your toe?" she asked him. "Is it really broken?" She inspected the cast. The darned thing looked real, but knowing Shamus, it could just be part of his costume.

"Not my toe," said Shamus. "A bone in my foot. The cuboid bone, if you really want to know. And does it ever hurt." He glared at her. "Jeez, you think I'd get a plaster cast put on my foot just to garner a few sympathy votes?"

Yes, thought Carmela, but she didn't say so out loud.

Rescue came in the form of Baby, who was dressed as Glenda, the Good Witch of the North.

"Welcome to my party, Munchkins," she said, waving her magic wand and spreading her arms wide. Then Baby grabbed Carmela and hugged her tight. "Do you need to be rescued?" she whispered in Carmela's ear.

Carmela shook her head no, then said, "What a fantastic party. And I can't wait to visit the buffet table. After printing up your menus, I'm pretty primed for the real thing."

Baby looped an arm around Carmela. "Then step right this way." She paused, looked at Shamus. "Care to join us?" From the tone of her voice it was obvious she didn't really care to have him tag along at all.

But Shamus shook his head and held up both hands in a gesture of surrender. "Pass. I'm going to find the bar and curl up with a Scotch and water."

"Tootles, then," said Baby, pulling Carmela away. When they were out of earshot, Baby gave Carmela a worried look. "I didn't invite him," she said vehemently. "Cross my heart. Del had some business thing going at Crescent City Bank, and one thing led to another . . ."

"Don't worry about it," said Carmela, waving a hand. "I've had practice aplenty in avoiding Shamus." *Of course, Glory's another story,* she thought to herself.

"Oh, Carmela, you're such a *modern* girl," laughed Baby. "So self-assured and self-sufficient. Now *that* one . . ." She pointed at Ava, who was posed in front of the marble fireplace and seemed to have gathered quite a gaggle of admiring men. "That one I worry about."

Swaying her hips and rolling her eyes, Ava was laying on her best Mae West swagger.

"I like my clothes to be tight to show I'm a woman, but loose enough to show I'm a lady," she told her admirers. Then she turned slightly, lifted a bare shoulder, and glanced back at them. "And I only like two kinds of men. Domestic and imported."

Zombies, witches, Venetian lords and ladies, Harry Potters, and a Queen Elizabeth, who had a five o'clock shadow under his white makeup, milled around inside the house and spilled out through the French doors onto the backyard patio. Notes from a string quartet could be heard as they played outside in the gazebo.

Just as Carmela was admiring a woman in a plumed and plunging cockatiel costume and edging toward the buffet table with Baby, Tandy Bliss came slaloming through the crowd.

"You've absolutely outdone yourself this year, Baby!" exclaimed Tandy. "I don't know how you do it!" Dressed in a cowgirl outfit complete with short skirt, vest, hat, and boots, Tandy enveloped the two women with hugs and dispensed a multitude of air kisses.

Once Carmela had extricated herself from Tandy's embrace, she finally allowed herself a longing gaze at Baby's main buffet table. To put it mildly, the arrangement was drop-dead gorgeous. Two giant candelabras, set at each end of the mahogany trestle table, blazed with claret-colored candles. A giant centerpiece of orange mums, bittersweet, purple grapes, curly willow, preserved oak leaves, and the glitter pumpkins she'd decorated sat in the middle. But the pièces de résistance were the main entrées of chicken jambalaya, baked shrimp casserole, and Cajun meatloaf that sat succulent and savory in gleaming brass food warmers. The piquant aromas of wine, seafood, garlic, sweet basil, thyme, Tabasco sauce, and cayenne pepper drifted up enticingly.

"Oh Lord," moaned Tandy. "Somebody hand me a plate."

"Will you look at those shrimp," marveled Carmela. "They're almost the size of bananas!"

The dessert table, of course, was a whole 'nother thing. Here Baby's caterer had worked some deft Halloween magic. A sheet of Plexiglas covered an open coffin where a skeleton wearing a tuxedo lay in quiet repose. Above Mr. Bones, out of reach of his bony hands, was a full complement of desserts.

A German chocolate sheet cake had been cut in irregular squares and tumbled onto a serving platter to look like clods of earth. Each "clod" was topped with green frosting, coconut grass, and, of course, brightly colored gummy worms.

A bowl of rice custard was accented with marzipan beetles.

Pralines shared a crystal plate with smiling chocolate bats.

And a colorfully striped plastic snake curled around the footed cake stand that held a Louisiana pear cake.

"What's that old Southern saying?" drawled Tandy, peering at the snake. "Red, black, yeller, kill a feller?"

"That's for the poisonous variety," pointed out Baby. "This one is red, yellow, black. Really quite harmless."

"So the saying should be red, yellow, black, y'all come back," laughed Carmela.

"Holy smokes, Carmela," said Tandy, as if she'd just remembered. "Did you know Shamus was here tonight? And his wacky sister Glory?"

Carmela nodded. "Already talked to Shamus. Glory I'll try to avoid."

"She always manages to make a scene, doesn't she?" said Tandy at the exact moment a woman's voice rose in a strangled, high-pitched cry of outrage.

"What the . . . ?" said Baby, as all three of them turned to see what was going on.

"I'm fine!" came a shrill, insistent female voice. "I told you that already. Can't I just *enjoy* myself?"

Carmela peered through the crowd and was shocked to see the designer, Chadron, trying to grasp the arm of a struggling blond woman in a red silk dress. Her words slurred as the blond pushed her way past them, fumbling in her matching handbag even as she tried to maintain possession of her flute of champagne.

"I just need some *air,*" the woman complained. "It's so hot in here I can't breathe." As she stepped out onto the back patio, she placed a cigarette between rouged lips and touched a tiny jeweled lighter to it. "So just back off!"

Chadron, still hot on the woman's heels, tried to grab her arm and wrest away the flute of champagne.

Then Carmela, Baby, and Tandy watched in horror as the glass slipped through the woman's fingers, champagne splattered down the front of her dress, and the champagne flute dropped to the ground.

"Damn," spat the woman as crystal shattered against brick and shards of glass flew everywhere. She stared morosely down at the demolished flute, then at her dress. "My dress is ruined, you idiot." All around them, embarrassed guests averted their glances and moved away.

"I'll design you a new dress," said Chadron, trying to pacify the woman, looking like he wished the earth would open up and swallow him whole.

"Did you guys catch that little scene?" asked Ava, suddenly rushing over to join Carmela, Baby, and Tandy. Still stunned, the three women just nodded.

"And do you have any idea how much one of those Baccarat flutes cost?" muttered Tandy under her breath.

"Lots," said Baby in a low voice. "But this little scenario has more drama than a soap opera. Kind of hypnotic to watch."

"If you like watching train wrecks," said Ava.

"So the woman is . . . who?" murmured Carmela, watching Chadron reach out to grasp the blonde's bare shoulder.

"His wife," finished Baby. "Angelique."

"I thought she looked a little old to be a model," said Ava. She and Carmela were edging out onto the patio, while Baby and Tandy dropped back.

"In theory," said Carmela, "they seem like they should be the perfect guests."

"Perfectly horrible," murmured Ava, as they watched the drama continue to unfold.

"Angelique, please . . ." began Chadron. Then he suddenly caught sight of Carmela and Ava watching them and forced a hesitant smile to his face. "Ladies, enjoying the party? And such a beautiful night?" He tried to sound hale and hearty, but his voice was tense, the expression on his face was one of sheer misery.

"Hey there," said Ava.

Angelique focused a cool, imperious glance at Carmela and Ava. "And who might you two be?" she asked. Angelique's blue eyes flashed angrily, her red silk dress with its plunging neckline revealed an acre of skin. Because of the spilled champagne her gown was plastered against her.

"Angelique," said Chadron, fighting for control, "I'd like you to meet Carmela and Ava. They're two very creative people who are helping with decorations at the atelier. Carmela owns Memory Mine, a scrapbook shop, and Ava is the owner of Juju Voodoo."

Angelique gave a cold smile. "The place where Amber was killed. I like this one

170

already."

Angelique's harsh words sent a chill up Carmela's spine. *What a horrible thing to say,* she thought.

Chadron looked almost apoplectic now. "Hush, Angelique," he hissed. "This is not the time nor —"

"Don't you hush me!" spat Angelique. "Amber was a bitch, and you know it. You were the one who —"

"Enough!" growled Chadron, grabbing roughly for his wife's arm and this time managing to hang on.

"Or maybe," said Angelique, narrowing her eyes at Chadron, "maybe you liked *la belle* Amber a little *too* much." She threw a triumphant gaze at Carmela and Ava, as if she'd managed to spill the beans on something she really shouldn't have. "At any rate," Angelique continued in a nattering, scolding tone, "it's clear you certainly don't make the smartest choices. In business or with women."

"That's for sure," muttered Ava.

Carmela gave Ava a sharp nudge, hoping to keep her friend's caustic wit at bay.

But Angelique was focused on Carmela. "What are *you* supposed to be?" she asked belligerently. And then, without waiting for an answer, said, "Spider-Man. How tedious.

You must have stayed up all night figuring that one out."

At which point Ava stepped forward and gently touched the fabric of Angelique's dress. "And I love *your* costume, too," she said in a silken tone as a sly smile danced at her lips. "I always enjoy watching the *Dark Shadows* reruns on the SCI FI channel. You ever catch those? With the witch Angelique. Blond, loud, and really nasty. She's quite the character — almost cartoonish."

Angelique's lips pinched together suddenly, and her face blanched white. From between clenched teeth she blurted out, "I need another drink." And without waiting for Chadron, turned and hurried toward the bar.

"Sorry, so sorry," said Chadron, flashing a weak smile at Carmela and Ava, then dashing off to catch up with Angelique.

"Wow," said Ava. "Isn't she a sweetheart."

"And Chadron seems so even-keeled and normal," marveled Carmela. "And talented."

"Maybe it's another case of opposites attracting," said Ava. "Kind of like you and Shamus."

"Maybe," allowed Carmela, although she wasn't thrilled to be lumped in the same category as those two.

■ ■ ■ ■

An hour later, dinner eaten, drinks imbibed, and countless friends greeted, Carmela and Ava found themselves back outside on the patio. They were seated on the cushioned bench of a giant garden swing, swaying gently, listening to a string version of *"Walkin' to New Orleans."* All around them the party continued to pick up steam.

"You know Jake Meraux asked me to go out with him," said Ava.

"Isn't he a little old for you?" asked Carmela. "I mean the man's got to be at least sixty."

"Sixty-two," said Ava. "But, you know, he's a big-time stockbroker, and he owns that gigantic house over on Chestnut Street."

"Hey, honey," said Carmela, "size isn't everything."

"Good point," said Ava, taking another sip of her drink.

"Carmela!" brayed a loud, brassy voice.

Carmela whipped her head around, expecting to see Angelique again. But her eyes fell on Glory. "Oh no," she murmured. "Not *another* scene."

Glory, the seams of her Mae West costume

still straining mightily, advanced on Carmela and Ava.

"What do you want, Glory?" asked Carmela. Both she and Ava stood up, ready to do battle if need be.

Glory's beady eyes gleamed wickedly. She clutched a tall tumbler in her hand that held a finger full of Scotch. Carmela knew Glory had easily downed five or six shots. Not good, since Glory also gobbled antianxiety pills like they were M&M's.

"I wanna talk to you about your divorce," said Glory. Only she slurred her words, so divorce came out di-force.

"Carmela's getting a di-force?" said Ava. "Fancy that."

"A hundred thousand and you walk away," said Glory. "That's the deal. A single lump sum payoff."

"Hah!" said Ava. "You think that's fair compensation for all the crap Carmela's had to put up with?"

"You stay outa this," slurred Glory. She turned wonky eyes on Carmela once again. "Whadya say? The hundred thou?"

"I think," said Carmela, "this discussion should take place in a lawyer's office and not at a Halloween party."

"Good point," chortled Ava. "Why negotiate when you're surrounded by evil-looking witches and devils, when you can sit in a lawyer's office that's filled with nasty, bottom-feeding —"

"That's enough," said Carmela calmly, putting a hand on Ava's arm and pulling her away. "Glory, this is something Shamus and I will work out. By ourselves."

"She really frosts me," grumped Ava.

"Me, too," said Carmela. "But it's not worth letting it get to you."

"Yeah," allowed Ava. "I suppose." But she wiggled her hips and fluffed out her boa anyway, doing her best to assert herself.

"Ava," said Carmela, "do you remember when we were at Moda Chadron yesterday, talking to Yasmin?"

Ava nodded. "Mm-hm."

"She told us that Amber had gone with Remy to a party in a mansion over on Iberville. Some fat cat's place."

"Yeah," said Ava.

"I talked to Baby earlier. She's thinking it might be Hubbell Turner's place."

"Who dat?" asked Ava.

"Hubbell Turner is a very prominent criminal defense attorney," said Carmela. "Which means he's already quite comfortable rubbing shoulders with some of our city's more notorious criminal element."

"So what are you thinking?" asked Ava. "That we should slip out the back gate and ankle over there? See what, if anything, is shaking?"

"Isn't it amazing," said Carmela, "how you can read my mind."

They eased their way along the tall hedge that lined Baby's backyard, heading toward a small opening. Just as the string quartet struck up a spritely version of "Blueberry Hill," both women stepped through the hedge into the alley. In an instant, darkness swallowed them whole.

CHAPTER 13

Click, click, click. Ava's stiletto heels clacked and echoed against the cobblestones.

"Can't you walk any quieter?" Carmela asked. Shadows circled them as they passed from one streetlight halo into the next. The night carried a gentle breeze, and music wafted from all directions. On this Saturday night, parties seemed to be happening everywhere in the Garden District. The faint tinkle of glass and muted bursts of laughter added to the sensation that they were somehow behind the scenes, peeking in on any number of dramas.

"How much farther?" asked Ava. Clearly she was having trouble walking some distance in her four-inch heels. "These shoes are made for posing, you know, not traversing the entire city."

"Just down here a bit more," said Carmela. "Baby said Turner's house backs up almost to the alley, and the back portico has tall, white columns."

As if on cue, party sounds erupted just ahead of them. And when Carmela and Ava peered around a gigantic clump of magnolias, they spotted the house.

"Columns," said Ava. "This has to be the place."

"And there's a party going on," remarked Carmela. "How convenient."

"We're certainly dressed to blend in," said Ava as they approached the back door.

"We are if it's a costume party," said Carmela. "If it isn't, we're just going to look extremely weird."

"We'll just say we're exotic dancers," said Ava. "Hired for the evening."

But just as Carmela's fingers brushed the doorknob, the door opened, and a tall man in a formal vampire costume came out. He smiled, fake blood dripping down one side of his mouth, and held the door for the ladies to enter.

A wave of hard rock music blasted their eardrums. "So much more subtle than Baby's party," Ava shouted above the din.

"And such classy decor," said Carmela, also raising her voice to a near shout. If she had to name a decorating style, it would be French bordello meets Frankenstein's laboratory. Red lights and flickering candles made the place look like an anteroom to hell. Costumed guests were draped across faux Louis XVI furniture, strangely garish modern art hung on the walls, smoke hung in the air. A suit of armor stood in one corner of the room, a cage with a full skeleton hung from the ceiling in the other corner.

"Someone overstayed their welcome," Carmela pointed out.

They moved through this family room of sorts into what must have been the formal dining room. A wrought-iron chandelier strung with orange pumpkin lights hung above a nonexistent table and chairs. A bar dominated one corner of the room. Guests milled about smoking, drinking, shouting, and halfheartedly dancing. A French prostitute looked like she might be on duty, a sailor looked like he hadn't regained his land legs yet.

"Want a drink?" asked Ava.

Carmela nodded, and they both bellied up to the bar and grabbed bottles of Abita Purple Haze, a local favorite.

Carmela pointed to a swinging door. "Let's see what their buffet table looks like."

"You know," said Ava, "I *could* eat again."

But when they pushed their way into the next room, they found a group of men sitting around a table, smoking and playing cards. Poker chips were stacked high, a pot of crumpled greenbacks sat in the middle of the table, blue smoke filled the room.

"Too rich for my blood," declared a man in a ten-gallon hat. He threw down his cards, clamped a cigar between his teeth.

The man across from him, dressed as a riverboat gambler in a vest and string tie, gave a self-satisfied grin and scooped the pot toward him. As he glanced around, his eyes met Carmela's.

"Remy!" she said.

Remy ignored Carmela as he snatched up the deck and began shuffling. His fingers handled the cards like a practiced Vegas dealer, but he had the sly arm movements and arrogance of a magician. All the time Remy's dark eyes never left Carmela's.

She wondered if Remy could be the one who left the errant poker chip at the scene of Amber's murder. Or had one of these other poker players been involved? Maybe even Hubbell Turner? The notion chilled Carmela, and she watched in fascination as Remy's fingers flipped and manipulated the cards, dealing out a new hand to the unsavory-looking lot that sat crowded around the table.

A geisha girl pushed past Carmela and

Ava and set a drink tray on the table. She bowed to each man as she handed him his drink.

Now Remy was focused solely on his poker game. He'd obviously dismissed or discounted Carmela.

"Let's get out of here," Carmela whispered to Ava.

Ava nodded, and they followed the geisha out, letting the music assault them once again.

"That was weird," said Ava. "Seeing Remy in there."

"Think one of those poker guys was Hubbell Turner?" asked Carmela.

Ava shrugged. "No idea. But this is definitely a wacky party. I'm picking up very strange vibes."

"Me, too," agreed Carmela. "Time to take off."

Threading their way toward the back door, Carmela noticed that the party seemed to have grown in size, was close to achieving critical mass. Music blared, people danced, women flirted, men groped.

Just as they tried to dodge around a clique of revelers who were making noisy toasts, a familiar-looking face loomed in front of them.

Carmela shook her head. Her eyes burned

from the smoke, her head was buzzing from the noise, and now this man was staring at them with hostile, piercing eyes. *Hostile, yes, but familiar, too,* she thought. Carmela glanced at Ava, who also seemed to be taken aback by this dark-skinned man with the manicured goatee.

"Excuse us . . ." began Carmela and then recognition dawned like a thunderbolt. She *had* seen this man before. At Cirque de Bella Luna!

"Santino!" exclaimed Ava at the precise instant the neurons in Carmela's brain fired and made the connection.

A sound rose in the back of Santino's throat, something that was a cross between an expression of dismay and a nasty growl.

Shivers ran down the length of Carmela's spine. She'd only intended to come here to satisfy her burning curiosity, do a drive-by snoop, so to speak. Now she was getting way more than she'd bargained for. Then, the same courage that had allowed her to leave Shamus seemed to kick in. And Carmela decided, *In for a penny, in for a pound.*

So she met Santino's hostile gaze with a look she hoped was equally fierce. "What are *you* doing here?" she demanded.

Ava's neck turned toward her like it was on a ball bearing. Clearly, Ava was shocked that Carmela had suddenly reared up and gone on the offensive.

Confusion played across Santino's face now. But he recovered quickly. "The same could be asked of you two."

"We're investigating," said Ava, bolstered by Carmela's big show of courage.

"Working for the *cops?*" taunted Santino. "Trying to frame me and my brother?"

"That couldn't be farther from the truth," said Carmela.

"We're trying to help, in case you hadn't noticed," said Ava.

Santino took a long pull on his beer, then stared at Ava. "Lady, your kind of help I don't need. You think having my wolves impounded is helping? You think ruining my working relationship with Cirque de Bella Luna is helping?" He shook his head angrily, narrowed his eyes. "Boy, are you two ever off your rocker."

"If Giovanni had been honest with us from the very beginning, none of that would have happened," said Carmela.

Santino gave a loud, derisive snort.

"Carmela's right," said Ava. "And we *do* care what happens. I kept Giovanni on at my shop, after all."

"So you can keep an eye on him," sneered Santino. "I know your type."

"Look," said Carmela, "the police are convinced that either you or Giovanni, or maybe *both* of you, were involved in Amber's murder."

"Amber," breathed Santino. His broad shoulders slumped, and he suddenly looked tired and defeated.

Carmela pressed on, using Santino's show of emotion to her advantage. "You cared about Amber," she told Santino. "I know you did. So you, of all people, should want her killer apprehended and brought to justice."

"If I find him," said Santino in a voice that was low and dangerous now, "I'll wreak my own brand of justice." He held up an index finger, brought his face in close to Carmela's face. "So don't be nosing around in things that don't concern you," he warned. "Someone could get hurt."

"Like Amber did?" said Carmela. "Tell us what you know, please!"

Santino shook his head like an angry lion and swore under his breath. "Enough!" he cried. He spun on his heel and crashed wildly through the crowd.

Five seconds later, Carmela and Ava were following him outside into the cool night air.

But Santino was already running across

the yard and slipping through the back hedge. He jammed his hand into his jeans pocket and fished out car keys. Then he was scrambling into a black Corvette.

"Santino, wait!" called Carmela.

But he'd already slammed the car door and was revving the engine. The motor purred like a tiger, and the wheels spun on the cobblestones, kicking up dust. Then there was a high-pitched squeal, and Santino was off, powering his sports car like a bat out of hell.

Carmela peered down the alleyway. *Now you see him, now you don't,* she thought to herself. "Should we try to follow him?" she muttered, but it was a halfhearted, pro forma question. Santino was long gone. She didn't have her speedy little sports car parked nearby.

Ava thrust out a leg. "Not in these, *cher.*"

"You know where he lives?" asked Carmela.

"Bayou," shrugged Ava. "Somewhere out in one of the bayous. But I don't relish wandering around in one of those tonight, do you?"

"Not in the dead of night," said Carmela. "For sure not in the dead of night."

CHAPTER 14

A jazz brunch at Bon Tiempe Restaurant was just about the finest way to kick off a Sunday morning. Housed in a crumbling old mansion in the Bywater district, Bon Tiempe exuded old-world charm. Antique chandeliers sparkled overhead, oil paintings crackled with age hung on brocade-covered walls, lush velvet draperies with fat tassels sectioned off various parts of the restaurant to create cozy, intimate dining nooks.

Quigg Brevard, the elegantly attractive owner, was dressed in his tux and standing at attention at Carmela and Ava's table, ready to take their order.

"Why are you honchoing this place today?" asked Carmela. "I thought since you owned the joint you'd at least have Sunday off."

"The weekend before Halloween is almost as busy as Mardi Gras," sighed Quigg. "We had parties up the wazoo last night. Kept us hopping until almost 3:00 a.m. Then half my staff was a no-show today, so we're running on . . . ha-ha . . . a skeleton crew."

"Well, I know exactly what I want," said Ava, setting the parchment paper menu down on the white linen tablecloth. "Eggs Sardou." Eggs Sardou was a delicious entrée of poached eggs on artichoke bottoms, set in a nest of creamed spinach and smothered with hollandaise sauce.

"Eggs Sardou, it is," said Quigg. He edged nearer to Carmela. "And for you, *mademoiselle?*"

"Do you still have the brioche French toast spread with cream cheese?" she asked.

Quigg nodded encouragingly. "With strawberries in brown sugar sauce. Is that what you want?"

"Please," said Carmela. With Quigg standing so close, she was beginning to feel slightly discombobulated. He was a tall man. Wide shoulders, dark hair, olive complexion, flashing dark eyes. A couple years younger, and he could pose for the front cover of a bodice-ripping romance novel.

"And may I suggest a Ramos Gin Fizz," he added.

"You may," said Ava. "But I'd prefer a Southern Bride."

A wicked grin creased Quigg's face as he

187

stared pointedly at Carmela. "So would I."

"What on earth is a Southern Bride?" asked Carmela, once they were alone at their table. "And why does Quigg Brevard look at me the way he does?" She fanned herself, managed a nervous smile.

"Ah," said Ava. "First of all, a Southern Bride is my new favorite cocktail. Gin, maraschino liqueur, and grapefruit juice. Sweet with a hint of tartness, just like me. Second, Quigg looks at you the way he does because he's seriously in lust."

"You think so?" asked Carmela.

"Oh yeah, *cher*," said Ava. "He's got it bad. You better hurry up and get that divorce from Shamus. Maybe pop up to Reno or something and hurry things along. A man like Quigg doesn't come along every day."

"You're probably right," murmured Carmela.

"You did that new catering promo piece for him, right?"

Carmela nodded. She'd put together a terrific scrapbook-style booklet using photos, menus, and a list of satisfied clients so Quigg would have a sort of show-and-tell book to send out when he was pitching bridal showers, wedding receptions, and corporate events.

"And you did his menus, right?" continued Ava.

"The dinner menu and the brunch menu," said Carmela. She had lightened up on the type, heavied up the paper, and designed a format that could be run off his own laser printer and inserted in Bon Tiempe's leather menu holders whenever Quigg decided to change an item. Which was pretty much every few days.

"You gotta go out with him," pronounced Ava. "You've already put your heads together. Now you gotta move on to the lips."

"I did go out with him once already," said Carmela. "He escorted me to a dinner party last year. Before I got cozy with Shamus again for the second — or was it the third? — time."

"But now you and Shamus are for sure kaput," said Ava. "So you've got to make a declaration of freedom and seriously start seeing Quigg."

"Let me think about that," said Carmela. She didn't want to rush into anything.

"Face it," said Ava. "The man's attractive, and he can cook like a dream. Did you ever have his chicken breast with sliced apples in root beer glaze?"

Carmela nodded. "To die for."

189

"There's only one other fine point a woman could want in a man," said Ava. Her face lit up with a loopy grin. "And that's if a man likes . . ."

"Shopping!" said Carmela, chiming in with Ava to complete her sentence.

"You got that right," said Ava.

Once they had their cocktails and brunch entrées in front of them, talk turned to their strange foray into Hubbell Turner's house last night.

"That was so weird seeing Remy there," said Ava.

"And literally running into Santino," added Carmela.

"And earlier, there was that strange scene with Angelique," said Ava. "Where she was acting like some kind of nutcase Barbie doll."

Carmela thought for a moment. "It was like . . . what do they call it when strange things seem to align? A triple witching moment."

"So what do you think?" asked Ava. "Have you developed any new theories as to who might have murdered Amber?"

"After last night," said Carmela, "Santino has definitely moved to the top of my hit list. Anyone with that much hostility and rage could definitely come unhinged. And where did he race off to last night?" Carmela rubbed her forehead. The encounter had been most unpleasant.

"Santino was definitely not thrilled to see us," said Ava. "And don't you get the feeling he's hiding something?"

"He not only acts hinky," said Carmela, "but he seems to have some kind of inner turmoil. So he could know something or somehow be connected. Not that we'll be able to pry anything out of him. I get the feeling he's probably gone into hiding."

"You think he could have been there that night? In the alley?"

Carmela exhaled slowly. "You mean was Santino the one who killed Amber and then tackled me from behind? Maybe. But . . . I just don't know."

"Maybe we'll never know," said Ava. "But if we don't figure something out, I get the feeling that Babcock is going to keep hounding Giovanni."

"And Giovanni's not saying much either," said Carmela.

"He could be covering for Santino," ventured Ava. She looked unhappy that her words sounded so disloyal.

"And Santino warned us to stay away from Giovanni," said Carmela. "Which means everything keeps looping back on itself."

"Very weird," agreed Ava.

"And how can you stay away from Giovanni if he's still working for you?" asked Carmela.

"Santino's just plain nuts," said Ava.

"Would you fire Giovanni?"

Ava shrugged. "My customers really seem to like him. And he brings in a fair amount of money. I guess I would hate to lose him. But I sure wish I knew if I could trust that boy."

Carmela and Ava fell silent as one of the white-coated waiters wheeled the dessert cart up to their table.

"Chocolate mousse," said Ava, always decisive when it came to selecting dessert. "With a couple dabs of whipped cream."

Carmela's eyes roved across the spread of goodies. "Fruit tart," she finally decided.

"So who else does that leave?" asked Ava. "In the suspect department."

"Remy doesn't exactly seem like the poster boy for good behavior," said Carmela. "And he did date Amber at some point in time. Or at least hung out with her."

"You think she liked a rough crowd?"

"I think that possibility exists," said Carmela.

"What about Chadron?" said Ava. "Although murdering his best model would seem to leave him with even more of a problem."

"It certainly isn't logical or rational," said Carmela. "Then again, murderers are none of the above."

"Maybe," said Ava, dropping her voice. "Maybe Chadron got a little *too* involved with Amber. And then he needed to somehow extricate himself from the relationship. He was afraid Angelique would find out."

"From the way Angelique was carrying on last night," said Carmela, "I think that cat's long since out of the bag."

"So Angelique had motive," said Ava. "But is she nuts enough to be a killer?"

"Nothing like a woman scorned," murmured Carmela. At this point, she was keeping everyone on her list of suspects. Maybe tomorrow she could talk to Detective Babcock and try to pry loose some of his suspicions on the various players. Maybe.

As coffee was poured, Quigg Brevard wandered back to their table.

"Everything to your liking, ladies?"

"Perfection," said Ava, playing the coquette. Then her foot connected squarely with Carmela's ankle, obviously nudging her to be a little more forthcoming with her praise.

"Wonderful, as always," said Carmela.

Ava smiled sweetly at her from across the table.

"You know," said Quigg, "I just signed the lease for a new space in the French Quarter."

"A new restaurant?" asked Ava.

"Yup," said Quigg. "Gonna call it Mumbo Gumbo. Remember, Carmela, I told you about my concept a while back?"

Carmela nodded.

"Where is it located?" asked Ava.

"On Governor Nicholls Street," said Quigg. "In the old Westminster Gallery space."

"Just a couple blocks down from Carmela," cooed Ava. "How convenient."

"I thought so, too," said Quigg, sliding away gracefully from their table.

"You didn't have to *kick* me," hissed Carmela, once he was out of earshot.

"You didn't have to do your impression of an Easter Island statue," Ava shot back. "Flirt with the man, will you? Show him you're interested."

"I'm not a natural flirt like you are," said Carmela.

Ava leaned back in her chair and stretched

languidly, allowing her cheetah-spotted tank top to ride up and expose an expanse of toned, trim midriff. "Sure you are. You just haven't released your inner you, yet. You've been suppressing it. Probably because of Shamus."

"Probably," said Carmela, just to be agreeable.

"I bet you'll unleash that tiger inside you when you hit the runway at Moda Chadron. Speaking of which, we still have to come up with a few more decorating ideas." Ava suddenly looked worried. "After all, *we'll* be on that runway, too, Halloween night. Got to make it look good!"

"The atelier or us?" asked Carmela. She was still unnerved by the idea of walking in a fashion show.

"Both," said Ava. "So think hard."

"We could bring in a fog machine," suggested Carmela. "To create a sort of ground mist over the runway." *And create a smokescreen effect so people won't notice me.*

"Very cool," said Ava. "What else?"

"What about . . . what about . . . tombstone rubbings," said Carmela.

"Huh?"

"Here's the deal," said Carmela, starting to gain enthusiasm for her idea. "We'll pay a little visit to one of the cemeteries tonight, pick out some of the more, er, interesting gravestones, and do tombstone rubbings. Then we'll laminate the rubbings onto foam core."

"Spooky," said Ava.

"That's the whole idea," said Carmela. "The rubbings are *supposed* to look spooky."

"No," said Ava. "I mean the idea of creeping around a cemetery at night."

CHAPTER 15

Despite the warm weather, the day had remained gray and overcast. A strong wind blew in from the Gulf of Mexico, adding humidity and the scent of brine to the air. The sun had attempted to break through the clouds several times, but gloom had fast descended.

Now, early evening, wrought-iron street-lamps glowed in the darkness, throwing little puddles of light throughout the French Quarter. In Carmela's apartment and across the courtyard in Ava's upstairs apartment, lamps burned brightly and hopefully in their windows.

Ava had phoned Carmela several times, pushing their departure time back. Every time she was ready to leave, a new problem seemed to crop up. So they weren't able to get away until seven o'clock that night.

"I'm so sorry, *cher*," said Ava as she scrambled into the passenger seat of Carmela's Mercedes. "Giovanni never showed up for his shift, so Miguel was in a blind panic. And for some reason the shop was super busy." She tossed her leather Coach bag on the floor at her feet, then kicked it out of the way, muttering, "Why does there always have to be a crisis?" Then she slouched down, tipped her head against the back of the seat, and sighed deeply.

"I guess Halloween just started early this year," replied Carmela. She put the car in drive and eased her way down the back alley, watching her headlights as they splashed along the cobblestones, trying not to think about what had taken place here just four short nights ago.

"To top it all off," said Ava, "my cash register locked up, two of my brand-new overhead lights popped, and then the circuit breaker sizzled like a cheap cheeseburger. Looks like pesky gremlins have been at work. Oh, and to top things off, mice have been nibbling at my love charms."

"Which ones?" asked Carmela.

"Little gray beasties."

"I mean the charms," laughed Carmela.

"The ones with rose petals and brown sugar in them."

"They do sound delicous," said Carmela.

"Jeez, maybe there's a full moon tonight."

Ava twisted her head and craned her neck to scan the night sky, but heavy clouds hung low and ominous, obscuring the view of planetary aspects.

"Well, it's been a veritable *cirque de canine* in my apartment," said Carmela. "First Boo and Poobah tipped over the wicker basket in my bathroom and had a Kleenex-shredding contest. Then Boo dug out an old mascara and decided to experiment."

"Uh-oh," said Ava.

"She unscrewed the wand and managed to drag it across the peach-colored coverlet on my bed as well as the white flokati rug."

"That's no way to land a job at the Chanel counter," said Ava. "She's got to learn how to handle makeup proper."

"I'll tell you what else," said Carmela. "She'll never make it as a graphic designer either. Graffiti artist maybe, but she's too much into freestyle for graphic design."

"Will it wash out?" asked Ava.

"Doubtful," said Carmela.

The two women rode in silence as Carmela negotiated traffic. At the convention center she cut down Poydras, then turned on Tchoupitoulas, just a few blocks from the Superdome. Both places had been open for events for well over a year now, and it was hard to imagine they had been the scene of so much misery and heartbreak during the dark days of Hurricane Katrina.

"We're headed for Lafayette Cemetery No. 1?" asked Ava.

Carmela nodded. Tucked in the Garden District, it was by far her favorite cemetery. Gothic-looking in nature, filled with tombs, mausoleums, crypts, and wall tombs, Lafayette Cemetery No. 1 was historic, highly atmospheric, and probably one of the most-visited cemeteries in New Orleans.

Of course, it had sustained terrible damage during Hurricane Katrina. Downed trees had completely collapsed the old wall at Coliseum and Sixth. A huge pile of debris had blocked the wrought-iron front gate, mud had smeared many of the tombs. And the place had been strewn with toppled bricks, fallen tablets, and damaged markers.

But like many other things, it was almost back to normal.

"Wish we had a little more daylight to work in," Ava fretted as Carmela pulled the car over to the curb. "I feel responsible for making us so late. Sorry."

"No need to keep apologizing," said Carmela. "I've got a big flashlight if we need it. And there are so many great graves, crypts, and markers here that getting a half dozen or so rubbings should be a snap."

They climbed out of Carmela's car, grabbed several rolls of white paper as well as a canvas tote full of craft supplies, and set off into the cemetery.

They walked slowly between a row of tilting aboveground tombs, gravel crunching underfoot. The scent of wilting flowers lent a slightly unpleasant note.

"Creepy," said Ava. "This place really does make you ponder the mysteries of death. And it's weird to think there are piles of dry bones just inches from us behind all these crumbling bricks."

"We're just lucky this place is under the watchful eye of a couple different preservation groups," said Carmela. "Do you know that twenty years ago some of the tombs were in such terrible disrepair you could actually *see* some of the remains?"

Ava crossed herself quickly. "Dear Lord, I don't like to think about things like that. Let's make this a quick trip, okay?"

"You own a voodoo shop, yet cemeteries make you nervous?" asked Carmela.

"That's because death is *real,*" said Ava. "Voodoo, at least my brand of voodoo, is harmless and make-believe."

"Okay," said Carmela, stopping suddenly and kneeling down. "Here's a good one right here."

Ava peered down skeptically. "Whatcha got?"

"Look at this head with angel wings sprouting from it," said Carmela. "And the inscription."

Ava squinted. " 'Behold and see, How Death has conquered me,' " she read. "Duh. Well that's for sure."

Carmela took a sheet of paper and spread it across the tombstone, taping it in position with strips of masking tape. Then she carefully ran a hand over the paper to ensure no bubbles or bumps would interfere with her rubbing.

"I think a charcoal gray would offer the most contrast on white," she said, selecting a piece of chalk.

"Wouldn't black work better?"

"First we'll get the words and details down," explained Carmela. "Then later, back at my shop, I can always use black to outline the letters and carvings, really make 'em pop."

"So you just use regular chalk?" asked Ava.

"Archival chalk. It's softer and will capture the best impression from the stone."

"Sidewalk chalk's not good enough, huh?" said Ava. She often drew fun little red and orange voodoo-doll images on the sidewalk outside her store. Helped to draw customers in.

"This chalk's better," said Carmela. "Watch." She bent over and started rubbing the chalk against the paper. She started off slowly, then moved on to bolder and larger strokes. Amazingly, the impression of the stone began to appear in even greater detail than it had originally looked to the naked eye. Cracks and fine lines materialized, making the flat sheet of paper seem almost three-dimensional.

Impressed, Ava asked, "Want me to scout the next one?"

"Go for it," Carmela told her.

While Carmela skillfully worked the chalk against paper, Ava wandered off, searching for another interesting tombstone.

A few minutes later, Ava's voice floated out of the gloom. "Got one over here," she called.

"What's that?" asked Carmela. She grabbed a spray can from her tote, popped the top off, and sprayed a thin film of fixative over the rubbing.

"There's a skeleton holding a Grim Reaper scythe and one of those weird-looking hourglasses."

"Excellent," said Carmela.

Ava's face suddenly popped up from behind the tombstone. "Want me to peel this paper off?" she asked.

"Give it a couple minutes," said Carmela. "Make sure it's dry." She grabbed another roll of paper. "Now, where's that next one?"

Ava pointed off into the darkness. "Over there, just to the right of the obelisk."

It would appear Ava had discovered the mother lode. There was a tomb with an outline of a running horse, one with the cryptic message, "Somebody's Darlings," and a tablet with a carved relief of an elaborate urn.

Carmela set to work. Taping up paper, easing her chalk across the ghostly images, spraying her fixative.

Ten minutes went by before Carmela realized she hadn't heard anything from Ava.

"Ava?" she called out.

Nothing. Not a single peep.

Louder this time, more insistent. "Ava?" Feeling the first stirring of nervousness now, Carmela tried to still her breathing, focus all her concentration on listening.

A twig snapped behind her.

Inhaling deeply, senses quivering on full alert now, Carmela clambered to her feet at the same time she spun about on the balls of her feet.

And saw . . . Ava staring back at her! Looking wide-eyed and very worried.

Ava put an index finger to her lips, silently warning Carmela to remain quiet. Then the two of them ducked behind a nearby mausoleum, and Ava whispered, "I think somebody has been following me."

"You're sure?" Carmela whispered back.

Ava gave an emphatic nod. "Every time I moved, they moved. I've been terrified, trying to work my way back to you."

Carmela nodded. Safety in numbers. Hopefully, anyway.

Grabbing her flashlight, Carmela turned on the high beam and flashed it across a row of graves. Whitewashed tombs looked like broken teeth in the beam of light. But as for anyone out there? Nothing.

"Let's pack up and get the hell out of here," urged Ava.

Carmela nodded. Absolutely. She grabbed for her rubbings, rolled them up quickly, and popped them into a cardboard tube. Then the two of them took off.

Just as they neared the front gate and were about to slip under the old wrought-iron arch, just as they had Carmela's car in full sight, there was a crunch in back of them and the distinct sound of human footfalls.

That was enough. The two women took off running. In midstride Carmela stretched out her arm, clicked the electronic key to unlock the doors, and they jumped into the car. Then it was another ten seconds before doors were locked, ignition turned on, and Carmela tromped her foot down hard on the accelerator.

Her little Mercedes, always voracious for a good sip of high-octane fuel, spun its wheels and hit forty-five by the time they'd traveled twenty feet.

"Close call," breathed Ava.

Carmela spread the rubbings out across the kitchen table and countertop. "I want to make sure these are completely dry," she said. "With all the humidity and —"

"And with that creep following us," said Ava, angrily.

"We didn't have time to finish as much as I'd have liked." Carmela tested the rubbings with a forefinger. "These are okay. Dry enough."

"And they look real good, too," added Ava. "Even though we risked life and limb to get them."

"Maybe it wasn't such a good idea to go into that cemetery at night," said Carmela.

"Very stressful," said Ava. "And you know what stress does to me."

Carmela peered at her. "Makes you hungry, right?"

Ava nodded emphatically, her dark hair bouncing. "But don't go to any trouble on my part. Just some toast or a dab of cottage cheese is fine."

Carmela opened the refrigerator, grabbed a carton of cottage cheese, and inspected it. "The expiration date on this says War of 1812."

"That's not good," said Ava.

"Tell you what," said Carmela. "I've also got red beans and rice and some seafood gumbo. Which would you like?"

"You know me," said Ava.

"I'll heat them both up," said Carmela, reaching up to grab pots and pans.

"And I'll pop the cork on a bottle of wine," said Ava. "Wait, you've got wine, don't you? I mean good wine, not that crappy swill that comes in a cardboard box."

Carmela grinned wickedly. "Cases of fine wine, actually. When I moved out on Shamus, I ransacked his wine cellar. Besides some pretty nice domestic stuff, a case of Pétrus and a case of Château Latour somehow found their way here."

"To the exclusive tasting room at Château Carmela," enthused Ava. "Attagirl. Nothing wrong with a little lateral transfer. Shows you got your priorities straight."

Boo and Poobah danced around Carmela's feet as she heated the food, then served it up in bowls. "Be good now, and you can lick these clean when we're done, okay?"

Two happy woofs told her they agreed.

"Have you thought about what kind of divorce settlement you're really going to ask for?" said Ava as they were eating.

Carmela groaned. "Figuring all that out seems so crass."

"Divorce *is* crass," said Ava. "It's a hard-nosed business negotiation. Two parties have to sit down and say, 'If you take this, then I get that.' "

"Sounds more like trading marbles in fourth grade," said Carmela.

"Good analogy," said Ava. She set her dish down on the floor, watched as Boo and Poobah shoved their furry snouts into it. "Too bad Shamus doesn't just keel over from a bad ticker or something. That way you'd walk away with the whole enchilada. With divorce you only get half the enchilada."

"Not really an enchilada then," said Carmela. "More like a *chili relleno.*"

"Whatever you do, *cher,* don't give the ring back. Even if you have to swallow it."

Carmela jumped up, turned on the TV set. "What I have to do is get a lawyer, that's the place to start."

"Get a nasty one," urged Ava. "Ooh, speaking of nasty . . ."

Kimber Breeze's head filled the television screen.

"Here we go again," sang Carmela, knowing this report would probably be another big sack of lies.

"To recap this ongoing story," said Kimber, adopting a serious face and staring straight into the camera as it tracked in for a close-up, "New Orleans police are still baffled over the death of a model this past Wednesday night. Strange bite and claw marks, along with as-yet-unidentified hair found on the victim's body, would seem to suggest a vicious animal attack. But crime scene investigators are not ruling out a human attack, either."

The scene switched to a clip of an elderly woman with a pinched face and gray, uncombed hair. "There's a werewolf running around the streets of N'Orleans at night," she shrilled. "And it wouldn't be the first time."

"Where do they *find* these people?" guffawed Ava. "Do aliens *bring* them? Are they rejects from the planet Zorak?"

Then Kimber was back, doing her best to look baffled as well as concerned. "There you have it, ladies and gentlemen. Some say a werewolf is prowling our city. The mysterious half-man, half-beast creature that has existed only in legend." Kimber paused, letting a few beats go by. "Until, perhaps, now."

Carmela grabbed the remote and flipped the TV off. "Anyone for silver bullets or wooden stakes?"

"Wooden stakes only work with vampires," Ava pointed out. "And even then I'm not so sure."

Carmela picked up her glass of wine, swirled it gently, then took a sip. "It would seem Kimber Breeze is doing her best to put forth the bizarre theory that a werewolf is stalking New Orleans." Carmela knew how ridiculous the whole thing sounded. In fact, Kimber's wild theory made her angry. But somehow, the whole notion plucked away uncomfortably at the limbic part of her brain, the reptilian brain that still carried a deep, primal fear of such strange and bizarre things.

And the idea of a strange beast terrified Carmela. After all, she hadn't forgotten the sensation of someone pushing her down and the nauseating feeling of hot breath on the back of her neck.

"She really is flogging this werewolf thing, isn't she?" laughed Ava.

"I'd like to flog her," muttered Carmela.

CHAPTER 16

"Are you going to take pictures at the funeral?" asked Ava. She was toying with Carmela's digital camera as they zipped along Highway 1, heading toward Hermitage, just northwest of Baton Rouge.

Carmela nodded, then reconsidered. "Well, maybe afterwards. Of the graveyard anyway. I understand it's quite old. Maybe I can get something we can use as wall decor to sort of augment the rubbings."

Ava studied herself in the rearview mirror, tilting her head left then right. "Do you think I'm gettin' crow's feet?"

"Nope," responded Carmela. She was watching the road more carefully now, looking for the turnoff.

"Bags under my eyes?"

"You look fantastic," said Carmela. "Better than fantastic."

"You know," said Ava, whispering as though she were revealing state secrets, "I'm not exactly a dewy-faced twenty-year-old anymore."

"Who is?" said Carmela.

Ava continued to scrutinize her face in the mirror. "But do I still look young enough to model? You know, my cheeks used to be as smooth as a baby's —"

"But you've already been selected to model," said Carmela, the corners of her mouth twitching. "You're the new face of Moda Chadron."

Ava sighed. "Such as it is."

St. Michael's Church was the oldest church in the small town of Hermitage. A small stone structure that looked like it had seen better times, the dark red stone was sorely in need of a sandblasting. But large, leafy trees surrounded the church and lent an air of peace and tranquillity. And a small whitewashed vicarage stood behind the church.

Carmela parked her car in the small parking lot. From there they could see people dressed in black heading toward the graveyard that adjoined the property.

"Has to be the place," said Ava, sounding none too chirpy.

Carmela nodded. "This is it." Since there was only a simple graveside service scheduled, she wondered just how religious Amber's family had been.

Joining the straggle of people, the two women walked toward the graveyard where a bronze casket rested atop a wooden bier. Bright green plastic grass surrounded it. Carmela shuddered. Funeral grass. There was nothing worse. Black metal folding chairs, looking aged and rickety, were set up in a semicircle around the casket, but nobody had taken a seat on them yet.

Ava nudged Carmela as they got closer to the grave. "Look at who all showed up," she murmured under her breath.

Carmela studied the crowd that shuffled nervously about in the vicinity of the casket. Chadron and Angelique were there, Chadron looking studiously sober, Angelique gazing about with open curiosity. Yasmin was there, too, along with three other young women who were so amazingly thin Carmela knew they just had to be models as well.

I'm not that thin, thought Carmela. *Ava's not even that thin. How on earth are we ever going to fit into Chadron's clothes?*

And Carmela caught sight of Gordon van Hees, too. He had moved over to chat quietly with Yasmin. Her short, dark hair made her look like she was wearing a skullcap, and her skin appeared almost translucent in the thin sunlight.

Nearing the group, Carmela nodded to Mr. and Mrs. Guste, who had just taken seats on the black folding chairs.

Margaret Guste daubed at her eyes with a tissue, then gave a slight nod toward Carmela. *Thank you,* she mouthed. Her husband sat next to her, staring straight ahead, not seeing the people or the event that was about to unfold before him.

Carmela's heart went out to him. To both of them. There could be nothing worse, she decided, than to lose a beloved child.

"The parents?" whispered Ava.

Carmela nodded. "The Gustes," she whispered back.

"That's right," said Ava. "She changed her name." She gazed around at the crowd. "Well, it's certainly a well-dressed group."

A minister clutching a prayer book took his place at the head of the casket. He cast sorrowful eyes about the crowd, then began. "We are gathered here today to pay tribute to our dearly departed sister, Amber Elizabeth Guste," he intoned. "May the good Lord give us comfort and strength as we grieve her death, for she was taken from us far too early in life."

Carmela sighed deeply and looked

around. The minister was very well-meaning, but his words were depressing rather than uplifting. Instead of focusing on an afterlife, he pressed on about Amber's untimely death and the misery that everyone had to be feeling. The crowd picked up on his melancholy words and seemed restless. Yasmin stared at Gordon, Angelique kept eyeing the gaggle of skinny models, and Chadron seemed to be staring at a dark figure who was standing away from the crowd, up on a slight rise between two thickets of palm trees. The man, whoever he was, had his back turned to the crowd.

Ava caught Carmela eyeing the figure, too, and murmured, "Who's that?"

"Not sure," Carmela said under her breath. And then the lone figure turned slowly and stared down the hill toward the gathering. "Santino," hissed Carmela.

Santino wore a black leather coat that hung past his knees. It was an article of clothing that seemed too hot for the day, but that didn't seem to bother him. He had his arms crossed casually, but Carmela could detect tension in his pose. Santino's long hair flowed down to his shoulders, and he seemed to glower at everyone as his eyes roved across the crowd.

"He looks pretty upset," said Carmela.

"The question is, what's he doing here?" asked Ava.

Then Santino's eyes fell on Chadron, and his stare turned into a disdainful sneer.

"Paying his last respects?" said Carmela.

It was Chadron who delivered the most heartfelt and meaningful eulogy of the day. His voice echoing through the picturesque graveyard, he talked about what a great talent Amber had been, what a shining star she surely would have become. At each compliment, Angelique rolled her heavily mascaraed eyes and tightened her lips, expressing her obvious displeasure. Yasmin, on the other hand, looked relaxed and radiant. She seemed to glow with the knowledge that she was now top model in the Moda Chadron house.

When the prayers had been said, when the wreaths and sprays of flowers had been laid tenderly atop Amber's casket, when final regrets had been conveyed to Mr. and Mrs. Guste, Carmela and Ava slipped off into the cemetery.

"This part is really old, *cher*," remarked Ava as they strolled among tilting markers that were covered in moss so dark and green it looked like velvet. "And look at the dates.

They almost go back to Louisiana Purchase days."

"It's very beautiful here," said Carmela. "Peaceful, too."

Live oaks draped in Spanish moss created a restful, highly atmospheric scene. A small reflecting pond contained dozens of tiny orange fish that seemed to dart in all directions when they ventured near. Beds of camellias and mums offered bountiful fall blossoms. And a tall marble statue of an angel, its face pitted with age, seemed to watch knowingly over nearby gravestones.

"Maybe Amber will really be at rest here," said Carmela, her voice catching in her throat. Her final memory of the girl was seeing her sprawled rudely in the alley.

"Let's hope so," agreed Ava.

"Did Santino leave?" asked Carmela, feeling a wave of sympathy for Mr. and Mrs. Guste, hoping Santino didn't walk down the hill and create some sort of nasty scene.

"Yeah, I think so," said Ava, gazing around. "At least I don't see him."

Just as Carmela had framed a shot of a granite headstone with a small lamb carved into it, Gordon van Hees stepped, literally, into the picture.

She lowered the camera, slightly startled.

"Oops," he said, backtracking fast, looking very embarrassed. "Didn't mean to do *that*."

"No problem," said Carmela. She reconfigured her shot, took the picture.

"You enjoy cemeteries?" he asked her. "I don't mean to imply that you're enjoying today's event, of course. Certainly not this terribly sad ceremony. But you are interested in their history and architecture?"

"Call me strange," said Carmela, "but I do."

"Nothing strange about it," said Gordon. "We live in New Orleans, after all. Which means we're surrounded by our cities of the dead."

"That's for sure," said Ava. "They're all around us."

"I'm curious," said Gordon, as Carmela took a couple more shots. "Are you perhaps thinking of using any of these pictures in the decorating scheme for Moda Chadron?"

"We're working on that," Ava told him confidently. "We have some wonderful designs cooked up. Very sophisticated stuff."

"Excellent," said Gordon.

"Actually," said Carmela, "I was thinking of incorporating a couple of these shots into a miniature theater I'm creating."

"Now *that* sounds interesting," said Gordon.

"No, I'm really kind of struggling with it," Carmela told him. "My little theater needs something; I'm just not sure what. Maybe some sort of photo backdrop or maybe just a snippet of marvelous fabric."

"You're talking to the right man," said Gordon, smiling. "I just happen to have access to yards and yards of the most incredible fabrics."

"I suppose you do," said Carmela, remembering the clothes and the luxurious fabrics she'd seen at Moda Chadron.

"And I'd be happy to . . . say, you don't stock ribbon at that scrapbook shop of yours do you?" asked Gordon. He scrunched up his face, looking slightly hopeful.

"Yards of it," said Ava, jumping in. "Carmela's got velvets, silks, beaded organzas, chiffons . . ."

"We absolutely must negotiate a trade, then," said Gordon. "Some of my fabric snippets for your ribbon. You see, Chadron is still laboring away on clothing and head-pieces for the Halloween Bash fashion show. He's got himself in a royal snit and has been absolutely *screaming* for purple velvet ribbon. I've been on the phone to our suppliers but . . ."

"Carmela can do purple," interrupted Ava. "As well as violet, amethyst, magenta, and everything in between."

"Talk about a lifesaver," enthused Gordon. He held up his right hand, pinched his index finger close against his thumb. "Chadron was *this* close to ripping my head off this morning."

"Oh my," said Ava. "And we're supposed to stop by later this afternoon for a fitting."

"Bring the ribbon in tribute," warned Gordon. "And maybe he'll spare your lives."

CHAPTER 17

"How was the funeral?" asked Gabby.

"Sad," said Carmela. "And relatively uneventful, thank goodness." She'd dropped off Ava, dashed home to let the dogs out, and had just pushed her way through the front door at Memory Mine. The door she'd had to have repaired following Shamus's nasty little snit fit. "How's business here?"

"Heating up," said Gabby, as she ripped open a FedEx box, gathered up the contents, and carried it all to the counter. "Oh, there's lunch if you'd like, a roast beef po'boy from the Pavillon Deli." Gabby was bent over the front counter now, happily sorting out their new shipment of stickers and foam stamps.

"Dressed?" asked Carmela.

"Yup," said Gabby. "The works. Mayo, tomatoes, pickles, *and* coleslaw. Oh, and Baby brought lemon icebox pie."

"Fantastic," said Carmela, as she threaded

her way through the store, heading toward her little office. "I'm famished."

"Hey cupcake," called Tandy. She was sitting at the craft table alongside Baby, working on a scrapbook page. "We heard you went up to Hermitage this morning. That poor girl's funeral."

"A sad business," said Baby. She pushed a wisp of blond hair behind an ear, revealing gleaming Chanel earrings.

"What's sad," said Carmela, slipping into a chair alongside Baby, "is that I'm not one iota closer to figuring out what happened that night."

Baby put a hand on Carmela's arm. "It's not up to you to solve this murder, honey. That's for the police."

"They don't seem to be any closer than I am," replied Carmela. "But, yes, Baby, I hear you. I know exactly what you're saying."

Now it was Tandy's turn to put her two cents in. She scrunched her face into a serious look and focused hard on Carmela. "And it's completely unfair that Ava's fortune-teller guy . . . What's his name?"

"Giovanni."

"That Giovanni dragged you even further into this mess," said Tandy. "You were just an innocent bystander who happened to be in the wrong place at the wrong time." She nodded hard, her tight curls bouncing as if to punctuate her sentence.

"Exactly," said Baby. "So have a slice of pie and forget about it."

"Thank you," Carmela told her friends. "Your words means a lot to me."

"You mean our criticism?" Tandy's laugh was slightly sheepish.

"No, your support," said Carmela. "I don't know what I'd do without friends like you."

"Honey," said Tandy. "We don't know what we'd do without this place!"

"We are scrapbook addicts," agreed Baby. "We should probably seek immediate intervention."

"And treatment," said Tandy.

"Check ourselves into a weekend scrapbook retreat," chuckled Baby.

"What are you two working on, anyway?" asked Carmela. She was heartened by her friends' kindness, could feel the damp cloud of Amber's funeral lifting slightly.

"Not much," said Baby. "But if you've got a new idea, we'd sure be open to it."

"*Do* you have a new idea?" asked Tandy, looking interested.

Carmela nodded. "I was going to save this project for my Dream Weaver classes, but it might be fun to take a test run."

"On what?" asked Baby.

Carmela stood up, slid out one of the drawers in her flat file, and pulled out two white cardboard templates. "They're templates for purses," she said, laying the pieces in front of Baby and Tandy. "I've got these two all ready to go." She paused. "Here's the thing. First you stamp and decorate them, which is a lot trickier than it sounds. Then you fold them up so they really look like a constructed handbag. See, I've already made dotted lines for folding. To finish them off, you add side tabs, a handle, and maybe a fancy closure."

"What's the finished size?" asked Baby. She was already folding her template, eager to get a sense of what her little purse would look like when it was finished.

"About eight inches long, six inches tall," said Carmela.

"A purse," said Tandy, slowly warming up to the idea. "For what purpose?"

"Decorated with beads and fibers, they make adorable gift bags," said Carmela. "For jewelry or candles. Or a piece of lingerie. Or maybe even some homemade cookies."

"I *love* the idea," said Baby. "And I already know what my design is going to be."

"What?" asked Tandy, still studying her template.

"I'm going to cover my template with pink and gold floral paper, then add gold trim, some beading, a bow closure, and a velvet ribbon handle. All in the same pink and gold colors, of course."

"Wow," said Tandy. "You sure figured yours out fast." She peered at Carmela. "A little help might be in order here, my dear."

"What if you stamped purple and lavender flowers onto the white card stock," offered Carmela.

"All over?" said Tandy.

"No, no," said Carmela. "Let a small field of white show through, particularly in the middle."

"I like that," said Tandy. "Then what?"

"Maybe punch in a couple eyelets and string purple beads for the handle," suggested Carmela. She got up from her chair again, started rummaging in another cupboard. "And use a purple bead with some of those crinkle fibers for a closure."

"Great idea," said Tandy. She rummaged in her craft bag, found a purple stamp pad, pulled it out.

"Here," said Carmela. She handed over indigo blue, mauve, and lavender stamp pads. "You're going to need these. Oh, and green, too. You want to use lots of jewel tones and stamp multiple layers. Try to achieve an almost stained glass effect."

"What are you going to do?" asked Baby.

"Eat lunch," replied Carmela. "And have some pie."

But just as Carmela took a bite of her po'boy, Gabby stuck her head in the office. "That Lieutenant Babcock is on line two," she said, wrinkling her nose.

Carmela picked up the phone. "What's going on?" she asked. "Who's topping your most wanted list today?"

"Still the usual suspects," Babcock replied mildly. "I understand you took a little drive this morning."

Carmela hesitated. How did he know? "How did you know that?"

"We had someone there."

"Someone from your department?" asked Carmela.

"No, someone from the CIA. Yes, from our department," said Babcock.

"Would that have been the skinny model with the gap-tooth smile or the lumpy guy standing at the back of the pack?" asked Carmela. Come to think of it, she *had* noticed someone standing off to the side.

"That information's confidential," said

Babcock.

"Did your guy see anything interesting?" Carmela asked, wondering if Babcock's guy, and she had to assume it was a guy, had spotted Santino.

"Not really," replied Babcock, causing Carmela to think that Santino might not have been seen.

"I wanted to ask you about the poker chip that was found near Amber," said Carmela.

"What about it?"

"Er . . . was it from one of the area casinos? Or do you think it came from one of those plastic home sets?"

Babcock exhaled loudly, obviously not pleased with Carmela's question. Then again, he was never thrilled by her questions. "That's confidential information," said Babcock.

"Then why did you call me?" asked Carmela. "Why do you *keep* calling me?"

"Do you have any idea where Santino is?" asked Babcock. He sounded like he might be gritting his teeth. "He seems to have dropped off our radar screen."

"No," said Carmela. "Then again, that's probably confidential information."

An hour later, Baby and Tandy were in the throes of making their little purses, and Carmela was ready to tackle the papier-mâché pumpkins for Moda Chadron. They'd gossiped about Baby's party, the upcoming fashion show, Carmela and Ava's good fortune at being selected as models, and the big celebration in the French Quarter two nights from now. Carmela figured she'd procrastinated as much as she could and now had to buckle down. So she dragged her papier-mâché pumpkins out from her office.

"You're doing more pumpkins?" asked Baby.

"For Halloween luminarias," said Carmela. "To line the runway at Moda Chadron."

"Good heavens," said Baby, "it feels like Halloween is over."

"That's because you had your big party early this year," pointed out Tandy. "But most people are just gearing up."

"I suppose they are," said Baby.

"Look at that daffy woman on WBEZ," said Tandy. "She's trying to whip everyone into a frenzy about werewolves." She glanced at Carmela. "Sorry, honey. I didn't mean to upset you."

"You didn't," said Carmela. She was busy painting her papier-mâché pumpkin with a coat of adhesive. "But I think that silly reporter might be upsetting a lot of other people."

"Kimber Breeze shouldn't even be on TV," said Gabby, coming over to join them. "She's only happy when she's stirring up trouble."

"That's called making headlines," said Carmela. "Garnering ratings."

"Didn't Kimber Breeze cause Ava to lose a lot of business?" asked Tandy.

"Actually," said Carmela, "I think Ava's shop has done *more* business in the wake of Kimber's wacky broadcasts."

Tandy shook her head. "Go figure."

Gabby slit open a package of gold foil and handed a piece to Carmela. It was thin, flimsy material and required a delicate touch.

Carmela put a finger to her adhesive, testing it. Perfect. Tacky, but no longer wet. She took the sheet of gold foil and applied it to the surface of the pumpkin. Then she worked the foil carefully, patting it, smoothing out wrinkles as she went along.

"That looks good," said Gabby.

Carmela eased another piece on, continued to smooth it gently. When the entire pumpkin was covered, she'd take a small dry rag and wipe it all over the surface. That technique would smooth out any final wrinkles, flake off any extraneous pieces.

Bang! Bang! Bang!

Gabby jumped, startled, and clamped a hand over her heart. "The back door," she stammered.

Carmela slid out of her chair, patting Gabby's shoulder to reassure her. "Probably Ava. Forgot her key."

But when she unfastened the latch and slid the door open a couple inches to peer out, two dark, piercing eyes stared back at her.

"Giovanni?" she said.

"What?" came Tandy's outraged squawk from behind her. "Who?"

"Don't let him in!" cried Gabby.

Carmela stared out at Giovanni. "It would seem you are persona non grata here."

"They don't know me," said Giovanni. "I'm really a pussycat."

"Sure you are," said Carmela. "A man who divines tarot cards and has a brother who keeps wolves. Just garden-variety hobbies. Whatever happened to stamp collecting or building model airplanes?"

"That stuff's for wusses," said Giovanni. He stared at Carmela. "So, are you going to let me in or not?"

"Not," said a voice behind Carmela. It was Gabby, looking more than a little concerned. "Do you want me to call 911?" she asked. "I've got it on speed dial."

Giovanni stuck his face closer to the door. "Boo," he said.

Gabby retreated a step.

"Can Carmela come out and play?" he asked in a wheedling tone.

"Don't be such an asshole," muttered Carmela. She pulled open the door, stepped out into the alley.

Giovanni stood there, his hands in his pockets, looking very tough-guy and urban in a black T-shirt, jeans, and brown leather jacket. "I need to talk to you," he said.

"Fine," said Carmela. "So talk."

"Santino was still very upset Saturday night. And I understand that when he ran into you and Ava he acted a bit rash."

"*He's* upset?" said Carmela. "Too bad. Lots of people seem to be upset these days." She stared at Giovanni. "You show up for work today? I heard you blew it off yesterday."

Giovanni shrugged. "Something important came up. But I was there today."

"Ava's not sure what to do with you," said Carmela. "She's impressed at how you handle customers, but she's not sure she can trust you. Then again, neither am I."

"What are you trying to say?"

"She doesn't want to fire you . . ."

"Fire me? Hey, I *need* that job!"

"Something is going on, *has* been going on for some time. And we've been trying our darnedest to help. But you haven't been completely up front with us."

"I'm sorry —" began Giovanni, but Carmela held up a hand.

"I don't want any more excuses," said Carmela. "Or smoke screens."

"You saw Santino this morning?" asked Giovanni.

"Yes, we did," said Carmela, remembering how he'd held himself apart from the crowd.

"That Lieutenant Babcock is looking for him again," said Giovanni. "Heck, the whole New Orleans Police Department is probably out looking for him." Giovanni glanced over his shoulder and scanned the alley nervously. "I gotta tell you, we probably do need your help."

"We've been *trying* to help," said Carmela, feeling frustrated, knowing she sounded like a broken record.

"The thing of it is," Giovanni rambled on, "you're smart. And Babcock will really *listen* to you . . ."

"What are you afraid of?" asked Carmela. "What's Santino afraid of?"

"You don't understand," said Giovanni.

"Because you haven't actually told me anything," snapped Carmela. "So start playing it straight, okay? Where's Santino right now?"

Giovanni shifted from one leg to the other. "I can't tell you," he said, then turned and walked quickly down the alley.

CHAPTER 18

At four forty-five, Carmela and Ava were hiking down Ursaline Street, on their way to Moda Chadron. Ava had come bouncing in earlier, all bubbly and excited about making a runway debut. Carmela decided not to tell Ava that Giovanni had stopped by. It would just ruin her fine mood.

"You know," said Carmela as they crossed to Royal Street, "I'm thrilled about doing the decorations for Chadron's big Halloween show, but I'm getting awfully nervous about this modeling business."

"Oh honey," exclaimed Ava. "It's going to be a piece of cake. All you have to do is strut down the runway looking sexy and fierce. When you get to the end, do a little signature twirl or wink or something, then walk back. Hey, how hard can it be if even a model can do it?" Ava giggled at her little joke.

"No," said Carmela, hunching her shoulders forward. "I'm serious. You've been in beauty pageants and all that, so this is no big whoop for you. But get me all gussied up, and I worry about traversing a city block without breaking a heel or twisting an ankle. Maybe they'll let me wear flats after all."

"Hah!" snorted Ava. "Good one. Designers rarely allow their models to walk down the runway in flats." Ava scooted out ahead of Carmela. "See, a woman *glides* in heels." Ava continued to demonstrate her grace as she floated down the sidewalk. "High heels show off the fine lines of a woman's form and help exaggerate hip movements."

"What if I don't want to exaggerate my hip movements?" asked Carmela. "What if my hips are exaggerated enough?"

"Then put one hand on your hip and rotate it backwards," suggested Ava. "Cheat the angle."

"You're suggesting I do Pilates while walking down the runway?" asked Carmela.

"Well, you've got to do *something* that approximates model-like posture," exclaimed Ava as they arrived at the atelier. "To be honest, I'm not all that crazy about my hips, either. I've actually been contemplating that hip-o-suction procedure."

"You mean liposuction?"

"Yeah, that's it," said Ava. They paused

outside the atelier, where the words Moda Chadron were lettered in gold on the glass doors, the looping letters forming an elegant, understated logo.

"Modeling," snorted Carmela as they stepped into an entryway with walls decorated in a gray suedelike fabric and gleaming white ceramic tile underfoot.

"At least try to extend your neck," Ava urged. "Pretend you're a graceful swan."

Carmela tried. And just about dislocated a vertebrae. "Ouch," she muttered as Ava pulled open the second set of doors and they stepped inside.

The interior of Moda Chadron looked as gorgeous as ever. Lights were turned low, soft music played, the clothing seemed to whisper at them from the racks.

"Do you know where we're supposed to go?" asked Carmela.

"The studio's upstairs," said Ava. "That's where all the action is. C'mon."

"Studio?" asked Carmela as they climbed the circular stairway. "Don't they have a changing room? Or maybe a locker room?"

Ava shook her head. "For Chadron and his dressers to fit dozens of girls and gowns, they need lots of open space. Plus, come Wednesday night, the hair and makeup people will be doing their thing, too. So it should be a real madhouse. Fun, actually."

"We'll be getting dressed in the middle of all that?" asked Carmela.

"That's how it's done, *cher.*" Ava pushed Carmela up the last couple steps. "So hustle your bustle."

Krisi Young was one of Chadron's dressers. A twenty-something with a pierced eyebrow and a mouth full of straight pins, encased in a skinny black knit dress. "Lose the bra," she mumbled to Carmela, pointing toward the offending object.

"No bra?" asked Carmela. "Whoa, I didn't agree to walk down a runway half-naked." Of course, all around her were half-naked models, posing, twirling, acting as though it was the most natural thing on earth.

Krisi spat pins into her hand. "Nothing must mar the lines of the designer's clothing." Her long blond hair was pulled high into a trendy bouffant psyche knot that bobbed with each subtle move of her head.

"What about *my* lines?" asked Carmela.

Krisi eyed Carmela's body, then grabbed a frothy dress off a rack and thrust it at her. "Here, try this."

Carmela studied the tiny floral dress as it hung limp on the hanger. To her it looked more like a halter top. "Is there more to it?"

she asked. "A skirt, perhaps? A jacket for coverage?"

Ignoring Carmela completely, Krisi grabbed a silver, shimmery number for Ava. Long and swishy, exactly her style.

"Ooh, I love it," cooed Ava. "But is this dress even my size?" She held it up to her, looking worried.

"Fitting means we make it fit," said Krisi, shaking her head. Then, as Carmela and Ava ducked behind a curtain that had mercifully been strung across part of the studio, Krisi muttered, loud enough for them to hear, "Amateurs."

"She thinks we're idiots," said Carmela, as the two of them undressed quickly.

"So what," said Ava with a shrug. "This is fun. Aren't you having fun?"

"No," said Carmela. "I'm standing here in my undies, some silly girl I don't even know is telling me to lose my bra, and I'm completely losing my nerve."

"Try on the dress, *cher*," Ava coaxed. "See how it looks. Keep an open mind."

Carmela's floral dress slithered over her head, then down over her hips.

"Oh my," said Ava.

"Bad?" asked Carmela. She was literally holding her breath. "Hideous?"

"No . . . it's a knockout!" declared Ava.

Carmela mustered her courage and stared at her image in the mirror. She couldn't believe what met her eyes. The short halter dress looked incredible on her. It hugged her waist, flared out over her hips, and made her legs look amazingly long. The pale peach color accentuated the highlights in her hair and made her skin glow.

"Audrey Hepburn, eat your heart out," giggled Ava. "That dress gives you a very feminine, gaminelike appearance. You look like you should be tossing coins into a fountain in Rome."

Carmela turned sideways. "But I do have a little . . . um . . . jiggle?"

"Tape," said Ava. "All you need is some judiciously placed tape."

Carmela looked squeamish. "You think?"

"Trust me," laughed Ava. "I know all the secrets. I used to compete in beauty pageants, remember?"

"So what are those deep, dark secrets, anyway?" asked Carmela, more than a little intrigued.

"Vaseline on the teeth so your lips slide easily into a smile. Preparation H on the face to smooth out wrinkles. Plastic wrap pulled tight around the old midsection to squeeze out that pesky water weight. And tape, lots and lots of tape."

"Preparation H?" giggled Carmela. "Seriously?"

"That's the down home treatment of choice," said Ava. "Today, of course, there's good stuff like BOTOX."

"Not sure how good that really is," murmured Carmela.

"Wait till we get really old," said Ava. "Then we're going to need all the plumpers and fillers we can get our hands on."

"I suppose," said Carmela, still eyeing herself in the mirror, stunned at what a dramatic difference a fine couture dress could make in a girl's appearance.

"Okay, my turn," said Ava. She shrugged her long gown over her head, smoothed it, and struck an artful pose that made her shoulders arch backward while her hips slid forward. "What do you think about this silver number?"

"I'm in awe," said Carmela. "You look like you're ready for New York Fashion Week!"

Pleased, Ava lifted a single eyebrow. "Really?" she drawled. "You're sure my ass doesn't look like the *Hindenburg*?"

"Not in the least," said Carmela. "It's gorgeous. In fact, this whole thing couldn't be working out any better," declared Carmela. "Now I'm positive the audience will be looking at *you* during the entire show."

"Ladies," said Krisi, grabbing the curtain and snapping it back fast. "We don't have all day!"

Carmela and Ava turned to face Krisi. Their inquisitor.

She studied them for a couple long moments, then Krisi's impatient frown seemed to morph into a look of resignation. "Not entirely terrible," she told them. "But we do have a lot of work ahead of us."

"Are you serious?" asked Ava, executing a little twirl. "I think this dress is perfect as is."

"Perfectly dreadful," said Krisi, tossing pairs of high-heeled sandals to each of them. "The neckline's too high, the straps need to be narrowed, and the draping's all wrong."

"I look that bad?" asked Ava, struggling into her shoes.

Carmela shook her head. *No.*

"Come, come," said Krisi, indicating for Ava to stand on a wooden platform. "So I can work on you. Make with the magic."

And thirty minutes later, Krisi really had made with the magic. Ava's dress looked flawless on her figure, and Carmela's short dress suddenly swirled about in an even more beguiling manner.

"I think I am having a little fun now," Carmela admitted to Ava. "Except for the fact that my feet are killing me."

"Pardon me," said Ava, addressing Krisi. "Are these the shoes we're going to wear Wednesday night?" Ava eyed the black stiletto sandals she was wearing with a touch of nervousness. She was used to a little more flash.

"No," said Krisi, jotting notes so the seamstresses could make their alterations.

"Can we please see the shoes we'll be wearing?" asked Ava.

"No," said Krisi. She finished with her notes, then turned toward the rolling rack full of clothes and grabbed two more dresses. "Here's your second change," she told the two women. "And hurry up, you two are taking forever!"

"Does it seem like we've been here all night?" asked Ava. She was climbing back into her jeans and T-shirt. Their dresses had been tugged and adjusted and draped and pinned until they couldn't take it anymore. Then they'd had to listen to Krisi lecture them about posture and runway pacing and study the rudimentary sketches that depicted potential hair and makeup styles.

"Of course nothing about hair and

makeup is ever carved in stone," Krisi had cautioned them. "If Chadron changes his mind a few hours before the runway show, everyone — and I do mean everyone — will just have to snap to and adapt!"

"I'm exhausted," said Carmela. "I feel like a torture victim from being stuck with so many pins, and my brain is spinning and sputtering inside my head. I never thought looking good required so much work. In my book, the book of Carmela, you take a shower, pat on a little makeup, and grab something from the closet."

"You just never did runway before," said Ava knowingly. She was tired, too, but was really getting into it. "That's the way —" she began. But just then the curtain parted, and Yasmin stuck her head in.

"Hey," said Yasmin, looking both gorgeous and vacant in a filmy, almost see-through outfit. "You guys seen Latsis?"

"What's a Latsis?" asked Carmela.

"Only the top hair guy in the entire southern United States," said Yasmin with a distinct pout.

"Not here," said Ava. She looked pointedly at Yasmin in her couture creation. "Nice dress. What there is of it."

A look of smug satisfaction crept across Yasmin's face. "In case you haven't heard,

I'm headlining the show. I'm top model at Moda Chadron now."

"Bully for you," said Ava. "And how long do you think that will last? I understand most models burn out by the time they're twenty-five. And I hear Chadron likes them young."

"I'm a lot younger than you," sniffed Yasmin. Her gaze shifted to Carmela. "Thinner, too."

"Listen here, little girl," began Ava in a threatening tone.

But Carmela interceded. "Yasmin, I'd like to ask you something. How well do you know Remy Chenier?"

Yasmin rolled her eyes. "Everyone knows Remy."

Ava clenched her hands as she stepped closer to Yasmin.

"We ran into Remy Saturday night," continued Carmela. She put out a hand, pushed Ava back.

"So?" Yasmin checked her manicure, clearly sending a message that she was bored with their entire conversation.

"So, Remy was dealing cards," said Carmela. "Do you know . . . is Remy a professional gambler?"

"What?" asked Yasmin in a flat tone, obviously not paying much heed to Carmela's questions.

"She asked if you knew whether or not Remy gambles," said Ava from between clenched teeth.

The tone in Ava's voice finally registered with Yasmin. She looked up at Ava, who was a head taller than she was and decidedly not waiflike. "I don't know that much about Remy," answered Yasmin. "He runs in a different crowd. Not *my* crowd."

"Yasmin!" called a voice.

Yasmin looked over and saw one of the dressers waving at her. "Yeah, whatever," she said under her breath, then took off.

"Such a little darling," said Ava in a snide tone. "A real pleasure to be around. If the dressers were smart, they'd use her head as a pincushion. It's certainly not doing anything else."

"I hear you," said Carmela. "Yasmin doesn't seem to know much of anything. Least of all what Remy is up to."

"Ladies," said Gordon van Hees, peering around a rack of dresses. "I trust the fittings went well?"

"Wonderful," gushed Ava. "I simply adore my dresses, and Krisi was a love."

"Tough love, anyway," muttered Carmela under her breath. Though getting insulted and stuck with pins hadn't been much fun, some parts of the evening had offered glints of amusement.

"Did Krisi tell you what we're going to do downstairs?" Gordon asked.

"You mean with the runway?" said Ava.

Gordon made a grand, theatric gesture. "I've decided to hang an enormous see-through piece of fabric between the front of house and the back desk. That way all the models can come capering down the stairs without being seen, then literally pop out onto the runway."

"So you'll have lights playing on the fabric?" asked Carmela.

"We're working on that," said Gordon. "Of course, your decorations are going to be key."

"You're gonna love them!" promised Ava. "Right, Carmela?"

Carmela nodded. "Very sophisticated. In keeping with Chadron's show."

"Excellent," said Gordon, waggling a finger at them. "Just don't keep me guessing too long."

"Oh," said Carmela, suddenly remembering the ribbon she'd brought along. "I brought some velvet ribbon for Chadron." She grabbed her handbag, unfastened the catch, dug around inside. "Here," she said, handing a plastic bag full of ribbon to Gordon. "I hope this works."

When Gordon saw what she'd brought, he literally beamed. "Oh my," he exclaimed. "Oh yes." A giant smile lit his handsome face.

"If Chadron needs more, I've got it," said Carmela, pleased. "Lots of it."

Gordon unfurled a roll of royal purple velvet ribbon. "Gorgeous. Chadron is going to adore this. He's been snarling all day about how he's unable to finish his headpieces. I told him I had something up my sleeve, but he didn't believe me. Thank you . . ." Gordon put a hand on Carmela's shoulder. "I can't tell you how much I appreciate your generosity."

"Have you seen my other boot?" asked Carmela. She was scrambling around, still trying to pull herself together. Now the studio was almost deserted.

"No, I . . . wait a minute," said Ava. "Here it is. Somehow it got stuck under the makeup table." She snuck a second glance at her watch, made a face.

"You have to be somewhere," said Carmela.

"I can wait for you," said Ava. "I just promised Miguel I'd be back at the shop."

"Go," commanded Carmela.

"You sure?"

"Please," said Carmela. "I'll be fine. I'm just a little discombobulated at the moment, but I'm sure I'll pull it together."

"Thanks, *cher*," said Ava. "See you tomorrow." She planted a kiss on Carmela's cheek and dashed off.

"Boots," muttered Carmela. "Why did I have to wear boots?" They were fashionable, oh-so-high, and looked very sexy when pulled over skinny jeans. But the whole boots-over-jeans thing wasn't always so easy to make happen.

Finally, after five minutes of tugging and tucking, Carmela did get herself back together. She grabbed her handbag, slung it over her shoulder, and dashed out the door into the hallway.

Lights had been turned low here, and she could barely see her way to the stairs. Carmela touched a hand to the wall, easing her way along.

But as she passed by what had to be Chadron's office, she heard angry, low voices coming from inside. Like a heated, mumbled argument was going on.

Someone arguing? Someone getting fired?

She stopped to listen, at the same time feeling slightly guilty about eavesdropping.

"That can't be possible!" roared a voice, seething with anger. The outburst was followed by a loud slam.

Carmela jumped at the sound.

Yipes!

She teetered unsteadily on her boots, put a hand out to steady herself, thumped against the wall.

"Who's out there?" demanded an angry voice.

Carmela could hear footfalls heading for the door.

Without waiting to find out what was going on, Carmela fled down the stairs and out into the night.

CHAPTER 19

Royal Street was almost deserted as Carmela hiked along. Not many people out, not many shops open on a Monday night. Probably, she decided, everyone was saving themselves for the big blowout on Wednesday. Then these same cobblestone streets would be filled with food booths, music stages, and cavorting witches, warlocks, vampires, and skeletons, all the die-hard party people who had no intention of waiting for Mardi Gras to put on a costume and were ready and willing to suit up for Halloween.

And the French Quarter was ripe and ready for the bash. Witches and goblins stood in doorways and skulked behind lampposts. Strings of skull lanterns grinned eerily from trees. Diaphanous ghosts floated from lines overhead. Cornstalks and pumpkins formed autumnal still lifes. Carmela was startled more than a couple times as she passed by strange, grinning faces, thinking them people instead of just part of the decor.

Easy, she told herself. *It's all just make-believe. Fabric and papier-mâché, just like the pumpkins I created.*

Pausing at the window of DeBordieu Antiques & Art Goods, Carmela peered in to admire a gleaming silver tray heaped with estate jewelry. The jewels were tumbled together in an elegantly haphazard way, as though a rich duchess had just come home from a late-night ball and tossed her fabulous jewelry into a dish on her nightstand. One ring in particular caught Carmela's eye. A wide gold band accented with a large green stone. Certainly not an emerald, but maybe a peridot or lemon citrine, she figured.

Carmela knew she'd have to sell a lot of albums, pens, paper, and embellishments to afford that little bauble. Still, it sparkled alluringly, an elegant piece of —

Whoosh-snap!

Carmela spun about, startled. All thoughts of the ring shattered like a soap bubble in the air. *What was that? What did I just hear?*

As her heart thudded heavily in her chest, her eyes searched the deserted street, trying to determine what had made that strange whooshing, flapping sound.

Whoosh-snap.

There it was again! Carmela searched shifting shadows that seemed to play tricks on her eyes and fill her mind with menacing images. Then, just as she was about to make a dash for it, she spotted a papier-mâché character across the street. A squat, green-faced witch whose ankle-length cape snapped crisply in the wind.

Carmela peered at the witch. The witch's hard, red eyes peered back. "I see you," Carmela said out loud, almost daring the witch to answer back.

But no ghostly answer floated back to her across Royal Street. There was only the muffled sound of piano notes from a bar up the street, the mournful toot of a tugboat sliding down a dark ribbon of Mississippi a few blocks away.

"Sheesh," Carmela said to herself, feeling more than a little foolish. "Why am I acting like such a scaredy-cat? In my own backyard at that!"

Striding purposefully down Royal Street now, Carmela set her course for home. She passed a few more antique shops, the Click! Gallery, where she'd once been invited to have a photo show, and the Blue Crab Restaurant. A long black limousine with smoked windows sat outside, no sign of its driver.

Rounding a corner, Carmela headed down St. Philip Street where, much to her unease, the mood seemed even quieter. Her footfalls echoed off the narrow sidewalk and reverberated against aged brick buildings.

Nervous. I'm still nervous.

A shudder ran down Carmela's spine. She decided she'd cut over to Dauphine Street at the next corner. There was a stretch of jazz bars along that street. Rough trade, but it would still be a comfort to have people close by.

Carmela quickened her pace. At the same time, a plastic bag skittered alongside her in the gutter. It fluttered and floated, almost keeping pace with her.

And there was something else, too.

What the . . . ?

Footfalls behind her.

Oh no.

Distinct footfalls that quickened even as her shoulders stiffened and she bent forward, intent on picking up the pace.

Now what do I do?

Carmela forced herself to breathe deeply and keep moving at a steady clip, even though every twitchy, frazzled nerve ending in her body was screaming, *Run!*

She knew if she could just make it around the corner, she'd be fine. She could duck into Boogie's Saloon or the Big Brass Note. But, unfortunately, that corner was still a long way away.

Carmela turned her head and glanced hurriedly over her shoulder. And was totally unprepared for what she saw.

Brown tufts of fur sticking awkwardly out from a dark face. A man's body but a . . .

A werewolf's head? This can't be happening to me! Carmela told herself as she suddenly broke into a shambling run. *There's no such thing as a werewolf!*

But the darned thing behind her, the bizarre creature that was definitely dogging her footsteps down this dark street, didn't act as though it had lumbered out of a 1950s William Castle horror flick. It acted like it was right here, right now, trying to run her down.

Carmela's boots pounded the cobblestones. Her knees and shins ached from the impact. Her breath came in ragged pulls. She ran past one alley, stutter-stepped as she thought to duck in, then decided it was way too dark, way too risky.

But what to do?

Her whole body shook from exertion, and her teeth chattered in her head.

A weapon! If I could just find a weapon.

Her eyes searched hungrily as she galloped past darkened storefronts.

And then, up ahead, a red devil lurked near a lamppost. A raised pitchfork was clutched in his gnarled hand, a wicked grin spread across his face.

As Carmela dashed by, she grabbed the pitchfork and ripped it from the devil's grasp.

Okay, now what?

Closer to the corner now, she gave it everything she could muster. Sprinted like her life depended on it, then spun around the corner.

Backpedaling now, stumbling a little, she skidded to a halt, knowing she had to make a stand. Gasping for breath, Carmela grasped the pitchfork in both hands, holding it like a baseball bat. Then she crouched down low, close to the building, ready to defend herself.

Carmela heard the werewolf's ragged, raspy breathing before she saw him. She cocked her arms, waiting for the perfect moment.

Then the werewolf spun around the corner, his furry head bobbing directly in Carmela's line of sight. She swung the pitchfork with all her might, like Barry Bonds going for the game-winning home run.

Crack!

The pitchfork connected solidly with the side of the werewolf's head. The werewolf let out a low moan, stumbled a few feet, then went down hard. Dazed, shocked, it lay there in the street, panting noisily.

Having him at a disadvantage now, Carmela sprang at him and whapped him hard again on the back of his head. "Take that!" she screamed.

"Shit!" said the werewolf, in a very un-werewolf manner. He tried to scramble away from her on all fours, but collapsed again with a loud "Ooof."

Carmela brought the pitchfork up, prepared to strike again. But now the werewolf was moaning, and his gigantic head seemed pitched at an awkward angle. A white streak of human skin appeared between his head and neck.

Carmela grappled in her handbag for her cell phone. Fishing it out, she managed to punch in 911. "Help!" she told the operator. "Someone just attacked me in the French Quarter! St. Philip and Dauphine! Send somebody! Now!"

"Ma'am, please stay on the line while I —" But Carmela had other things to do. The werewolf had just rolled over.

Grasping the end of the pitchfork, Carmela braced herself, then sank the tines of the pitchfork into the werewolf's stomach. The tines weren't that sharp, but they pushed into the werewolf's pudgy stomach.

"Ouch! That *really* hurts!" complained the werewolf.

"Who are you?" Carmela demanded. "What the hell do you think you're doing?" Anger and frustration burst within her. She jabbed murderously at the werewolf again. "You idiot!" she screamed.

The werewolf flopped about on the pavement, then two arms reached up to either side of its ungainly head. Slowly, the werewolf mask or head or whatever it was came off.

"You!" screamed Carmela.

Harvey, Kimber Breeze's cameraman, stared sheepishly up at her from the pavement.

"What were you *doing!*" Carmela shrilled. "What were you *thinking?*" She could barely resist the urge to poke him again. "Did Kimber put you up to this?"

Harvey moaned as blood dribbled down the side of his face. "Please stop shouting," he implored. "I think I'm really hurt."

A siren shrieked in the distance. Help was on the way.

Still Carmela didn't let up. "Tell me what's going on," she demanded. "Did Kimber stage this whole thing?"

Harvey nodded miserably. Obviously, this had not been his intended outcome.

"Kimber Breeze and her whole rotten TV station are in deep trouble," said Carmela, a cold fury suddenly replacing her red-hot rage. "They want a story? I'll *give* them a story!"

Red and blue lights pulsed as a squad car rounded the corner and screeched to a halt. Two uniformed officers jumped out. While one dealt with a moaning Harvey, the other rushed up to Carmela.

"You okay?" the officer asked her. His name tag said Dutrey. He was a tall, skinny African American with an exceptionally kind face.

Carmela nodded. "I am now." She pointed her pitchfork at Harvey. "That idiot was chasing me."

"And you hit him," said Officer Dutrey, taking in the situation.

"I'd like to hit him again," snapped Carmela.

"Ma'am," said Officer Dutrey, "are you okay? Were you harmed in any way?"

"Kimber Breeze and her pack of idiots at the TV station are behind this," Carmela told Dutrey through clenched teeth. She could feel herself beginning to lose it. "All because of poor Amber's murder in the alley behind Ava's voodoo shop and —" Carmela stopped, put a hand to her mouth. She knew she was rambling. "Give me a moment, okay?" she asked.

Dutrey nodded. "Take all the time you need, ma'am."

Walking a few paces on badly wobbling legs, Carmela told herself she had to calm down, that she was probably babbling on without making any real sense.

Forcing herself to take deep, cleansing breaths, the kind she and Ava had learned about in yoga class but never really practiced, Carmela watched as Officer Dutrey talked on his phone and made an abrupt hand gesture at Harvey.

Carmela seemed to exist in a dreamlike state for the next five minutes or so. Until another car, a plain red Chevy Caprice, rounded the corner at top speed. As it rocked to a stop, Carmela noticed the twirling red light on its dashboard. Then the driver's door was flung open, and Detective Edgar Babcock climbed out.

Carmela took one look at him and started to cry.

CHAPTER 20

"Viewership," snarled Carmela, curled on the chaise lounge in her apartment. "This whole crappy werewolf stunt was about luring in viewers and advertisers. Kimber Breeze, idiot that she is, thought she'd try to scare me to death. Or scare me into giving some ridiculous interview that would hustle up more interest in her stupid werewolf story."

"She almost succeeded," said Ava. She was focused intently on Carmela, trying to force-feed her a praline.

Detective Babcock was watching both of them with slight amusement. After he'd transported Carmela home and withstood the onslaught of two welcoming dogs, he'd hustled across the courtyard and narrated the whole sordid scenario to Ava. Ava, of course, had been overcome with worry and rushed right over to take care of Carmela.

"If you can't eat a praline, *cher,* at least

try a chocolate chip cookie," urged Ava. She'd dug some cookies out of the frozen depths of Carmela's freezer and had already wolfed down half a dozen of the frozen discs herself along with a glass of Chardonnay.

Carmela shook her head. Now that she'd harnessed her anger, she was trying to make it work to her advantage. "I'm not in a sugar mood, what I want is . . ."

"Something salty?" asked Ava. "How about a nice chocolate-dipped pretzel?"

"I think what she really has a taste for is revenge," said Babcock mildly. They were all seated around Carmela's small dining room table. Boo and Poobah had picked up on the tension in the room and were now dancing and snorting at their feet, vying for attention.

"Not revenge, but justice," said Carmela, finally able to focus her thoughts. "I want to take very specific legal action against Kimber Breeze and WBEZ-TV."

"Can she do that?" Ava asked Babcock. He was amusing himself by paging through one of the glossy gossip magazines Ava had left at Carmela's.

"Sure," Babcock responded. "In fact I wish she would."

"How would she do that?" asked Ava.

"The police have already made an arrest,

so that's the beginning of a criminal action right there. Now Carmela is free to launch a civil suit, too."

"So she needs . . . what?" asked Ava. Then answered her own question by saying, "A lawyer, I suppose."

Babcock nodded. "That would do the trick." He turned the gossip magazine slightly, squinting at the centerfold story.

"Do you have a lawyer?" Ava asked Carmela.

Carmela shook her head no.

Ava pulled the boatneck collar of her yellow knit shirt down over her shoulders as she thought for a moment. "You're probably not gonna like this, *cher,* but Shamus is the one with good connections to lawyers. Heck, there are probably dozens of lawyers just hanging around that big old bank of his. Working on their briefs or tortes or whatever it is lawyers work on."

"Rattling their sabers," muttered Babcock.

"Yeah, probably," Carmela responded. "But, Ava, I really don't want to get Shamus involved in this. I don't want him poking his big nose in *anything.*"

"I understand that," said Ava. "You don't want to be *personally* involved with Shamus any more than you have to. The man is a skunk and a cad and a philanderer. But I see this as a completely different issue." She grasped Carmela's hand, gazed anxiously into her eyes. "You could have been seriously hurt tonight, *cher.* If you don't take some sort of major action right away, Kimber Breeze could continue with her bizarre tricks, maybe hurt somebody else."

"Good point," said Babcock. He'd lobbied to call Shamus in the first place and had been immediately shot down by Carmela.

"You think?" asked Carmela.

Ava nodded. "You said you want justice. Shamus and that big old bank of his have got plenty of money to buy you some good old-fashioned justice."

"It's the Southern way," added Babcock.

"You think I should call him," said Carmela, ignoring Babcock's remark.

"Yes, I do," said Ava. "Appeal to the gentleman that's buried within him. Get him to ride to your rescue like a knight astride a white horse. Besides, Shamus is already ticked off at Kimber Breeze for putting his little door-kicking performance on TV. So he's probably *motivated.*"

"Aha," said Carmela. Deep down, she knew Ava was right. Shamus was a self-proclaimed take-charge dude. Her little incident tonight would be infinitely appealing to him. "I suppose I should call him now."

"There's no time like the present," said Ava.

Carmela sighed. "All right. You win." She got up, squared her shoulders. "This is gonna take a while. You two gonna stick around?"

They both nodded. Babcock reached for another magazine.

"Okay," said Carmela, heading for the bedroom where she'd have a little privacy. "Wish me luck."

Shamus was outraged. "You what?" he screamed.

"Got chased," Carmela told him again. "By a werewolf. Stalked, really." Shamus, she was beginning to believe, suffered from AADD, adult attention deficit disorder. More and more, she had to repeat things to him.

"And you hit him with what?" barked Shamus.

"A pitchfork."

"A pitch pipe?"

"Pitch*fork*," shouted Carmela. "You know, like a devil carries."

"Devil?" said Shamus. "Like in *the* devil?"

"Have you been drinking?" asked Carmela. "Or have squirrels just been gnawing your phone line?"

"No," said Shamus, huffy now. "It's just such a bizarre story."

"Of course it is," said Carmela. "The thing is, will you help me? Can I count on you to sic one of your good old boy lawyers on Kimber Breeze and her scummy TV station?"

"Hell yes," said Shamus, always up for a good squabble. "I've been itching to get back at those assholes. I'll phone one of my attorneys tonight. Probably Dewayne Jeffson. Dewayne's one tough sumbitch. He'll be burning up the lines to WBEZ as well as the FCC."

"That's exactly what I was hoping for," said Carmela, heartened now. "Thank you, Shamus."

"You're welcome, darlin'." He paused. "You know, this shit wouldn't happen if we were still together."

"Sure it would, Shamus. It'd just be different shit."

"Don't say that. We had a good thing going. Still could if we wanted to."

"Shamus . . ." pleaded Carmela.

"Hey, honey, are you really okay?" he asked. "Physically, I mean." A note of interest crept into Shamus's voice. "Maybe I should come over there, babe. Spend the night. Offer a little husbandly companionship and comfort."

"Your offer is duly noted," said Carmela. "But not accepted."

"You sure?" he asked.

"Oh yeah," said Carmela.

"I told you," squealed Ava. "Shamus to the rescue!"

"Excellent," said Babcock, once Carmela revealed the full outcome of her talk with Shamus.

"Shamus's *lawyer* to the rescue," corrected Carmela. "Big difference." She started to yawn, tried to suppress it, wasn't very successful.

"You're tired," said Ava. "I better toddle off." She stared pointedly at Babcock. "You coming too? *Detective?*"

"In a minute," he told her.

Now Ava was hesitant. "Well . . . okay. I suppose." She paused at the door. "Call if you need me, Carmela. Or if you just want to jabber."

"Night night," said Babcock.

"What?" said Carmela, once Ava had finally left. *"What?"*

"A couple things," said Babcock. "And then I'll get out of your hair."

Uh-oh, she thought, then stared expectantly at him.

"We can't find Santino anywhere."

"Why are you bringing *that* up?" Carmela asked.

"Because it's all related," Babcock explained patiently. "Giovanni working at Ava's shop. Santino's disappearance. WBEZ's werewolf fiasco tonight. It's like an intricate Chinese puzzle."

Carmela sat in silence for a few moments. Then she said, "Giovanni told me that Santino was going into hiding." She pushed a strand of hair out of her eyes. "But I don't know where."

"I hate to tell you this," said Babcock, "but when people go into hiding, that's generally a sign of guilt." He rolled up one of Ava's gossip magazines, the one that said "Angelina's New Love" on the cover in forty-eight-point type, obviously intending to take it with him.

"I'd be in hiding, too," said Carmela, "if the cops thought I murdered someone."

"Look," said Babcock, pushing his chair back from the table and getting to his feet. Boo and Poobah immediately stuck their furry muzzles against his knees, hoping for a final ear tug. "All I'm saying is it's great that you're a nice and generous person who cares about Giovanni and Santino. But you need to be careful. How well do you really know these brothers, anyway? Why are you putting yourself at risk for them?"

"I didn't know I was," stammered Carmela. "Until tonight."

CHAPTER 21

The phone rang before Carmela's coffee-maker had concluded its morning sputtering and muttering and trickled out its hearty blend of chicory brew.

"Let's hope this is good news," Carmela told Boo and Poobah as she plucked hot rollers from her hair and bent to snatch up the phone. "Hello?"

"How are you feeling?" Shamus asked, worry shading his voice.

"Not bad. Running a little late." A hot roller slipped through her fingers, and Carmela watched it bounce under the bed. Boo dropped to her tummy like a new Army recruit doing push-ups, stuck a paw under, and batted around, trying to fish it out.

"You're going in to work today? After what happened last night? Babe, you should stay home," Shamus commanded. "Take it easy."

"I'm fine," said Carmela. "Besides, it's going to be a busy day." She looked at herself in the mirror, decided her hair looked a little like an artichoke. *Needs some gel or mousse or something.*

"My little entrepreneur," sighed Shamus. "Always thinking business."

And where were you when I really needed business advice? wondered Carmela. *Out snapping photos or wining and dining one of your little bimbettes.*

"I have a present for you," said Shamus. "Turn on your TV."

"Huh?"

"Turn on WBEZ," urged Shamus. "Right now."

Carmela turned on the TV, flipped the channel to WBEZ. The morning anchor was just wrapping up the news. "Yeah. So?" she said. Then Carmela watched in awe as a graphic of a werewolf face suddenly flashed on the giant blue screen behind him.

"We have an apology to issue . . ." began the anchor.

"Shamus!" squealed Carmela. "What's going on? Is this for real?" She watched, stunned, as the anchor extended a formal apology for what the station termed "an ill-advised werewolf stunt."

"I told you Dewayne Jeffson was lawyer enough to fry their asses," chortled Shamus. "Don't you love it?"

"I can't say I'm not pleased," said Carmela. "Oh, Lordy, they're not going to mention my name, are they?"

"Not to worry," laughed Shamus. "Your involvement last evening shall go unmentioned."

"And what about Kimber Breeze?" asked Carmela. "Any repercussions for her?" She glanced down, saw that Boo had successfully retrieved the plastic roller and was munching contentedly on it. She snatched the roller from the dog's jaws.

"Dewayne took care of her, too," said Shamus. "Suspended from on-air work until further notice."

"Wow," breathed Carmela. Ava had been right on. Shamus's connection to the Crescent City Bank chain really did give him the clout to make things happen.

"What do you think?" Shamus asked in a wheedling tone. "Did I do good?"

Carmela dropped the phone to her chest. Why couldn't Shamus have been this take-charge and decisive in their marriage? she wondered. Why couldn't he have come to her rescue a year or two earlier?

"You did great," she told Shamus, wondering if there was any possible way she could retain Dewayne Jefferson as her divorce attorney.

■ ■ ■ ■

Just as Gabby was restocking the wire racks with paper, just as Baby and Tandy were finishing up their purse projects, just as Carmela was arranging an assortment of their new eight-by-eight-inch albums, Ava came galloping in, hair flying, blouse open a few buttons too many, worry still written across her face.

"Honey, are you okay?" she exclaimed. A swathe of auburn hair swirled about her creamy shoulders, making her look like an eighteenth-century heroine in a Regency novel.

Tandy turned toward Ava, an inquisitive look creeping across her thin face. "Pray tell, why wouldn't Carmela be okay?" she asked.

"Are you kidding!" exclaimed a very out-of-breath Ava. "After last night?" She stared at Carmela, who suddenly looked very uncomfortable. "What? You mean you didn't tell them about last night? Your harrowing chase through the French Quarter? That awful werewolf stunt?"

Carmela shook her head. She'd been hoping she wouldn't have to go into it all over again. But now Ava was fanning the flames, and it looked like she was the one who was probably going to get burned. Or at least outed. Once again.

"Werewolf!" screamed Gabby.

"What on earth happened?" cried Baby.

Tandy's eyes narrowed to mere slits. "Oh my gosh!" she squealed suddenly. "This has something to do with that werewolf stunt WBEZ apologized for this morning, doesn't it!"

So Carmela told her story, singing and dancing the whole thing like she was pitching a TV commercial to a bunch of marketing executives. Making silly faces and adding sound effects, trying to convey that last night's goings-on had been far more amusing than frightening. And, the funny thing was, in the cold, clear, rational light of day, the whole darn thing *did* seem awfully silly.

A shiver ran up her spine. *Yeah, right,* she thought, reconsidering. *Running through the French Quarter, that wacko breathing down my neck. Exactly my idea of fun.*

Thirty minutes later, friends had been reassured, and a tentative calm had been restored in Memory Mine. Ava gave Carmela a quick hug, reminding her she'd be back at five, then dashed back to Juju Voodoo. Gabby was busy at the front counter. Tandy and Baby were busily stringing colored glass beads for their purse handles. And Gordon van Hees sauntered casually into Memory Mine.

"Can I help you?" Gabby greeted him from behind the front desk with her customary warm smile.

Gordon looked toward the back of the shop, saw Carmela, raised his hand in a friendly wave. "I'm here to say hi to the boss," he told Gabby. "In fact, I brought a little something for her."

Carmela hustled up to the front of the shop. "Hi," she said, meeting Gordon halfway. "I hope you're not worried about the decorations, because they're almost ready."

As he gazed about Carmela's shop, the friendly smile on Gordon's face morphed into an approving grin. "Not anymore," he told her. "Now that I actually see your place. Your little scrapbook shop is quite fantastic. A veritable treasure trove."

"We're probably not all that different from your studio at Moda Chadron," laughed Carmela. "Except we deal in paper and paint and glue sticks."

"And we deal in fine fabrics, of course." Gordon took the fancy chocolate-colored box that was tucked under his arm and handed it to Carmela. "Dear lady, a small repayment for the ribbon you brought over yesterday. Which Chadron highly approved of, saving both my sanity and my scrawny neck."

"Good heavens," said Carmela, accepting Gordon's gift. They moved up to the front of the store where she set the box down on the counter, removed the lid, peeled back several layers of tissue paper.

"Oh my!" said Gabby.

Nestled inside the gift box was a gorgeous array of fabric and lace. Swatches of Chinese silk, fine linen, Georgette crepe, *toile,* Mechlin lace, and reticella lace.

"Is this organza?" Carmela asked Gordon, fingering a rich piece of purple fabric.

He touched it gently, too, and nodded. Then indicated another piece of shiny gray fabric. "And this is silk douppioni. Donatella used it for a skirt last season."

"I can't accept this," said Carmela. "It's too much." She pushed the box toward him as if to give it back.

Gordon pushed the box back toward her. "For your little theater," he told her. "The one you told me about? The one that was so sorely in need of curtains or a backdrop?"

"My theater," Carmela said. "Yes, I did mention that to you, didn't I?"

"May I see it?" asked Gordon.

"I'll get it," said Gabby. She reached down, grabbed the small paper theater, set it on the counter next to the fabric.

"Oh," said Carmela. "I guess introductions are in order. This is Gabby, my assistant."

Gordon shook Gabby's hand. "I'm Gordon van Hees, Chadron's assistant," he told her, even though he was really a partner.

"You have no idea how much I adore Chadron's clothing," said Gabby. "So romantic but modern, too. My husband bought me one of Chadron's wrap blouses for my birthday."

"May I say," said Gordon, grinning, "that your husband has exquisite taste."

"Well, thank you," said Gabby, more than a little dazzled.

"As you can see," said Carmela, turning her paper theater so it faced Gordon, "my little creation seems to lack a finishing touch."

"Ah," said Gordon, "your *Theatre de la Vampyr.* You do have a love of the macabre."

"Ya gotta love it," laughed Carmela, "living in New Orleans."

"Well said," replied Gordon as he studied the little theater from all angles. "It is lovely, but you were right when you said it might need an extra snippet of lace or something."

He indicated the fabric in the gift box. "May I?"

Carmela nodded.

"I think . . . this," said Gordon, selecting a piece of silvery lace. "As an overlay to your purple velvet backdrop."

"Lovely," said Carmela, enchanted. Gordon was right; the effect would be spectacular.

"And perhaps some of this gold organza for side curtains. You have such a strong black and purple theme going on, maybe a counterpoint is in order."

"I think he's right," said Gabby. She gazed expectantly at Carmela. "You, too?"

"Perfect," breathed Carmela. "Now it's really taking shape."

"Actually," said Gordon, "A couple tassels, and I think you're finished. By the way, I adore your castle turrets with the little gargoyles on top. You're quite an *artiste*."

"Did you want to show him your rubbings and photos?" Gabby asked. "Because I just finished mounting everything."

"Why not?" said Carmela.

Gabby pulled a stack of large foam core boards out from behind the counter. "I think you're really going to like these," she told Gordon, then held up one of the rubbings so he could study it.

Gordon took a step back and stared at it for a few seconds, and Carmela wasn't sure what was going through his brain.

"Wonderful!" he proclaimed suddenly.

"And here's one of her photos, too," said Gabby, holding up another board. "Enlarged considerably."

"One you took yesterday?" Gordon asked. "At Amber's funeral?"

Carmela nodded.

"Very moving," said Gordon. "The images are so stark and modern. You managed to drop out the gray tones and thus convey a certain gritty intensity."

"More like a screen print," said Carmela, which was the effect she'd been going for.

"These will all line the walls?" asked Gordon.

"With gossamer ghosts overhead," replied Carmela. "And a couple strategically placed fans to make them flutter."

"And the pumpkins," said Gabby, thrilled their work was being so well received. "Don't forget to show him the pumpkins."

Carmela put one on the counter.

"Adorable," said Gordon. "And these will function as luminarias, I take it?"

"At the last minute we'll insert tiny tea lights," said Carmela. "Should add the perfect glow to your runway."

"To show off a remarkable collection," added Gordon as his cell phone suddenly shrilled. He pulled it from his jacket pocket. "Yes?" he said. "The insurance company? Absolutely, put them through."

The rest of the day flew by in a blur. The bell over the door tinkled constantly as customers entered in a never-ending stream. It was also, Carmela decided, her day for selling fancy paper.

A regular customer from nearby Chalmette came in looking for lace paper to use as an overlay for wedding invitations. Carmela dug out several varieties of Rakushishi or "falling water" paper for her. This lovely paper was created by placing a freshly made sheet of paper over a stencil and then blasting it with water. Bits of paper were worn away until a lace sheet emerged.

Then two of Baby's friends, who also lived in the Garden District, asked for "something unusual." Carmela showed them her batik and veneer papers, but they really got excited when she dug out her Cloud Dragon paper. This was thick, textured Japanese paper imbedded with beautiful, coarse fibers.

"Whew," said Gabby, when they had a brief interlude between customers. "This is shaping up to be a record day for sales."

"About time," said Carmela. They had hung on by their fingernails long enough. Now things really felt like they were getting back to normal.

"I can't believe you found time to finish your little theater," said Gabby, indicating Carmela's little *Theatre de la Vampyr.* "In between meeting the demand for rubber stamps, textured papers, and colored tags."

"I pretty much had to if I want to put it on display in the front window," said Carmela. "After all, tomorrow's the big day."

"Good point," agreed Gabby.

"You know," said Carmela, squinting at her tiny masterpiece. "If I took a quick photo of my theater and converted it to a slide, we could project it on the fabric that's going to hang as a backdrop for Chadron's show."

"So your *Theatre de la Vampyr* would be magnified like about a hundred times?"

"Yeah," said Carmela, still noodling her idea. "That's the general idea. Think it works as a backdrop?"

Gabby grinned, then hummed the *Twilight Zone* theme.

"Really?" said Carmela. "It's not too strange?"

"This is Halloween," said Gabby as the

phone on the front counter sounded. "And I think you just found the perfect image." She reached for the phone. "Hello?" Gabby nestled the receiver against her chest and said to Carmela. "It's for you. Margaret Guste?"

"Amber's mother," said Carmela, hesitating. She didn't really want to talk to the woman, didn't have anything more to say, except *I'm so sorry.* "Okay, I'll take it." Carmela put the phone to her ear. "Mrs. Guste? Hello, how are you?"

"As well as can be expected," came Mrs. Guste's somber reply. "But I wanted to thank you for coming to Amber's funeral yesterday. It was greatly appreciated."

"We were happy to be there," said Carmela. Then, when she realized what she'd said, hastily amended her words. "Well, not *happy,* but we certainly wanted to be part of things."

"Yes," said Mrs. Guste. "I know what you mean." She cleared her throat. "I know you've spoken with the police several times. Particularly that detective . . ."

"Edgar Babcock?"

"Yes," said Mrs. Guste. "I was wondering if you'd heard anything new."

"Not really."

"Or if you remembered anything more

281

from that night?"

"I wish I had. Truly. I've racked my brain about it and keep coming up empty. Sorry."

"You're a dear to even talk to me," said Margaret Guste.

"No problem," said Carmela. "Really."

"Tell me again why we're paying this little visit?" asked Ava as they hustled along the street. It was quarter past five, and Carmela and Ava were headed for Grand Folly Costume Shop.

"Return your costume," said Carmela.

"We could have done that any time," said Ava, clacking along beside her in four-inch heels. "What else is on your agenda, my dear? Talking to Remy Chenier, perhaps?"

"Maybe," said Carmela. "If he's even working today. Did you have a chance to ask Giovanni what he knew about Remy?"

Ava made a zipping motion across her lips. "Yeah, but he's not saying anything, *cher.* I'm surprised he even came to work today."

"You think Giovanni's starting to become a liability?"

Ava nodded. "Yeah, probably. Maybe. Still, I'd like to get to the bottom of all this."

"So would I," agreed Carmela. "And, truth be known, I still haven't crossed Remy off my list of suspects." They turned a corner together, dodging a group of street artists who'd set up easels. The artists were trying to capture a pair of Caribbean-colored Creole cottages on canvas. "Mrs. Guste called me just before you came by."

"Amber's mother?"

Carmela nodded.

"Sad," said Ava. "What'd she want?"

"She asked if I'd heard anything new," said Carmela. "But I think she really just wanted someone to talk to."

Remy Chenier was slumped behind the cash register as Carmela and Ava entered the Grand Folly Costume Shop. He glanced up at them, recognition flickering in his dark eyes. His wardrobe hadn't changed much, except today he wore an aged Pantera T-shirt on his skinny frame.

"Hey," said Ava.

"You two," he snorted. "Back again?"

"Just returning a costume," said Carmela pleasantly.

"You don' need it for the big party in the Quarter tomorrow night?" he asked in his Cajun accent.

"Oh, we'll be there," said Ava. "Just in different costumes."

"What's wrong?" Remy sniggered at Ava.

"That fat lady scare the bejeebers outa you?"

Ava draped her Mae West costume across the front counter and leaned in toward Remy. "Nothing scares me, sweetheart."

"Oooh," said Remy, pretending to be cowed by her. "Then why you run away so fast Saturday night? Afraid of a little slumming?"

"Not at all," said Carmela. "We just bumped into a friend of ours. Santino."

Remy squinted at them. "You girls know Santino?"

"Sure," said Ava. "He's a great guy. Hey, you've been to my shop; you know that Santino's brother works there."

"Yeah, yeah, the one who tells the fortunes," laughed Remy. "So good with the cards, too. Yeah, sure. I partied with him a few times. We'd go to dat old place in the swamp, have ourselves a good old time. A *brosse.*"

"You'd go drinking?" said Carmela.

Remy brightened. *"To konprann?"* he asked. You understand?

Carmela nodded. "Some. A little." Her father had been part Cajun.

"Brosse," laughed Remy. "And make the *veiller.*" A drinking binge and lots of talking with friends.

Carmela edged closer to the counter, her heart thumping a little harder. "You mean at Santino's place?"

"Yeah, yeah," said Remy. "That old camp house he got on Kawanee Road. Haven't been there for a while, of course, but we had ourselves some pretty wild times out there. Drink and play cards all night, sleep it off, maybe do a little fishing for redfish or speckled trout." He grinned. "Then start drinkin' and do it all over again."

"You're talking about his place down south," said Carmela, taking a wild guess.

"By *Au Bayou*," said Remy. "Don't know what it look like now, of course. Could still be laid low from the hurricane."

"No," said Carmela. "I heard it was okay. Came through just fine."

"Dat good," said Remy, gathering up Ava's costume. "Maybe I'll see you girls down there sometime."

Carmela favored him with a broad wink. "You never know."

Outside on the sidewalk, in the cool of the evening with yellow gaslights flickering on around them, Ava shrugged and said, "Well, that was no help. Remy said something about a Kawanee Road, but that could be anywhere. He was never really specific about where Santino might be holed up."

"Yeah, he was," said Carmela.

"Huh? What are you talking about?"

"He said *Au Bayou.* That's a Cajun reference to Golden Meadow. Below Galliano on Old Highway 1."

"You know that for a fact?" asked Ava, impressed.

"Yes, I do."

"So . . . what?" said Ava, obviously impressed. "We're gonna take off and go exploring?"

"Wouldn't you like to put this whole thing to rest?" said Carmela. "Once and for all?"

"Well . . . yeah," said Ava. She paused, hands on hips. "So, when?"

"Tonight," said Carmela. "Right now."

CHAPTER 22

A globular yellow moon slipped out from behind a swash of clouds, illuminating the gravel road and the Spanish moss that hung down from live oaks like clothes on a wash line. Clumps of mangrove stretched verdant tentacles, the bayou reaching out to test the very road that snaked through its inhospitable terrain.

Then Carmela's car dove beneath another canopy of trees, and the darkness and silence of the bayou seemed to close in. A blue sheen reflected off the brush and ground foliage, lending an almost electrical feel.

"Are you sure you know where you're going?" Ava asked. "I think we've passed that same stunted tree three times now."

"I'm not completely positive where we're headed, but I'm pretty sure we're in the general vicinity," replied Carmela. They'd taken Highway 90 down from New Orleans, cut south on Old Highway 1 at Raceland, then hit Golden Meadow. Now they were bumping along on Kawanee Road, a tentative gravel road that didn't look all that promising.

"Sure is desolate out here," remarked Ava.

"Our real piece of luck was getting hold of somebody at city hall," said Carmela. Indeed, she had called the Golden Meadow Town Hall just after they'd left the costume shop, pretending to be a mortgage loan officer from Crescent City Bank. While Ava had noisily shuffled papers as a convincing sound effect, Carmela had launched into a rambling mumble about annual percentage rate, points, and earned equity, saying they had Santino Stavrach's loan application in hand with the Kawanee Road address listed as collateral property, but were unclear on specifics.

The bored, somewhat harried woman in the office had furnished them with Santino's actual street address. Fourteen twenty-two Kawanee Road. MapQuest had narrowed the address down somewhat, but it was still a mighty big area with narrow roads that seemed to loop back on each other.

"Santino's place is in Bayou Grisgris," said Ava. "Had to be, huh?"

Carmela nodded. Gris-gris was another

name for voodoo.

The road twisted and turned again, and both women weren't sure which direction they were headed now. The moon bounced from the right side of the car to the left. Insects splattered the windshield.

"This car's gonna need a couple trips through the Tidy Wash when we get back," remarked Ava. She sniffed the inside of the car. "Maybe me, too."

The headlights swept around a curve, then suddenly reflected into a glimmering pair of eyes at the side of the road.

"Did you see that?" asked Ava. "What was it? Fox? Dog?"

"No idea" said Carmela.

"You know," said Ava. "Last night when we were having our fittings, that woman Krisi actually made me feel fat."

"Join the club," said Carmela. "Only I'm in the fat and short club."

"You're barely a size eight," said Ava. "And I'm a . . ." She gave an indistinct mumble.

"A what?" asked Carmela.

"What I was thinking of doing," said Ava, "was getting one of those fun house mirrors. You know, the kind that makes you look real skinny? Like a string bean?"

"For what purpose?" asked Carmela. Ava

was already skinny.

"Why . . . to feel good," said Ava.

They drove on, both women scanning their side of the road for anything that might reveal an address. Or, for that matter, that indicated this part of Lafourche Parish was even inhabited.

A mule deer capered across the road in front of Carmela, and she pumped the brakes hard, sluicing into the oncoming lane, spitting gravel. "Whoa," she said, slowing to a crawl. "Almost hit him."

Ava pressed a button and lowered the passenger side widow. The chirp of crickets, drone of insects, twitter from night birds, and occasional bark of an alligator seemed to blend into one overpowering cacophony of sound. "Whew," said Ava. "It's like the sound out here magnifies then beats down on you. Even the air feels oppressive."

"In here, too," said Carmela. "I have the AC on, but it doesn't seem to be doing much of anything. Certainly not spitting cold air." She accelerated again, but this time kept her speed in check. "It's the vegetation. With all the rain and hurricanes, everything has grown back more lush than before."

"Mother Nature repaired Louisiana faster than FEMA and the Army Corps of Engineers," said Ava. "Whoa . . . what's that?" Carmela's headlights had caught the reflection of something.

"Mailbox," said Carmela. She slowed to a stop, put her car in reverse, backed up a few yards. "Can you see an address?"

Ava peered into the darkness. "The numbers are kinda peeled away, but it looks like . . . maybe 1409?"

"We're looking for 1422," said Carmela.

"So we're getting close."

"Looks like." Carmela slowly depressed the accelerator, and they coasted forward. "So, just up ahead maybe?"

They both hunched forward, scanning the road ahead. Sweeping around another turn, they bumped across a narrow bridge, listening to the rumble of the boards under the tires. Dark water and woods spread out on either side of them.

"Okay, what was that?" asked Ava. Carmela's high beams had caught another quick flash of something up ahead.

Carmela slowed down again. "A driveway," she said. "Excellent."

"Turn in," said Ava.

Instead, Carmela switched off her headlights and negotiated a tight U-turn.

"You're taking no chances," said Ava, who seemed ready to go cowboying in.

"I want the car aimed in the right direction in case we need to make a fast getaway," said Carmela. "I'm also going to turn off the dome light before we get out and leave the doors unlocked."

"Yes, ma'am," said Ava, saluting Carmela, then pulling on a black baseball cap.

Carmela hesitated. "You think I should leave the key in the ignition, too?"

"Sure," said Ava. "Unless you think that mule deer's gonna sneak back and take your car for a joyride."

They both emerged from the car, and Carmela circled around to the passenger side. "You see anything?" she asked, listening to her engine tick down, feeling darkness ooze around them.

As they let their eyes grow accustomed to the night, Ava whispered, "Lookit. A Vette." About ten feet in, a black Corvette was snugged near a copse of mangrove.

"That's Santino's car, right?" said Carmela as they creeped closer.

"I think so," said Ava. "It sure looks like the car he made his wild escape in." They continued down the narrow path. "And I can see why he left it parked back there." Ava tugged to lift up a foot. "Mud." A rotten egg stench rose around her. "Putrid mud."

"We're in the bayou," said Carmela. "You have to expect a little mud and stink."

"But these are Italian shoes," moaned Ava.

Carmela kicked a leg out in front of her, revealing a pair of black high-top Keds.

"Not fair," said Ava. "You've been out here before; you knew what to expect."

Carmela gazed into the inky darkness, knowing how dangerous and hostile a bayou could be. "No. Not really."

"So . . . what's the plan?" asked Ava.

"We came here to check on Santino, so I'm going to keep going," said Carmela.

"Then so am I," said Ava.

They slogged another fifty feet through mud and wet reeds until they came to a metal gate.

"Who do you suppose he's trying to keep out?" whispered Ava.

"How do you know he's not trying to keep something in?" Carmela whispered back. She put a foot on the bottom rail, boosted herself over. Ava followed.

Now they were deeper into the bayou. Owls hooted, bats fluttered overhead, stands of bald cypress and tupelo poked toward the sky.

"There's a kind of boardwalk over here," said Ava. She pulled one foot then the other from sucking mud, scraped them in turn against the dry wood.

Carmela nodded. Shamus had a camp house in the Baritaria Bayou, and there was a boardwalk much like this that extended around his property.

They clumped along for another twenty yards, happy to have solid boards under their feet, then Ava said, "Uh-oh, another fence."

Just to their right, a wooden fence with vertical slats seemed to rise out of the swampy forest. Six feet high, sturdy-looking, with dark green moss crusting the lower portion.

"I could boost you over," suggested Ava.

"Then how do I get back again?" wondered Carmela.

"Good point. Okay, you go up, straddle the fence, and then pull me over. That'll work on the reverse trip, too." Ava bent down and laced her fingers together.

Carmela stepped lightly into Ava's proffered hands, then skittered up the fence. Throwing one leg over, she straddled the top plank. "Now you," she called. Ava took a running start, grabbed for Carmela's hand, and scrabbled for purchase. Two seconds later, they sat facing each other.

"I feel like Humpty Dumpty," said Ava.

Carmela looked around. "See that hay

bale down there?"

Ava nodded.

"We can pull that over and use it to get back out."

"Great," said Ava. "But first we have to get down."

"On three?" said Carmela.

Both women swung their legs over the fence and got ready to launch.

"One, two, three," called Ava.

Both made a soft landing.

"That wasn't so bad," said Ava. She tested the ground. "It's not as wet over here. Kinda spongy but not quite as soggy."

"And there's the camp house," said Carmela. She could just make out a small wooden building though the trees. Two small windows that let out a faint scrim of light, a front porch covered with a corrugated metal roof. A couple smaller outbuildings stood nearby.

"So Santino lives way out here all by his lonesome," said Ava. "Definitely a strange dude."

"Uh . . . Ava?" said Carmela.

"Talk about a loner," continued Ava. "I'd go half-batty if I —"

"Ava," said Carmela in a voice that was low and suddenly tense. "We're not alone."

Ava brushed dust from the knees of her

slacks. "What do you mean we're — ?" She suddenly straightened up. "Oh shit. Carmela, honey, tell me that's your stomach growlin'."

"It's not my stomach."

Ava reached for Carmela's hand, Carmela gripped Ava's hand, just as a large gray wolf slipped out of the dark and approached them.

"Don't move," hissed Carmela.

"I don't think I *can* move," whispered Ava as two more wolves circled in behind the first.

The first wolf moved in closer, wrinkling his muzzle, baring long, white canine teeth.

"Santino has other wolves," stammered Ava. "Imagine that."

And no one will ever know, thought Carmela, *if this all goes very, very bad.*

The alpha wolf continued to move closer. When he was four feet away, he extended his narrow snout as if to sniff Carmela.

Maybe he smells Boo and Poobah, Carmela hoped with a wild burst of optimism. *Maybe he'll think we're friendly. Compadres.*

The wolf bared his teeth even more.

Maybe not.

"You see that tree over there?" whispered Carmela. The two other wolves had continued to circle around, heads low, working in tandem to cut off their escape to the hay bale and over the fence.

Ava gave a shuddering nod.

"We're going to back toward it."

"Won't they follow us?"

"I don't know," said Carmela through clenched teeth as they shuffled gingerly toward the tree.

"We're like Lucy and Ethel," said Ava. "In trouble again."

"Got some 'splaining to do," agreed Carmela.

The alpha wolf stared at them, cocked his head, as if wondering what they were up to.

"Nice wolfy," cooed Ava.

"Shh," warned Carmela. She was watching the alpha wolf closely, saw the comprehension of what they were about to do suddenly dawn in his eyes. "Run!" shouted Carmela.

They broke for the tree in unison, slamming into the base, scrambling madly for footholds.

"Faster!" urged Carmela. "Get your butt up here!" The alpha wolf had flung himself after them, hitting the base of the tree a few seconds behind them, biting and jumping wildly. Frenzied now, white foam dripped from both sides of his mouth. Definitely not a pretty sight.

"I'm trying," yelled Ava. "But my foot's caught on something. I think my shoe . . ." They both looked down, saw that the chunky heel of Ava's right shoe was caught squarely between the wolf's jaws. Ava squirmed, kicked harder, allowing the shoe to release from her foot. Then she flung herself upward, breathing heavily.

Twelve feet up, they paused.

"Can wolves climb trees?" asked Ava.

"I don't know," said Carmela. "I don't think so. I think tree climbing requires opposable thumbs."

"Bears climb trees," Ava pointed out.

They moved up another five feet, then gazed down. One of the smaller wolves appeared to challenge the alpha wolf for the prize he held in his jaws, but the large male shagged him off, whimpering, pacing, clutching Ava's shoe, still hoping to get at them. Then, upset at his inability to scale the tree, the wolf took his anger out on Ava's shoe. He ripped off a strip of leather, spat it out, began gnawing on the heel.

"That's a Franco Sarto," Ava called down. "Italian. Forty-five ninety-nine on sale at Saks."

"I don't think he cares," said Carmela.

Before Ava could protest any more, a wooden door swung open on a nearby shed.

"Nero!" called a rough voice.

Carmela nudged Ava, hoping they wouldn't be seen. "Santino," she whispered.

The wolf tossed the shoe aside and cocked his head.

"Nero. Come," Santino commanded.

The wolf gazed up into the trees and made a desultory jump at the lower branches.

"Nero, quit playing around. Come!" Santino's voice had taken on a sharp, angry tone. He stepped out of the shed, peered into the darkness. The other two wolves looked at him, as if ready to answer his command. Nero looked down at his shoe.

Carmela and Ava held their collective breath.

"Caesar, Cleo, come."

The two smaller wolves loped toward Santino and stood point at his side.

"Nero. Come."

This time Nero obeyed. He walked over to Santino and stood in front of him, staring.

"Kennel up," said Santino.

Nero, Caesar, and Cleo slowly walked into the shed. Santino continued to gaze out into the pen.

Carmela could hear her own heartbeat thudding in her ears. *Don't look up, don't look up,* she prayed.

Then the moon slipped behind a cloud, and shadows closed in. Santino turned and walked into the low barn, pulling the door closed behind him.

Ava and Carmela let out slow breaths. Carmela held up an index finger. *One minute,* she pantomimed.

Hunkered in the tree, swatting at insects, they kept their eyes focused on the shed but heard nothing. Nothing moved in the pen, either.

"Thank goodness they're well trained," said Carmela.

"Yeah," said Ava. "They've got great manners. So friendly and eager to play. I wish I would've brought one of Boo's squeaky toys."

Carmela slithered down from the tree. "We better get out of here."

Ava came down after her. "For a few minutes there, what with all the climbing and shouting and scrambling, it felt like we were in a summer action movie."

"You got that right. C'mon."

"Wait, let me get my shoe."

"What's left of it," muttered Carmela.

"Jeez," said Ava, picking up a very sad-looking shoe. "Muddy, shredded, and a gob of wolf poop stuck to it. There's no way I can return these suckers now."

"Doggone that Saks," said Carmela. "And their unreasonable return policy."

They ran to the hay bale, upended it, and rolled it a couple times until it was right at the fence. Carmela stepped up, then hesitated.

Hair!

She wasn't about to exit this wolf pen until she'd collected a sample of the wolf's hair. Dashing back to the tree, she felt around gingerly. Surely, when the alpha wolf was flinging himself against the bottom of the tree some of his long gray hair had rubbed off against the bark, right?

Carmela's fingertips edged across rough bark, gouges, and scratches, reading the topography of the tree, searching for a few hairs, a tuft, anything.

The tip of her index finger brushed against something downy and soft.

Got it, she thought to herself with grim satisfaction. She plucked the little bit of hair that was stuck in the bark and shoved it in her pocket.

"Come on!" hissed Ava. She was waiting at the top of the fence. "What's taking so long? You want those wolves to come back for their midnight snack?"

Carmela leapt up and over the fence. "I wasn't about to leave this place empty-handed. I grabbed a hunk of wolf hair," she said triumphantly.

"A souvenir for your scrapbook?" asked Ava.

"Evidence," said Carmela.

CHAPTER 23

"Happy Halloween," chirped the WBEZ weatherman as he stood in front of his chroma-keyed weather map. "New Orleans will start the morning on the cool and crisp side, then a warm front is going to sweep in and take us all the way up to a balmy seventy-five degrees by late afternoon. Perfect for all you trick-or-treaters who plan to walk the walk and a great forecast for the big Halloween Bash in the French Quarter."

"Isn't it nice Kimber Breeze isn't on the news anymore?" Carmela asked Boo and Poobah as she hurried to get ready. "The big bad lady got fired. Can you say *fired?*"

Boo cocked her head. "Frrrrrow!" she growled.

"Very good," said Carmela as she slithered into a black bouclé skirt, then wound a silk scarf around the neck of her black turtle-neck. "Improve that diction a little, and I think you've got a good shot as morning anchor on WBEZ."

Boo wagged her curly puffball tail. Poobah barked an enthusiastic response, his ragged ear flopping wildly.

"And because today is Halloween, I have a very special treat for you guys."

Both dogs cocked their heads, listening to her.

"You're going to spend the day at Daddy's house. Isn't that a wonderful idea?"

"Ruff, woof," came their answering barks.

The fact of the matter was, Carmela had a million and one things to do today. Drop her so-called evidence off with Lieutenant Babcock, check in at Memory Mine, try to keep up with all their customers' needs, then grab Ava and decorate Moda Chadron. And since she was modeling tonight in Moda Chadron's fashion show, she figured she probably wouldn't be getting home until well after ten o'clock. Taking Boo and Poobah to Shamus's house was the best idea she could come up with on the spur of the moment. Besides, next to Fourth of July, with its booming, hissing firecrackers, Halloween was the next-hated holiday by dogs. All that doorbell ringing and flapping of costumes was just too much for most pups.

Shamus greeted them at the door wearing a

Tulane sweatshirt, khaki Bermuda shorts, and his white cast. His hair was tousled and wet from the shower. If Carmela didn't know better, she would think him heart-breakingly attractive.

"Come on in, you wild mutts!"

Boo and Poobah stretched their necks up and danced around, toenails clicking on the parquet floor, eager for Shamus's hearty pats and ear tugs. Carmela could see they were still crazy over him. Go figure.

"You want to come in, too?" Shamus asked, hobbling a few steps backwards.

"No," said Carmela. Even though he looked collegiate and rather endearing, she wasn't eager to spend time in the house she'd lived in and then been kicked out of. "How's your foot?" she asked.

Shamus immediately looked pained. "Still hurts. Throbs, in fact. The doctor gave me some anti-inflammatory pills, but the stupid things just made me sick. So I switched to some over-the-counter junk, but that didn't do a darn thing. Now I'm trying Naprosyn. You ever take Naprosyn? The directions said take one, but I was really hurting so I took three, and I think they might have made me a little woozy."

"Information overload," said Carmela, holding up a hand. "I really just want to drop off the dogs and get going." She paused. "You still have some of their food here?"

Shamus nodded, looking hurt at being blown off. "The dry stuff and the canned shit. The stuff that looks like liver pâté. Kind of tastes like it, too."

"You *tasted* it?"

Shamus shrugged. "Whatever."

"Well, don't give Boo too much canned food," warned Carmela. "It's awfully rich, and she's keeping an eye on her girlish figure." *Aren't we all?*

"Yeah yeah yeah," said Shamus. When he wasn't the center of attention he was easily bored. "Don't worry. I'll be here till noon, and then Earlene comes in at one. She can let the dogs out again and feed them late afternoon. I'll leave a note." Earlene was Shamus's cleaning lady, who was actually very good with the dogs.

"You're not planning to drive, are you?" Carmela asked. Shamus did look a little wonky from the drugs.

"No, no, Sugar Joe's picking me up." Sugar Joe was heir to one of western Louisiana's major sugarcane plantations and one of Shamus's old frat rat drinking buddies. Nothing ever changed with Shamus, Carmela decided.

306

"Good old Sugar Joe," said Carmela. "What's he up to?"

"Just opened a fancy cigar club on Dauphine Street down in the Quarter. Calls it Club Stogie. We're gonna swing by and have us a smoke before we head over to the Pluvius den."

"So you're still going to ride on the float tonight," said Carmela.

"Hell yes," said Shamus. "Got to do my civic duty."

Carmela knew Shamus's civic duty extended to partying at the Pluvius den in the Central Business District, recklessly imbibing any number of bourbons while actually on the float, then winding up at Antoine's or Galatoire's for fine wine and a megacalorie meal.

"Fun," said Carmela. She figured if she was lucky she'd have time to guzzle a Slim-Fast. Then again, she probably needed to be a little lean and hungry to fit into her dresses tonight.

"And I'd like to see your fashion show, too."

"You don't really have to do that," said Carmela, instantly on the alert. "In fact, please don't do that."

"But you're my wife," whined Shamus.

"Not for long," said Carmela, marveling

at how fast Shamus could switch from good old boy upbeat to soon-to-be-ex whine meister.

Shamus shook his head sadly. "Where did we go wrong?"

"Not *we,* Shamus. *You.*"

"And where exactly did you get this?" Lieutenant Babcock demanded. He scowled at Carmela, sighed deeply, then held the little plastic baggie containing the wolf hair up to eye level and peered at the contents with what seemed like mounting suspicion.

"I really can't tell you," said Carmela, trying to avoid eye contact with him, which was next to impossible since they were standing in the middle of the Eighth District Police station at Royal and Conti. She was also not unaware of the fact that more than a few men had brushed past her accidentally on purpose.

"Why can't you tell me?" Babcock asked.

"Could you please just analyze it?" replied Carmela. "As you can see, it's obviously animal hair."

"But what kind of animal?" asked Babcock.

Carmela gazed at him in frustration.

"Look," said Babcock. "We can't just take anything people bring in off the street and run it through our mass spectrometer or gas chromatograph. It's way too risky. For all we know, we could be fooling with Ebola or bird flu virus."

"Oh come on," said Carmela.

"Or end up disclosing the McDonald's secret sauce recipe," Babcock added with a smirk.

"Which is basically Thousand Island dressing," said Carmela. "Where do you live? Under a rock?"

"I'm just saying it's important to adhere to police protocol. Testing unknown substances is a drain on tax dollars."

Carmela stared at him for a few seconds. "It's not an unknown substance. It's wolf hair."

"*What?* Where did you get it?" Now Edgar Babcock looked beyond suspicious. He seemed downright cranky, in fact.

Carmela shook her head.

"If you don't tell me the circumstances," said Babcock, "I'm certainly not going to test it." He folded his arms across his chest.

Carmela folded her arms and waited.

Babcock didn't budge.

"Okay, okay," relented Carmela. "Ava and I took a little trip into the bayou last night looking for Santino."

"Tell me you're kidding." Babcock's face

had blanched a pasty white.

"Not at all. We went to his camp house —"

"*Camp house!* How on earth did you find that?"

"Remy Chenier sort of told us," said Carmela, hedging. "In a roundabout way."

"That low life," snarled Babcock. "And, once again, *you're* the one getting the information!"

"Anyway, we climbed over this fence —"

"I'm not hearing this," said Babcock, pursing his lips.

"— and found out, much to our surprise and wonderment, ha-ha, that Santino had a couple more wolves stashed there."

"What!" Now Babcock's face was a blotchy red. "Those animals were confiscated!"

"Not these little darlings," said Carmela. "So long story short, we got chased up a tree and escaped with our lives and this little bit of hair. Oh, and Ava lost a shoe."

"Huh?"

"A big bad wolf ate it." Carmela let her explanation sink in. "So the thing is, if you would actually condescend to analyze these hairs, they might possibly match the hairs found on Amber, and this case would be closed."

Babcock put a hand to his cheek and rubbed it. "I can't begin to tell you how out of line you are. And I really resent the fact that you're jumping to conclusions like this."

"No," said Carmela. "I may be jumping over fences and bounding up trees, but I am not jumping to conclusions. I'm only . . . uh . . . hoping for some kind of resolution."

"Resolution," echoed Babcock, cocking a wary eye at her.

"Justice," said Carmela. "Isn't that what we all want?"

"Sure," said Babcock. "But resolution and justice aren't always the same thing."

"Can you just analyze the hairs?" asked Carmela. She was tired of verbally jousting with him. "*Will* you?"

Babcock held up the envelope and jiggled it. "It's your tax dollars."

Carmela let loose a deep sigh. "So bill me."

"Have you been busy?" Carmela asked as she slipped into Memory Mine.

Gabby glanced up from the front counter, a look of supreme frustration on her face. She seemed to be waiting on three customers at once. Another dozen or so were crowded in the middle of the store, shopping, and it looked like Tandy was demonstrating a paper folding technique to two women at the back table.

"Sorry," murmured Carmela. "Dumb question." She tossed her purse behind the counter, fluttered over to assist her customers.

One woman was looking for a scrapbook album that had both a silk cover and a drop-in frame. Carmela had albums that fit the bill perfectly. In a selection of four different colors, in fact.

Two other customers wanted fibers and colored brads. Carmela pulled those from a nearby drawer.

Another woman was desperate for plastic project folders to organize all her paper and photos. Carmela plucked those from a shelf and put them in her hand.

The morning continued nonstop until finally, blessedly, everything seemed to settle down. Only two customers were left in the shop, and they were busily sorting through the wire racks that held the twelve-by-twelve-inch paper, choosing and selecting, building little stacks for themselves.

"Another big day," said Gabby. She was shoving fifty dollar bills into their secret spot under the counter.

"Sorry to be so late this morning," said Carmela.

"Sorry to look so panicked when you walked in," replied Gabby. "We just got hit with a tidal wave of customers."

"It was sweet of Tandy to pitch in," said Carmela.

"What?" called Tandy from the back table. She was just finishing up her purse project.

"Sweet of you," said Carmela. "Thanks for the help."

Tandy waved a hand. "No problem. It was kinda fun."

"Excuse me," said one of their paper customers.

"Yes?" said Gabby.

"Ephemera. I keep hearing about it as the newest thing, but I'm not sure exactly . . ."

"Carmela?" said Gabby. "Do you want to . . ."

"Ephemera is and isn't new," said Carmela. "It's new as a kind of hot topic in scrapbooking and collecting, but it's really about old things."

"Explain please," said the woman, looking even more interested.

"The term, ephemera, is meant to define something short-lived or transitory. Particularly paper documents. And by that I mean sheet music, vintage postcards, old maps, tourist brochures, antique valentines, catalog pages, and such."

"I get it," said the woman, nodding.

"Some people love to incorporate ephemera into their scrapbooks," said Carmela. "There was a woman in here last week who was doing a scrapbook for her future daughter-in-law. She mixed photos of her son as a child with things like his old report cards, his Captain Midnight manual, a book report, and some old postcards he had sent from camp."

"What a wonderful idea," said the woman.

"Of course," said Carmela, "you can use just a piece or two to enhance a scrapbook page. An old valentine juxtaposed with a wedding photo, an antique playbill with a school play, an old map for a scrapbook page detailing a vacation."

"Do you have any . . . what would you call it? Like faux ephemera paper?"

"We do," said Gabby. "Paper and stickers. Let me show you what we've got."

Wondering if there really was a can of Slim-Fast in her little refrigerator, Carmela wandered back toward her office. Just as she got there, the back door flew open and a gust of wind whooshed in, sending a few scraps of paper flying.

"You ready, *cher?*" It was Ava, looking excited and primed for the rest of the big day. "I got my car parked out here stacked to the gills with skulls and ghosts. You got the tomb rubbings and the other junk?"

"Give me a minute," said Carmela, "and we'll load it all up."

"Time to roll," said Ava, gleefully. "Gotta get that place decorated and then get gorgeous for tonight!"

CHAPTER 24

White, gauzy ghosts fluttered from tall ceilings. Skulls grinned from perches throughout the shop. Miniature skeletons danced atop racks of designer clothes. Moda Chadron was slowly being transformed from a high-fashion atelier into an elegantly haunted fashion house.

"That's right," said Ava, "move that rack of clothes a little more toward the left." She turned toward Carmela and rolled her eyes. "Getting these scrawny little salesgirls to do anything is like pulling teeth. They're no help at all!"

Carmela glanced at one of the sales associates who was leisurely plucking a speck of lint off her perfect chocolate brown sweater dress. "Did you really think they would be?" she asked.

"When we took this project on, Gordon promised we'd have plenty of cooperation," said Ava. "I see you working and I see me working and maybe some of these lighting and special effects guys. But certainly not them."

"I think they're saving themselves for tonight," said Carmela. "So they have enough strength to lift a pen and write orders."

"Hey lady." One of the workers tapped Ava on the shoulder.

She whirled around. "What? What!"

He held up his hands. "Take it easy. I'm on your side."

Ava peered at the logo and name that was embroidered on his blue denim shirt. "What do you want, Charlie from Set Worx?"

"You wanted blue and red bulbs in the overheads?" he asked.

Ava nodded.

"Done," he told her. "Plus the runway's pretty much knocked together, and Seth is rolling out the black vinyl covering now. Oh, and the chairs are in position, and the backdrop is hung."

Ava looked around. "You're right. Good work."

Charlie squinted at her. "Bobby still has to test the fog machine."

"Now?" said Carmela.

Bobby, a muscular-turning-to-flab assistant, shambled over to join them. He touched his cap, snapped his chewing gum. "Yes, ma'am. These machines are damned hard to control. No telling how much fog they'll spew out if they ain't adjusted just right. You could get anything from thin ground fog to thick pea soup."

Ava looked pained. "We have to make sure the setting is absolutely perfect. A little fog rolling over the runway is nice and atmospheric, but we don't want so much that the models or clothes are obscured. Even their shoes have to be clearly visible."

Bobby stuck to his guns. "That's why we should test it."

"Right," said Ava. "Okay."

A silly grin crept across Bobby's pudgy face. "We really should use a live model."

Ava looked at Carmela, Carmela looked away. "Okay," said Ava. "I'll do it."

"I'll crank up the music," volunteered Carmela. She grabbed the CD Gordon had handed them earlier, the same CD Moda Chadron had used for their New York runway show, and popped it in the boom box. She hit Play, and the room suddenly filled with a sexy backbeat and the bluesy wail of a saxophone.

Charlie dimmed the lights, Bobby bent over his fog machine, and the other workmen stopped what they were doing. All eyes were focused on the runway.

Ava burst through the center of the hanging scrim, head high, hands resting gently on hips. One of the white chiffon ghosts was draped around her shoulders. She strutted down the runway, dead on with the music, the chiffon fluttering enticingly around her. Fog rolled across the runway in thin, diaphanous tendrils lending a gossamer feel to the spectacle.

"Perfect," murmured Carmela. But watching Ava's sensuous stride put fear in her heart that she could never appear this confident.

At the end of the runway, Ava stopped, cocked one hip out, and held her pose. "Well?" she said. "Did it all work together?"

A spatter of applause answered her.

"Thank you, gents," she said, dimpling prettily, almost reverting to her Mae West mode.

"If I shoot a strobe light straight down the runway, the mist will really be perfect," Bobby told her.

"Then do it," said Ava. She stepped off the runway, looked pointedly at Carmela. "Whadya think? Everything look okay?"

"*You* looked gorgeous," laughed Carmela.

"Not me," said Ava, gesturing around at the lighting, fog, and decorations. "This stuff. Our stuff."

"Almost there," said Carmela. "With a little more work on our part. I was thinking of using fabric paint to create gold stars and silver moons on the black vinyl."

"Great idea," said Ava. "And you're still going to project your *Theatre de la Vampyr* image on the backdrop?"

"Got to talk to Bobby about that," said Carmela. "But, yes, that's the general idea."

"And we still need to hang the tomb rubbings and photos," said Ava.

"Let's see if we can get some of these workers to help," said Carmela. "Have them string fishing line through the foam core and suspend everything from the ceiling."

"Gee, I sure hope we have time to eat something before we get ready," said Ava. "There's no way I can manage tonight's big runway show on an empty stomach."

Carmela's cell phone shrilled in her purse. "I don't think I could do it on a full stomach," she said, as she dug for her phone. "Hello?

"Carmela."

"What?"

"Edgar Babcock here."

"Oh." She edged away from the end of the runway, trying to find a little privacy. "What's up?"

"Those wolf hairs you brought in this morning?"

Carmela felt a shudder run down her spine. Here it was. The mystery solved.

"Not a match."

"What?" she said, not believing her ears. "*Not* a match?"

"That's what I said."

The breath eased out of her like a balloon deflating. "I thought Santino might be guilty," she murmured. She wasn't sure whether to be angry or grateful.

"Doesn't mean he isn't guilty," said Babcock lightly.

"But we don't have proof that he is," said Carmela.

"You're catching on," said Babcock. "See, the way this law enforcement stuff works is you try to find motives, witnesses, and evidentiary proof *before* you go rushing in to accuse people."

"You're a fine one to talk," said Carmela. "You thought Santino was guilty from the get-go."

"And you charged in to defend him based on the word of his fortune-telling brother." A sudden burst of music from the boom box drowned out some of his words. "Where are you, anyway?" asked Babcock. "Sounds like you're standing in the middle of some crazy carnival."

"Close," said Carmela. "I'm helping set up a fashion show for tonight. At Moda Chadron. And it does have certain elements of the bizarre."

"So, what are you going to do next? Try to get some clippings from Giovanni's beard?"

"You're not helping things," said Carmela.

"And you are?" Babcock shot back.

"Oh my goodness!" exclaimed Gordon van Hees. "This place looks absolutely amazing!"

"You like it?" asked Ava. It was late afternoon, and she and Carmela had just finished supervising the hanging of the tomb rubbings. The final piece in their decorating scheme.

"I adore it," Gordon gushed to Ava. "You're a veritable magician, a conjurer!"

"Carmela did an awful lot," admitted Ava.

"We're a good team," said Carmela.

"You two ladies just have talent dripping from your little fingers," extolled Gordon. "And the projection on the runway backdrop is just too much." He gazed at the image Bobby had managed to project perfectly. "The lovely *Theatre de la Vampyr*. Could anything be more moody and *perfect?*"

"It was a last-minute brainstorm that happened to work," said Carmela. "Once my theater was finished, thanks in part to you."

Gordon van Hees dropped his voice to a conspiratorial tone. "You know, ladies, I've been highly skeptical of this entire show all along, worrying about the appropriateness of the Halloween venue and the fact that Chadron had to design yet another collection. But now I think we just might pull it off! Every single chair has been spoken for, stringers from two major fashion magazines are coming, and the TV stations have promised us full coverage."

"How's Chadron holding up?" asked Carmela. "Isn't most of this resting on his shoulders?"

"Dear Chadron is upstairs in the throes of another major hissy fit," said Gordon. "He's trying to make final adjustments to the collection as well as orchestrate the various changes for the models. Of course the hair and makeup stations are being set up, too. So the entire studio is a veritable madhouse."

"Sounds like fun," enthused Ava.

"Gulp," said Carmela.

"Santino didn't do it," said Carmela. She and Ava were out in the back alley, lounging on top of a wooden crate. Ava was smoking a cigarette, one of the two per day she allowed herself. Carmela was spooning up strawberry yogurt from the half-eaten carton she'd found in the refrigerator in the back room at Moda Chadron. Probably, she decided, some model's daily allotment of food.

"That was the call you took before," said Ava. "Babcock."

"Yup," said Carmela. "He had the wolf hair analyzed, and it wasn't a match to the stuff found on Amber."

Ava stretched languidly. "Face it, *cher,* you fought the good fight. Gave it the old one-two."

"And came up empty," said Carmela.

"Nobody expects you to be Angela Lansbury," said Ava. She inhaled deeply, blew out. "I know what I'm gonna have to do, though."

"Fire Giovanni?" Carmela knew it was coming.

"Yup," said Ava. "Just too many unknowns."

"Agreed," said Carmela. "You pretty much have to." She didn't feel good about Ava's decision, but what could she do?

Ava looked pensive. "Giovanni and Santino are tied in to this somehow, but darned if I can figure out how."

"Maybe it's exactly what they say it is," said Carmela. "Maybe they simply knew Amber. Maybe we're reading too much into their relationship with her."

"Maybe," said Ava. "But it's probably time for us to just back away from this. Let the police do what they do best."

"Funny," said Carmela. "That's exactly what Baby said to me a couple days ago. And I wasn't buying it."

"Are you buying it now?"

Carmela gazed into the empty yogurt container, still feeling a little empty inside. "I don't think I have a choice."

CHAPTER 25

Halloween festivities in the French Quarter were in full swing. Roman gladiators, pirates, witches, magicians, twenties flappers, fairy princesses, and Egyptian pharaohs rubbed shoulders and mingled together in Jackson Square and in the crowded, narrow streets. Revelers who were fortunate enough to gain entry to the infamous second-story balconies pressed up against wrought-iron railings and rained down beads and plastic doubloons upon the heads of those who milled below.

Food booths served up steaming *geaux* cups filled with shrimp gumbo, boiled crawfish, jambalaya, Cajun sausage, soft-shell crab, turtle soup, and sticks of corn bread.

Five different music stages featured groups playing Dixieland, jazz, zydeco, soul, and blues.

Actors portraying stalking zombies, damsels in distress, fortune-tellers, and troubadours roamed the French Quarter, interacting with the crowd.

"Vampire cams" played live footage of the kaleidoscope of wild goings-on across the Internet.

The torchlight Halloween parade rumbled down Bourbon Street, then snaked through the narrow streets of the French Quarter. The men of the raucous Pluvius krewe hoisted drinks and tossed bronze werewolf doubloons from their float to wildly enthusiastic crowds who screeched and screamed with delight, calling out the traditional Mardi Gras cry of, "Throw me somethin, mista."

But Shamus only rode half the parade route this year. Once they hit Royal Street, he slipped off his float and clomped his way into the Moda Chadron atelier. Here, among whispers and soft music, flickering candles and ghostly delights, the fashion elite of New Orleans waited for the event of the season: the unveiling of the new Moda Chadron collection.

"I can't do this," Carmela whispered to Ava.

"What?" said Ava as she struggled into her long, silver dress. "You mean you can't change in front of all these people?" The modesty curtain of two nights ago had not been hung this evening.

"No," said Carmela. "I mean all of *this*." She swept her hand around to indicate the frenzy of models, fitters, assistants, hairstylists, and makeup artists that were jammed into the second-floor studio. "I'm not right for this. I'm simply not a model."

"Don't be silly, *cher,* you look fantastic," soothed Ava. She reached out, gave a gentle tug on the neckline of Carmela's dress, pulling it a tiny bit lower, revealing a little more cleavage. "You look fresh and beautiful and very, very stylish in that dress."

"And I'm short," said Carmela. "Shorter than all these . . . these giraffes."

"Just slip into that pair of four-inch stilettos, darlin' and you'll be right up there with the tall girls."

"Not sure I can walk in them," worried Carmela. She stared at the teetery sandals she'd been given and made a face.

"You'll do fine," Ava assured her.

"Ladies?" asked a harried male voice. "Everything okay?" Chadron, flanked by his fitter, Krisi, and another assistant, was carefully scrutinizing Carmela and Ava.

"Couldn't be better," Ava told him. "We're just waiting for hair and makeup."

"Juan can take this one now," said Krisi,

barely looking at the two women. She reached out, gave a hard yank on the bodice of Carmela's dress. "Your neckline needs to be *much* lower." Then she grabbed Carmela's elbow and propelled her toward one of the makeup tables.

"Really," said Carmela, "just slap on a little lipstick and mascara, and I'll be good to go."

Krisi plopped Carmela down in front of a mirror surrounded by incandescent lightbulbs. "This one needs special attention," she instructed the makeup artist as she caromed away.

Juan Caldera, twenty and bronzed-skin gorgeous, raised his carefully plucked brows in twin arcs and studied Carmela. "Hmm, I see what she means." He cocked his head as his eyes continued to scan Carmela's face like a laser beam. "Good bone structure and I simply *adore* those interesting blue-gray eyes of yours. But why don't we try to bring out your brows a little more. And maybe do something about that slightly yellow cast under your eyes."

Carmela peered anxiously into the mirror. "I have yellow under my eyes?" Her worried reflection stared back.

Juan pursed his cupid-shaped lips and met her eyes in the mirror. "Not a lot, nothing a little schmear of green corrector can't fix."

"I usually just smooth on a little foundation," said Carmela, as he spun her chair around. "Then go with some blusher."

"Uh-huh," said Juan as he squeezed five different shades of liquid foundation into the palm of his hand. "But tonight we're going to make you *stage* ready." He took a fat, flat brush, daubed at his palette, blending and customizing a shade just for Carmela. "Trust me, sweetie, you're going to love this."

"I love it!" Carmela exclaimed fifteen minutes later. She stared into the mirror, not believing it was really her staring back.

"Told you," sang Juan.

"What did you do?" marveled Carmela. "Better yet, can I take you home with me?"

"We just needed to pop your brows and cheekbones," said Juan. "And smooth out your skin tone and add some lush color to your lips. I used a plum-colored stain, but a rich berry color would have worked just as well. You have very good lips, by the way."

"Thank you," said Carmela. "I mean thank you for everything." Krisi was back at her elbow now, plucking at the neckline of her dress, being irritating once again. "This is really great!"

"Come *on,*" insisted Krisi. "Try to get over yourself. The show starts in twenty minutes, and we still have to do something with your hair. You certainly can't walk the runway with your hair looking like a plucked chicken!"

"I thought I looked pretty good," said Carmela. She decided she was definitely walking better in her four-inch heels now. Probably had something to do with her newly discovered cheekbones and lush lips.

Krisi rolled her eyes as she plunked Carmela down into the hairstylist's chair. "Do something," she implored Latsis Sevan. "You're the master. You're the one who gets paid the big bucks."

Latsis, skinny, olive-skinned, and barely thirty, held up a lush piece of blond hair. "We do piezes, no?"

"No," said Carmela.

Ignoring her, Latsis quickly back-combed the hair on the top of Carmela's head, clipped in the piece, and smoothed it over. "Nize," he said.

Carmela cocked her head, gazed in the mirror. Not bad. The extra hair did give her a somewhat glammed-up fashion-model look. Hmm.

"Put in me-ore, yez?"

"You have an interesting accent," said

Carmela, still amazed at her ever-evolving appearance.

"Yez, ma'am," Latsis answered as he worked quickly to pin in a second piece.

"Where are you from originally?"

"Heah and there," answered Latsis. "I lif in diffront countries."

"South America?"

"Once or twize. Central Yoo-rope, too."

"Great," said Carmela, giving up. She watched as Latsis Sevan pinned in two more hairpieces and a row of braids.

When he was finished, Latsis stood back and smiled at her. "Like Jez-ca Seempson, no?"

"No," said Carmela, studying herself. "Well . . . maybe."

"Now your headpiece."

Carmela sat entranced as Latsis twirled a grapevine around her greatly enhanced locks, tucked the ends in delicately, then wove in two opera-length strands of pink pearls. As the pièce de résistance, Latsis added tiny sprigs of purple and green grapes.

"Complete!" he announced.

Carmela swiveled her head, testing her ability to move. Not too bad.

As if reading her thoughts, Latsis Sevan

warned, "Keep head up. No lookeeng down!"

"Right," said Carmela, rising up out of the chair, feeling slightly transported. As though she couldn't possibly be this exotic, ethereal creature that stared back at her from the mirror.

"Oh my Lord!" exclaimed Ava. "You look so beautiful I barely recognized you! I mean . . . well, you've always been beautiful, *cher,* it's just that you look extra amazing tonight. Like a real model!"

"Thank you, Ava," said Carmela, giving an instinctive bob of her head. Then, when she felt things begin to shift on top, straightened up again.

"And your posture's so ramrod straight," raved Ava. "You're really feelin' it, huh? Really getting into it?"

"You know," said Carmela. "I just might be."

They paused at the top of the stairs, where Krisi was stationed. Wearing a headset so she could communicate directly with the runway, she was lining up the models, getting them ready to head down the circular stairway, then out onto the runway.

"You. Carmela person," Krisi hissed. "Go!" She gave Carmela a nudge, looked as though she would have preferred to boot her down the stairs.

Carmela descended the circular staircase, trying not to let her heels catch on the carpet, listening as the insistent beat of the music increased in volume with each step she took.

Finally she was standing behind the backdrop of fabric. Chadron held up a hand, indicating for her to wait. Angelique stood next to him, holding a clipboard, looking petulant and unhappy.

"Don't screw up!" Angelique hissed at Carmela.

"Thanks for the vote of confidence," Carmela whispered back, suddenly determined to go out there and knock everybody's socks off. Then, as a model slipped back through the curtain and headed upstairs, Chadron gave her the high sign. Go!

A flash of lightning and a roll of thunder greeted Carmela as she stepped out onto the runway. Pumpkin luminarias lit the way; underfoot were the stars and moons she'd painted. And directly out there, in the dim light of the atelier, over one hundred faces were focused entirely on her.

Spotlights blazing, fog rolling, Carmela strutted her way down the runway, lifting her knees the way Ava had coached her, pretending that she was walking a straight line. The skirt of her dress flounced and swished, her shoulders swayed, she thrust her hips forward and leaned back slightly.

A deafening cheer rose from the audience. She ventured a quick glance down and saw the enthusiastic faces of Baby, Tandy, and Gabby in the audience. She grinned, continued her bump-and-glide strut. Reaching the end of the runway, Carmela dropped her right shoulder, put her left hand on her hip, slid to a stop, and posed. And there, directly in front of her, was Shamus staring up at her. His eyes shone as he applauded wildly and called out her name. She caught his eye briefly, noted that Glory was sitting alongside him, looking grim-faced and determined.

Yes, she thought to herself. *And don't I look good? Maybe even better than good.*

Then it was time for her return walk, gliding, moving carefully because now was not the time for a major mishap. The back curtain with its projection of the *Theatre de la Vampyr* drew closer, and then Carmela was ducking through it, finished for now.

"Wonderful," said Chadron, motioning her out of the way, so Yasmin could take her turn. Ava waited to go on after her.

"Shamus is out there," Carmela whispered to Ava.

"I know," Ava whispered back. "He came clomping in like Frankenstein with that cast on his foot. What a putz, huh?"

Carmela would have loved to wait and watch Ava, but she had to hustle back upstairs and change.

Then, barely five minutes later, she was back downstairs, moving to the thump-bump of the music, gliding down the runway in her second dress of the evening, feeling that she wasn't doing so badly after all.

Krisi met her at the top of the stairs. "There's been a change. Chadron's added a couple more pieces to the show, and you're going to wear one of them."

"Who me? No, no way."

"Yes, you," said Krisi, spinning her around.

"What if it doesn't fit?" protested Carmela.

"We'll make it fit," snapped Krisi. "Besides, the fabric's got a touch of Lycra, so it'll stretch. Hopefully a lot." She propelled Carmela into a far corner where a full rack of clothes was parked. "The sleeveless chiffon with the stand-up collar. He wasn't going to show it at all, but now he's changed his mind, so hurry up and get into it." Krisi barked her orders even as she unzipped the back of Carmela's dress and pushed her behind the rack of clothes.

"But I —" protested Carmela.

"This one," said Krisi. "There's a shawl that goes with it, too. I'll run get it."

"Listen," said Carmela, "I really don't think —"

But Krisi had already disappeared.

Reluctantly, Carmela shucked out of her short blue tunic and reached for the gown Krisi had indicated. It was a beautiful piece. Gray silk chiffon dotted with free-form daubs of pink, peach, and white that looked like they had been hand-painted onto the fabric.

But as Carmela pulled the dress off its velvet hanger, she saw a fluttering piece of paper attached to the metal clothes rack. It had one word printed on it: "Amber."

Whoa.

I'm supposed to wear this dress? thought Carmela. *A dress that had been intended for Amber?* This was weird. Beyond weird. In fact, seeing Amber's name on the sign almost felt like an unlucky omen to Carmela.

"Krisi?" she called out tentatively. Then peered out from behind the rack and looked around. Nobody there. She supposed they were all downstairs watching the show from the wings.

Carmela blew out air as she stood there holding the dress. *Now what?* she wondered. And answered herself. *Stop being a ninny, and just put it on.* She'd surprised herself thus far by actually having quite a bit of fun. So this wasn't the time to start screwing things up. This wasn't worth getting all bent out of shape over.

"Carmela?" called a male voice. "I've got your shawl."

Carmela finished shimmying into the gown, then came out from behind the rack of clothes to find Gordon van Hees standing there. He looked harried and distracted.

"Come on, come on," Gordon urged. "Turn around and let me zip you up. They're all waiting downstairs."

She complied, then turned around to face him. "Do I look okay? There isn't a mirror here . . ."

"Nice," said Gordon in a perfunctory tone. "Lovely." He made a few quick adjustments. "Now hold still."

Carmela complied as Gordon draped a matching silver-gray shawl around her shoulders.

"Perfect," he told her.

The shawl felt warm and almost tickly.

Carmela reached up and fingered the material. It was amazingly soft and luxurious. "This is very elegant," she said. "What kind of . . . ?"

"Qiviut," said Gordon. "A type of musk ox down. Very rare, very expensive."

Carmela gave a halfhearted smile. Something had just pinged deep inside her brain. The confidence she'd felt flowing through her for most of the evening seemed to be slowly ebbing away.

Now what's wrong? Carmela asked herself. Why was she suddenly weirding out like this?

"Head forward a bit," Gordon instructed her, "so I can adjust the back of this stand-up collar."

While Gordon reached both arms around her, fussing at the back of her neck, Carmela found herself staring down at a large pair of dressmaker's shears that hung from a blue ribbon around his neck.

"Almost got it," mumbled Gordon.

They were stainless steel, with jagged edges. *Serrated edges,* Carmela thought to herself. In fact, they looked almost like animal teeth.

Then the tickle of the downy-soft shawl against her bare skin nudged something deeper inside Carmela's brain.

A rare type of fur or fiber . . . could it have been this qiviut down? And serrated scissors could probably wreak terrible damage on human flesh! Would look just like teeth marks. Oh no . . . !

CHAPTER 26

Carmela reached up and tentatively touched the shawl. "This fiber . . . the qiviut or musk ox. It's . . ."

"Yes?" said Gordon. His voice sounded icy, cautious.

Carmela knew something had changed between them big-time. Gordon van Hees was suddenly no longer the hale and hearty, hand-kissing, good-natured fellow of a day or two ago. Now he was staring at her as though she had just peered into the depths of his soul.

"I'd better get downstairs," Carmela told him. She was shaking but tried not to show it.

Gordon grabbed her arm and held her in a viselike grip. "Just a minute. I'm not sure this is going to work after all." He fished a headset from his jacket pocket one-handed, clicked it on, spoke into the tiny microphone. "Chadron? This last number's not working at all. You heard me. Just go ahead and finish the show with whoever's down there." He clicked off before Chadron could reply.

"Let me go," said Carmela, trying to pull away from his grip.

"I told him not to drag this outfit out," muttered Gordon between clenched teeth. "I *warned* him."

"I said let me *go!*" Carmela tried to wrench her arm away again, but Gordon held fast.

Then he lifted his eyes to stare at her. "I think you and I are going to have a little chat."

"Not necessary," said Carmela. "In fact, I really —"

"Shut up!" screamed Gordon. He grabbed the shawl, let it slip farther down around Carmela's shoulders, then cinched it tight and yanked her toward him. Her arms successfully pinned against her sides, Carmela fell forward, off balance, and could do nothing more than launch a verbal protest as Gordon towed her out of the studio and down the hall into his office.

"Stop it!" she screamed. "Let me go! Ava! Chadron! Anybody!" But the music was so loud, the applause so thunderous, that no one could hear Carmela's shrieks for help.

"Sit down." Gordon shoved her roughly into a dark green club chair. "Let me think!"

"You killed her, didn't you?" said Carmela, so angry now she was shaking. "You killed Amber."

"Shut up," said Gordon. "Shut up, shut up, shut up!" He slid the top drawer of his desk open and pulled out a pistol. It was dull gray, short and ugly.

Carmela shut up.

Gordon's hard eyes stared at her. "What a little snoop you are. Wouldn't give up, would you?"

She lifted her chin, met his gaze. "There's no way you're going to get away with this."

"You're a strange girl, too," he muttered to himself, as if going over something in his own mind. "Why would you even care about a little twit like Amber?"

"Somebody had to," said Carmela, almost to herself.

Gordon stared at her with fiendish eyes. "But it was all so perfect," he hissed. Almost absently he fingered the steel shears strung around his neck. "The teeth marks, the animal hairs, the silly white dove. All pointing to Giovanni."

"Or Santino," said Carmela.

Gordon favored her with a smile that was sharklike in its ferocity. "That would have

343

been fine, too. Just A-okay with me. Didn't matter who took the fall. They both knew Amber, both were a little overprotective of her. Perfect suspects, really."

"You're crazy," said Carmela. She stated it flatly; there was obviously no arguing over it.

"I just didn't count on you being such an *incredible pest!*" Gordon's voice had continued to rise until he screamed the last two words at her. Then he suddenly sprang to his feet and grabbed a leather attaché that sat on a nearby credenza. He opened another office drawer, grabbed a pack of papers. In his frenzy, he seemed to have almost forgotten about Carmela, until she shifted in her chair.

He grabbed for his gun, pointed it directly at her. "Let's go," he growled.

"Where?" she asked.

He gestured toward the door. "Out."

Carmela stood up, trying not to let her knees shake so much. "I should change," she said. She was suddenly aware of the strange sounds Gordon was making in the back of his throat. A sort of . . . *growl!*

"Not necessary where you're going," Gordon murmured. He pulled open the door, jammed the gun into Carmela's ribs. "Move. Downstairs. And don't think I won't pull this trigger. I'll kill you if I have to. I'll shoot your little voodoo shop friend, too, if she dares get in my way. Blow a hole clean through her pretty little chest." This last threat was accompanied by more growling sounds.

"Leave Ava out of this," hissed Carmela.

"Then *move!*"

They edged their way downstairs, Carmela trying to descend as slowly as possible, while Gordon pushed and shoved and muttered at her, trying to hurry her along. As they made the final turn on the circular staircase, Carmela inhaled sharply. There, at the bottom of the stairs, stood Kimber Breeze! Her face was a hard mask framed by her pouf of blond hair; she wore one of her trademark red suits.

"I've been waiting for you, Carmela," said Kimber. Hate fairly burned in her eyes. "I came to see you fail miserably."

"Wow, Kimber," Carmela exclaimed with nervous false heartiness. "Great to see you."

"Get lost, lady," snapped Gordon, "we're busy here."

"And even if you don't fail," threatened Kimber, "I'll make sure the TV footage we get tonight portrays you as an awkward, stumbling clod. I've got my cameraman in the audience just waiting to shoot you."

"To shoot me," said Carmela. "Ha-ha, you and everybody else."

"Shut up!" said Gordon.

"Besides, I thought you were suspended," said Carmela, doing her best to continue stalling. Hoping someone, anyone, would come along and see her plight.

Kimber bared her teeth. "By tomorrow morning my agent will have my suspension lifted, and I'll be back on air. Needless to say, the station adores me. I garner great ratings, and that's all that really matters!"

"Get rid of her," muttered Gordon. His pistol jabbed harder into Carmela's back.

"Sorry, Kimber," said Carmela. "I'd really love to stick around and chat show biz with you, but I'm a little *involved* right now."

Kimber's eyes narrowed, suspecting a trick. "You're going to walk the runway right now?" she asked.

"No, we're actually on our way to a party," said Carmela. "A wonderfully bizarre Halloween party."

"What are you talking about?" asked Kimber, clearly befuddled.

"I think maybe we should *all* step out into the back alley," said Gordon, between clenched teeth.

"Yeah, c'mon along, Kimber," invited Carmela, her mouth suddenly feeling dry as cotton. "We'll tell you all about it. I've got a great news story you can break."

Gordon marched Carmela behind the sales desk, down the passageway that led past customer dressing rooms, and straight toward the black metal door that led out into the back alley.

Kimber dogged them every step of the way. "What's going on?" she demanded. "You're not going to get out of this, Carmela. You're going to talk to me whether you like it or not!"

"Sure, Kimber," said Carmela, nervously clenching and unclenching her hands. "No problem." Kimber had shouldered her way past Gordon and was standing right next to Carmela as they reached the sliding door that led to the back alley.

"Open it," ordered Gordon.

Carmela reached out, undid the latch on the black metal door, and began to slide the heavy door open.

At the same time, Gordon extended his hand high above him, then brought the butt of the gun crashing down on Kimber Breeze's head. As he caught her squarely on the back of her head, Kimber let loose a low groan, her eyes rolled back in her head, and she crumpled slowly to the floor.

Carmela reacted in an instant. Though the

door was barely open, she slithered out fast. Gordon grabbed for her but was only able to pull the shawl from her shoulders.

Outside in the dark alley now, Carmela grasped the outside frame of the metal door and struggled frantically to slide it closed behind her.

Just when she had inches to go, Gordon's hand poked out and waved the gun about wildly.

"Open this door!" he demanded, even as the gun continued to waggle in his hand.

Eyes darting about, Carmela snatched up a hunk of wood. It was part of a two-by-four board that had been used to construct the raised runway. If she could just wedge it in somewhere and hold him off . . .

A loud gunshot erupted, and a metallic *ping* echoed off the nearby Dumpster!

"Gordon, you maniac!" screamed Carmela. "Don't shoot!" She grasped the piece of wood in her hand, brought it crashing down on top of Gordon's wrist!

"Aaaaagh!" His scream pierced the air as the gun clattered to the pavement.

Quick as lightning, Carmela kicked it away. Then she slid the door the rest of the way closed and wedged her hunk of wood against it.

Gordon pounded away from the other

side. "I'll get you for this, Carmela!" He wasn't just growling now, he was gnashing his teeth!

Carmela looked left, then right, then dashed up the dark alley. She knew the wood she'd wedged in the door wouldn't hold for long. She had to get out of there and find help!

Emerging on Orleans Street, Carmela found herself smack up against a wall of moving, partying people. "Help!" she cried. "Somebody call the police!"

A man in a tattered hobo costume who was guzzling beer from a *geaux* cup stopped to leer at her. "What are you? A damsel in distress?" He was grinning and weaving in place. "Love your costume! Love your act!"

"Does anybody have a cell phone?" she asked, staring into a sea of masked, indifferent revelers.

"Carmela!" came a harsh scream from down the alley.

Damn.

It was Gordon. Somehow he'd fought his way out!

Carmela spun left. Maybe if she circled around and dashed in the front door of Moda Chadron, she'd be okay. Safety in numbers and all that. Surely, Gordon wouldn't attack her in front of dozens of witnesses, would he? But first she had to get to Royal Street!

Gathering up her long skirt in both hands, Carmela bobbed and wove her way down the street. But it was hard going through the packed crowd, and her four-inch sandals caused her to stumble more than once.

Stopping to lean up against a lamppost, Carmela bent down, undid the buckles, and kicked her sandals off. Glancing up, she saw Gordon's red face bobbing toward her through the crowd like an angry balloon. He didn't have the gun anymore, but his long stainless steel shears dangled menacingly from around his neck!

Carmela lurched down the street and around the corner, heading for the front door of Moda Chadron. Dodging people, constantly glancing back over her shoulder, she was filled with fear that Gordon was going to catch her, would drag her into a narrow alley and rip her throat open like he had poor Amber's!

And would anyone help? No, they'd probably think it was simply playacting! They'd probably circle round them and applaud!

Finally flinging herself against the double doors of Moda Chadron, Carmela grappled for the doorknob. But the door was locked!

She beat frantically on the glass. "Let me

in!" She felt like a moth in the night, beating its wings futilely against a screen door.

Carmela put an ear to the door, heard the crash of music, the peal of thunder. They were just getting to the grand finale where all the models would parade onstage. All except her.

Gordon's head bobbed even closer! She could see him coming at her through the crowd! What to do?

Carmela threw back her head and screamed. "Ava! Shamus! Anybody!"

She allowed herself another quick glance back. Gordon was twenty feet from her now and closing in. She watched as he ripped the scissors from around his neck and jammed his fingers through the loops, brandishing them like a weapon!

Carmela grasped the doorknobs and rattled them with all her might.

"Let me in! Please!"

And, lo and behold, one door opened slowly. A puff of white smoke rolled out, then a head followed. A familiar-looking head at that.

"Shamus?" cried Carmela. She was stunned to see him.

Surprise spread across Shamus's boyish face as he suddenly recognized her. He held his just-lit cigar in one hand, his lighter in the other. "Carmela?" he said, his expression changing from one of recognition to puzzlement. "What on earth are you — ?"

She threw herself against him, pointing up the street. "Being chased," she gasped. "Gordon." She was panting so hard she could barely catch her breath.

Shamus dropped his cigar, let his Dunhill lighter clatter to the tile floor of the entry. Then he grasped Carmela under the arms and swung her around behind him in one smooth motion. Then, with his bad foot, he kicked the door shut.

"But he'll just —" began Carmela, just as the door crashed open and Gordon appeared.

Wild-eyed, spitting with rage, Gordon charged through the front door of Moda Chadron like a bull gone mad. The deadly shears were clutched tight in his right hand.

Without hesitation, Shamus stuck his foot out, the broken foot with the cast on it, catching Gordon completely unaware and tripping him right at knee level.

A sick, snapping sound echoed in the entryway followed by Shamus's high-pitched scream of pain.

At the same time, Gordon cartwheeled wildly. Caught in midcharge at full velocity, unable to recover his balance, Gordon stumbled badly. His arms flailed out, but to no avail, and he crashed face-first onto the tile floor.

"Dear Lord," whispered Carmela. She peered around Shamus, who was bent over, moaning, and clutching what had to be a broken *leg* now. And stared, saucer-eyed, at the spread of red blood that oozed across the floor. "Dear Lord," she said again, "I think he fell on his own scissors!"

CHAPTER 27

"Gordon killed Amber," Carmela said for about the fortieth time.

She was sitting on a folding chair at the end of the runway. Lieutenant Edgar Babcock was hastily scrawling notes in his wirering notebook, while Gordon van Hees's body lay swathed in black plastic in the rear of an ambulance. He wouldn't be departing in a flurry of lights and sirens; it was all over for him.

The atelier was empty now, save for Shamus, Ava, Chadron, and, for some strange reason, Krisi. Shamus wore an inflatable splint on his leg, compliments of the same EMTs who had bundled up Gordon.

All the customers had been hustled out the back way into the alley, where Angelique and Chadron's salesgirls were writing orders like mad, and the models were serving flutes of champagne. For some bizarre reason, the fashion show attendees all thought this grand conclusion in the alley was part of the Halloween program. They'd swallowed the hasty announcement Chadron had made at the end of the show hook, line, and sinker.

"We know Gordon killed Amber," Babcock said to Carmela. "The scissors will undoubtedly match what we thought were bite marks on her neck. When we get that shawl tested, there's a good chance the hairs and fibers will match those found on Amber's body."

"What a scumbag!" spat Shamus. He'd persuaded one of the EMTs to give him a painkiller, and he looked happily loopy again.

Only Krisi seemed mournful. "Gordon fell on his own sewing shears," she muttered. "Such a tragic ending."

"He was a real fashion victim," declared Ava.

"Giovanni and Santino are innocent," murmured Carmela. "So's Remy."

"I know, *cher,*" said Ava. "Try not to think about it. Just try to relax."

Carmela stared pointedly at Edgar Babcock. "The question is, why did Gordon kill Amber?"

"Yes," said Chadron, sounding pained, "when she was so clearly contributing to our bottom line."

Babcock held up the leather attaché that Gordon van Hees had dropped earlier at the back door. "From the papers we found in here, I'm guessing a couple reasons. First, Gordon was up to his ears in gambling debts. Banks, loan sharks, casino tough guys were all coming after him." Babcock focused his gaze on Chadron. "And he was embezzling from your company, too. Thousands and thousands of dollars. There's pretty much a paper trail here that will attest to his theft."

Chadron put his head in his hands. "Angelique was always on my case," he moaned. "No matter how many orders we wrote, we never seemed to come up profitable. We could never get out of the red!"

"You were profitable," said Babcock. "Trust me."

"But I'm ruined all the same," said Chadron. He looked like a broken man.

"Not if we write enough orders tonight," said Krisi.

"They're probably writing double orders on Glory," quipped Ava.

Carmela digested all these revelations, then said, "But why on earth kill Amber? She didn't have any money, did she?"

"Insurance," said Babcock, as if that one

word explained it all.

"Our insurance?" asked Chadron, puzzled.

"*In*surance?" said Ava, putting the emphasis on the first syllable.

"You ever hear of key person insurance?" Babcock asked the group.

Shamus was beginning to bob his head in the affirmative. "Absolutely. Lots of companies have it. Common practice these days."

"Gordon van Hees had taken out almost a million dollars' worth of insurance on Amber," said Babcock. "More than enough to get him back in the black. A lot more, considering what he stole from here."

"And I *trusted* that man to handle the business end," murmured Chadron. He was still so shocked he was almost quaking.

"So Gordon killed Amber for the money," said Carmela. "Not out of anger or passion."

"People can be awfully passionate about money," said Babcock.

"You can say that again," said Shamus.

"Nobody asked you," snapped Ava. Then her anger softened when she remembered how Shamus had literally stepped in to save Carmela. "Sorry, Shamus. If it hadn't been for you . . ." Tears oozed from Ava's eyes. "Poor Carmela would have . . ." She reached over, gently pinched a loop of pearls that had come loose from Carmela's headpiece, and tucked them back in.

"Excuse me!" screeched a woman's high-pitched voice.

Kimber Breeze suddenly staggered through the front door, a white gauze bandage protruding from the back of her head. Her hair looked like a crazed rat had made a nest in it, her eye shadow had dissolved into raccoon eyes, her mascara streamed down her face in dark rivulets.

"Do you know there's a *dead body* in that ambulance out there?" Kimber shrieked. "I thought the EMTs came rushing over to take care of *me!*"

Babcock held up a hand. "Go back outside," he told her. "Keep quiet, don't talk to anyone. I'll get to you in a few minutes."

"How dare you," snapped Kimber. "I could have my camera crew —"

Ava stood up, edged her way boldly toward Kimber. "Why don't you put a cork in it, honey," she said. "Or crawl back under a rock. Nobody really cares about your problems."

"Oh yeah?" snarled Kimber.

Ava reached into her handbag and pulled out a pocket mirror. She turned it toward Kimber and held it in front of her face.

"What the . . . ?" began Kimber. Her hard

expression crumpled, her voice dropped to a pathetic whine when she saw her own reflection. "Oh my! I guess I do need a . . . a touch-up."

"Or a fire hose," said Ava. "And FYI . . . if you're looking to enter a costume contest with that hag thing you've got going, the judging's taking place in Jackson Square."

Kimber slunk out the door as Ava waggled her fingers at Kimber. "Lotsa luck, toots."

"You're a hoot, Ava," said Shamus. He was definitely feeling no pain.

"Excuse me," came a man's tentative voice.

They all turned to see who'd shown up now.

Now Giovanni's dark form stood in the doorway.

"Giovanni," said Edgar Babcock. "We have some questions for you."

Giovanni nodded. "No problem."

Carmela blinked. "What are *you* doing here?" she asked Giovanni.

"Ava called me," he said in a soft voice.

Carmela whirled to face Ava. "You did?"

"I thought it was only fair to let him know he's officially cleared."

"I am?" said Giovanni. "Really? Santino, too?"

Now everyone turned to stare at Edgar

Babcock. He gave a reluctant, somewhat pained nod. "Yes, yes, I suppose you're both cleared." He pointed a finger at Giovanni. "But we still need to talk."

Giovanni bobbed his head. "Yes, sir."

"And we have to get Shamus to the hospital," said Babcock in take-charge fashion.

"I'm fine," said Shamus. Krisi had given him a glass of champagne, and he was sipping it slowly. *No problema.*

"Yes, it is a problem," said Carmela. "We need to get your leg X-rayed, find a good orthopedist, and have a cast put on. Plus you're taking pills and drinking champagne. Would you prefer to get hauled off to the hospital or a treatment center?"

"Hospital," said Shamus in a small voice as Ava pried the drink out of his hand.

"Then let's go," said Carmela. She clambered to her feet, hooked her thumbs under the bodice of her strapless gown, and pulled it up.

"We need those dresses back," said Krisi.

Carmela and Ava both stared coolly at her.

"Fat chance," said Ava.

"I thought models got to keep the clothes," said Carmela. She wasn't sure that was correct, but it sounded like a nice perk.

"I suppose we could make an exception," said Chadron slowly.

"Where is she going to wear a one-of-a-kind couture gown like that?" huffed Krisi.

"I think Carmela has a few ideas," murmured Babcock. His eyes slid over to Carmela, appraising her, no longer giving her his suspicious cop look.

Carmela caught Babcock's glance. In fact, it was more of an admiring look. Like that of a potentially interested suitor.

Yes, Carmela decided, she could think of quite a few places where she could wear a fancy couture dress. There were always holiday parties in the Garden District, and Mardi Gras was just months away. Quigg Brevard had asked her to a fancy ball not so long ago. She'd declined. But next time he asked — and Carmela knew there would be a next time — she was going to say yes. And, now that you mention it, Edgar Babcock was awfully nice-looking, too . . .

SCRAPBOOK, STAMPING, AND CRAFT TIPS FROM LAURA CHILDS

Take a Spin with the Color Wheel

You probably learned about this in grade school, but a color wheel can be enormously helpful in selecting colors when it comes to paper, backgrounds, type, and design. For example, according to the color wheel, if you are using red as the primary color in your scrapbook layout, the most complementary colors would be red-orange and red-violet.

Tie a Pretty Ribbon

Ribbons look great on scrapbook pages. Here are a few ideas!

Use ribbon to frame a photo.

Create a woven ribbon montage.

Punch holes or insert eyelets in your page, then thread a ribbon through.

Stamp on ribbon.

Add bows to your page.

Hang charms and tags from ribbons.

Count Your Blessings

Have you ever thought about creating a Count Your Blessings album? You could include scrapbook pages about your family, friends, church, and the various volunteer organizations you belong to. Include inspirational phrases, poems, and affirmations, or create the entire album as a prayer journal.

Make a Mosaic

When you have so-so photos that may not stand up to being the main image on a page, cut off slivers and create a mosaic. Or take nine so-so photos, reduce or crop them tight, and organize them three across and three down, à la a crossword puzzle.

Mementos, Please

Use vellum envelopes on your scrapbook pages so you can include small mementos like ticket stubs, postcards, souvenir brochures, etc.

Put Photos in Your Headlines

Consider using die cuts or smaller die-cut photos as part of your scrapbook page headline. An example would be "Home is where the ♡ is."

Cook up a Recipe Album

Putting all your favorite, time-tested recipes in a scrapbook album makes a great gift for a young bride-to-be.

FAVORITE NEW ORLEANS RECIPES

Big Easy Peanut Butter Pie
1 pkg. (8 oz.) cream cheese, softened
1 cup sugar
1 cup peanut butter (chunky or creamy)
2 Tbsp. melted butter
1 cup heavy cream
2 Tbsp. vanilla
1 premade graham cracker crust
1/4 cup chocolate chips
1/4 cup chopped peanuts

Beat cream cheese until smooth. Add sugar, peanut butter, and butter, and continue to beat. In a separate bowl, whip heavy cream with vanilla. Combine the two mixtures, then pour into crust. Freeze for at least 2 hours. To serve, melt chocolate chips and drizzle over top, then sprinkle with chopped peanuts.

N'Orleans Bourbon Balls

1 cup vanilla wafers (reduced to crumbs)
1 cup pecans (very finely chopped)
1 1/2 Tbsp. light corn syrup
1/2 cup bourbon
2 Tbsp. cocoa
Confectioners' sugar

Mix vanilla wafer crumbs, pecans, corn syrup, bourbon, and cocoa together in a food processor. Then form mixture into small balls (you may need to put a little butter on your fingers) and roll in confectioners' sugar. Store in refrigerator in tightly covered container. Wait at least 24 hours before serving to let flavor develop. These can also be frozen.

Bayou Black Bean Soup

2 Tbsp. butter
1 small onion, chopped
2 cans black beans (16 oz. each)
1 cup chicken broth
1 cup salsa

1 lime (the juice of)

Melt butter in medium saucepan, sizzle chopped onions until golden. Add in black beans, chicken broth, salsa, and lime juice. Simmer for 20 minutes. To serve, top with a nest of shredded cheese or a dollop of sour cream.

Momma's Sour Cream Muffins
1/2 cup butter (softened)
1/2 cup sugar
2 eggs
1 cup sour cream
1 tsp. vanilla extract
2 cups all-purpose flour
1 tsp. baking soda
1 tsp. baking powder
1/4 tsp. salt

Cream butter and sugar together, then add in eggs, sour cream, and vanilla, and mix well. Mix in flour, baking soda, baking powder, and salt, and beat well. Pour batter into 10 to 12 well-greased muffin cups. Bake at 375° for 20 to 22 minutes, depending on your oven. Top with whipped cream or serve with jam. Or use the topping recipe below:

Momma's Sweet Muffin Topping
1/4 cup finely chopped pecans
1/4 cup brown sugar
1/2 tsp. cinnamon

Mix together and sprinkle on muffins while still hot.

Cajun Meatloaf
2 Tbsp. butter
1/2 large onion, chopped
1/2 cup green pepper, chopped
1 tsp. salt
1/2 tsp. pepper
1 tsp. Tabasco sauce
1/2 tsp. cayenne pepper
1/2 tsp. thyme
1/4 tsp. cumin
1 lb. ground beef
2 eggs, beaten
1/2 cup bread crumbs
1/2 cup ketchup
1 tsp. Worcestershire sauce

Melt butter in heavy skillet over medium heat, then add onion, green pepper, and spices. Stir frequently for 8 to 10 minutes. In separate bowl, mix together ground beef, beaten eggs, bread crumbs, 1/4 cup of the ketchup, and Worcestershire sauce. Add the sautéed onion, green pepper, and spices to the beef mixture and gently combine every-thing. Put into a 9"×5" loaf pan and bake for 20 minutes at 375°. After this first 20 minutes of baking, spread the remaining 1/4 cup ketchup on top and bake for 40 more minutes. (Note: You can, of course, adjust spices to taste.)

Party Perfect Rice Custard

6 eggs
3 cups milk
1 cup sugar
1 tsp. vanilla
1/2 tsp. salt
1 1/2 cups cooked rice
1 cup golden raisins
Sprinkle of nutmeg

Butter a 2-qt. casserole dish. Break eggs into casserole dish and beat well with a fork. Add milk, sugar, vanilla, and salt, then blend well. Add the rice and raisins and stir till well-mixed, then sprinkle with a touch of nutmeg. Place casserole dish in shallow pan of water and bake, uncovered, for 1/2 hour at 350°. After this first 1/2 hour of baking, stir custard well, making sure to break up any chunks. Then continue baking for an additional 45 minutes.

Louisiana Pear Cake

4 large pears, peeled and diced
1 Tbsp. sugar
3 eggs
2 cups sugar
1 1/4 cups vegetable oil
3 cups flour
1 tsp. salt
1 tsp. baking soda
2 tsp. vanilla extract
1 cup pecans, chopped
1 cup raspberry preserves
1/4 cup hot water

Mix diced pears with 1 Tbsp. sugar and let stand for 5 minutes. In a separate bowl, beat eggs, remaining sugar, and oil at medium speed. Combine flour, salt, and baking soda, then add to the egg mixture. Add in vanilla and beat at low speed until mixture is well-blended. Fold in the pears and chopped pecans and blend gently by hand. Pour mixture into a greased and floured 10″ Bundt pan. Bake at 350° for approximately 1 hour or until wooden pick inserted in cake comes out clean. Cool for 10 minutes in pan, then remove cake from pan and transfer to a serving platter. Combine raspberry preserves with hot water to form a sauce, then drizzle over cake and serve immediately.

Southern Bride Cocktail
1 1/2 oz. gin
1 dash maraschino liqueur
1 oz. grapefruit juice

Shake ingredients in a cocktail shaker with ice, then strain into a cocktail glass.

Quick 'N' Easy Red Beans and Rice
2 Tbsp. butter
1/2 cup onion, chopped
1/2 cup green pepper, chopped
1/2 cup celery, chopped
2 cans red beans (15 oz. each)
1/2 lb. sausage (already cooked, cut into 1/2" slices)
1 can tomato sauce (8 oz.)
1 tsp. Worcestershire sauce
1/4 tsp. ground red pepper
1/4 tsp. hot pepper sauce
3 cups hot cooked rice

Melt butter in large, heavy skillet, then add onion, green pepper, and celery. Sizzle on medium heat for 3 to 4 minutes. Add beans, sausage, tomato sauce, Worcestershire sauce, red pepper, and hot pepper sauce. Stir together, cover, then reduce heat. Simmer for 16 minutes. Serve beans over cooked rice.

Lemon Icebox Pie

2 eggs
1 can (14 oz.) Eagle Brand sweetened condensed milk
1/2 cup lemon juice
1 premade graham cracker crust

Beat eggs well, then add in condensed milk and lemon juice and beat again. Pour into crust and put in icebox to chill until firm. Serve with your favorite whipped cream or whipped topping.

ABOUT THE AUTHOR

Laura Childs is the bestselling author of the Tea Shop Mysteries and the Scrapbooking Mysteries. She is a consummate tea drinker, scrapbooker, and dog lover, and travels frequently to China and Japan with Dr. Bob, her professor husband. In her past life she was a Clio Award–winning advertising writer and CEO of her own marketing firm.

We hope you have enjoyed this Large Print book. Other Thorndike, Wheeler, and Chivers Press Large Print books are available at your library or directly from the publishers.

For information about current and upcoming titles, please call or write, without obligation, to:

Publisher
Thorndike Press
295 Kennedy Memorial Drive
Waterville, ME 04901
Tel. (800) 223-1244

or visit our Web site at:

http://gale.cengage.com/thorndike

OR

Chivers Large Print
published by BBC Audiobooks Ltd
St James House, The Square
Lower Bristol Road
Bath BA2 3SB
England
Tel. +44(0) 800 136919
email: bbcaudiobooks@bbc.co.uk
www.bbcaudiobooks.co.uk

All our Large Print titles are designed for easy reading, and all our books are made to last.